PRAISE

"In *A Time To Go*, LaVine Rathkey tells a compelling story of the full range of immigrant experience: the transatlantic voyage, trancontinental travel, rural and urban settlement, and the struggles encountered on a wilderness farm. The characters evoke compassion, and sometimes anger. A good read of an era without the safety nets of labor laws, health insurance, and entitlement programs."

—Barry Ostrom, a Monmouth writer

"A *Time To Go* will bless you as you read about the adventures of a family living their daily lives under extreme difficulties. The children discover their strengths and forgive their weaknesses to become adults with strong family values."

—Faith Ministrie

"An amazing saga of one man's family as they leave England for the wilds of Canada. Young Amy Watts and her nine siblings cope with extreme cold, inadequate housing, and crushing emotional pain. This story tears at your heart and leaves you wanting more."

—Sandrea Scott

"Following Amy's story, one cannot help but be captivated and enthralled with her courage as she endures the many heartaches life throws at her in Canada. In spite of it all, Amy grows up a wonderful person."

—Cindie L. Shatto-Vinson

"The author's characters are fully developed and they evoke powerful emotions in the reader. LaVine Rathkey's touches of humor are a delight. The book is hard to put down. The writer's style makes the reader want to know what happens next."

—Leonard Colen

A beautifully written story of love and courage as the Watts family conquer the challenges of a a hostile environment.

—Teresa Heitzman R.N., M.B.A.

A TIME TO GO

To Birdie,
   Thanks for all your
encouragement + faithfully
answering all my e-mail

   Blessings
      La Vine Rathbey

A TIME TO GO

*From England to the
Wilds of Canada*

LaVine Rathkey

Tate Publishing & Enterprises

Published by Tate Publishing & Enterprises, LLC
127 E. Trade Center Terrace | Mustang, Oklahoma 73064 USA
1.888.361.9473 | www.tatepublishing.com

Tate Publishing is committed to excellence in the publishing industry. The company reflects the philosophy established by the founders, based on Psalm 68:11,
"The Lord gave the word and great was the company of those who published it."

Published in the United States of America

ISBN: 978-1-61663-715-6
1. Fiction / Historical
2. Fiction / Family Life
10.08.30

DEDICATION

To all the descendants of Frederick Watts. And to those souls everywhere who are in awe of the brave pioneers that carved homesteads from the wilderness.

Acknowledgements

To thank everyone who helped and gave me encouragement while writing this story would undoubtedly require another book.

Foremost, I want to thank Carol Gutmann for her faithful recording of history as told to her by her grandmother, Amy Gladys Watts Rathkey, and other close relatives of Frederick and Edith Watts. Without her meticulous documentation this book would not be possible.

Thanks also to my sister-in-law, Dorothy Schattenkerk, who said, "Go for it!"

To my Creative Writing Class, and teacher, Jane LaMunyon, for your faithful critiques, suggestions, and encouragement. I'd like to mention everyone by name, but it frightens me I might unintentionally leave someone out. To all of you, thank you so much! I do want to thank Len for physically showing me how Leslie climbed down from the train seat. It saddens me Keith is no longer with us. He encouraged me greatly and would have loved this book.

To all the amazing staff at Tate Publishing and Enterprises. Your kindness and help from first contact to last is so appreciated. Always you are patient and courteous. A special thank you to my editor, Sheridan Irick, for her helpful suggestions in polishing this manuscript.

Last, but not least, Eldred, thank you again for your unfailing support on this journey. Your patience, and long-suffering are incredible. And thank you, too, for bringing me into your wonderful family. No woman ever had a more wonderful mother-in-law.

THE WATTS FAMILY

Father: Frederick Watts born June 23, 1871 in Thorpe-le-Soken, Essex, England

Mother: Edith Annie (Rampling) Watts born November 13, 1873 Ipswich, Suffolk, England

1. Stanley Reginald WattsIpswich, Suffolk, England July 7, 1892

2. Frederick Cecil WattsIpswich, Suffolk, England October 28, 1893

3. Dorothy (Dolly) May Watts Ipswich, Suffolk, England April, 11, 1896

4. Amy Gladys WattsIpswich, Suffolk, England August 3, 1898

5. Percy Claude WattsColchester, Essex, England October 27, 1900

6. Eric Ralph WattsColchester, Essex, England September 3, 1901

7. Charles Leslie WattsColchester, Essex, England October 29, 1902

8. Edith Anne WattsHampshire, Borden, England February 6, 1904

9. Norah Elizabeth WattsBad Shot, Lea Surrey, England August 16, 1905

CHAPTER I

Amy Gladys Watts sat beside her paternal grandmother on the solid oak bench, hands folded sedately in her lap; she tried hard to imitate the proper woman beside her. It was not easy for a seven-year-old whose feet lacked inches of reaching the floor. The sermon seemed unusually long and Amy couldn't help squirming, just a little. Then a bit more. Grandmother Watts frowned, but kept her chin firm and eyes straight ahead as she reached over and pinched Amy on the arm.

Only a kind look from her brother, Reginald, kept Amy from crying. Reg, in his white surplice, appeared angelic from his place in the choir. Amy bit her lip, blinked away the tears and centered her attention on the robed pastor behind the high pulpit. His sonorous voice boomed out, "We're going to pray for the Watts' family—they're leaving England for a new beginning in Canada."

Father had caught the fever of others wanting the opportunity to homestead on their own land. In 1906 many areas in Canada were largely unsettled and the lure of sections of rich untried ground was not to be denied.

The service finally over, Amy joined hands with her older sister, Dolly, as they walked to Grandmother and Grandfather Rampling's brick house for the last Sunday dinner they would have with them. Father and Mother followed; Mother carrying baby Norah.

"Grandmother, isn't it exciting? Just think, we're going across the ocean. Father says we'll do well in Canada; I think we'll have a big house with lots of rooms. And I might have my very own bed," said little Amy in a breathless rush.

"Humph! I declare, you're the beatin'est child for dreamin.' Most likely you'll be lucky to have a pallet on the floor. No doubt you'll be scratchin' and clawin' for your very existence." She looked even more austere, and placed a piece of fried chicken on her granddaughter's plate.

A stern look from her father, and Amy ducked her head and remained quiet. Children were to be seen, not heard. But he couldn't silence his mother-in-law and she continued to upbraid and admonish. "Fred Watts, I don't understand why you have to drag your family off to God-only-knows-what when you have a secure home and family here. What's wrong with men that they can't be content with what they have?"

A beseeching look from her daughter, Edith, only deepened the onslaught. "Rob me of my precious daughter and my grandchildren, will you? You've no mercy, lad." *Or sense God gave a goat, for that matter.*

"Well, ma'am, I reckon Edith's told you, Norah will stay with my mother, and then her Aunt Polly and Uncle James will take her until I can arrange to come get her. The SS *Lake Champlain* sails Friday. We're booked, and they won't wait. Neither will they let us board with a child broken out with eczema. The doctor confirmed it." He sighed. "I hate leaving her behind.

I do! But, I can't miss this opportunity. We're going now."

⁖

Amy cried as she said goodbye to her school chums, but most thought it terribly exciting to be going on such an adventure. "You're favored!" they said, as she hugged her girlfriends for the last time. Thoughts of hardship hadn't entered their minds.

That night she could scarcely sleep for anticipation of the trip that lay ahead. Almost before daybreak, Amy crawled from the feather bed she shared with Grandmother Watts and dressed quickly. She pulled a wooden stool to the dresser and climbed up to look in the mirror. Pleased with her reflection, she hopped down and turned to the woman behind her. "Grandmother, look at my cheeks. Aren't they rosy?"

The old woman glared, and then slapped her across the face. "Pretty is as pretty does! Now get on with you. I need to get dressed."

The child resembled her mother, a handsome woman with curly fair hair and twinkling blue eyes. She also possessed her loving and forgiving nature. Amy brushed tears from her eyes. It would be a long time before she forgot the lesson of the morning, and a long time before she looked in another mirror.

⁖

Amy could scarcely believe the time for them to go had actually arrived. Suddenly it didn't seem like such a fun venture anymore. Tears ran down her mother's cheeks.

Her older sister sobbed. The little boys stood stiff as soldiers. They didn't cry, but their eyes were as round and luminous as Grandfather's watch. Reg, the oldest sibling, looked as if he'd swallowed a rock. Father, known as a "bit of a lad," for his short height, wiped his eyes. Grandmother Watts dabbed at tears with her apron and handed a bag of lemon drops to Amy. "Now don't forget to share," she admonished.

They all kissed baby Norah, who was now howling, one more time as Grandmother Rampling held the seven-month-old in her arms. Amy reached in her pocket for a hankie and blew her nose. She didn't like it that her baby sister had to stay behind; but Aunt Polly and Uncle James were kind, and they did love little Norah.

All the aunts, uncles and cousins were assembled on this momentous occasion to wish them God-speed and a safe journey. Everyone called, "Don't forget to write."

Amy watched as her mother turned to give her baby sister one last hug and kiss. Tears rained down her mother's cheeks and she trembled until Grandmother put an arm around her and whispered something in her ear. Father scowled, but there were tears in his eyes too. It scared Amy to see her parents so sad. She reached for Dolly's hand and squeezed hard.

The train ride across England soon made Amy forget her tears. She and her siblings kept their noses pressed to the glass as they watched the countryside slide past. There were so many new and exciting things to see, large farms with animals running about, and more rivers and bridges than Amy could count. The children gazed in awe as they entered the city; tall buildings and ornate mansions loomed everywhere.

"England is beautiful," said Mother. "I'm glad the children are getting to see this part of it before we leave. Though I suppose the younger ones won't remember the land of their birth." Edith sighed and wiped a tear from her eye.

"We have plenty of time," Father declared. "I'd like to show you some of the city before we go to the ship." He instructed the driver of their cab to take them on a tour.

Amy giggled when her mother's head drooped and she nearly fell asleep to the familiar clip-clop of the horse's hooves against the cobblestones. Too excited herself to ever sleep, Amy had trouble sitting still, but she knew better than to squirm.

The cab drew up to a flower-rich park with immense green lawns, small ponds with brightly colored fish, and continuous brick-lined walkways. "All right, children," Father said. "You may get down and run about a bit, but stay within our sight." Edith smiled at him as she took his arm and strolled the sun-dappled paths. "Fred, I must thank you," she said. "This is exactly what our children need before we board the ship."

The inevitable couldn't be delayed forever and they made their way to River Mersey and the many adjoining wharves that appeared to run on without end. It seemed a miracle in itself to find the SS *Lake Champlain*. Six members of the Watts family stood on the dock and stared up at the huge vessel that was to be their home for the next two weeks.

If two-year-old Annie, and four-year-old Leslie weren't impressed no one noticed. Annie stuck a thumb in her mouth and clung to her mother's skirt. Leslie, far more interested in the seagulls circling the wharf, turned his back.

Reg, a teenager, not wanting to seem too impressed, and hoping to scare his sisters said, "Is that the old tub we're going on? Think she'll make it all the way across the Atlantic? Maybe we'll end up in Davy Jones locker." He gave a meaningful look to little sister Amy, the most vulnerable of his siblings.

Before he could continue with taunts, Father silenced him with a stern look.

Dolly, her eyes wide and frightened, moved closer to her mother and whispered in her ear. Mother looked startled and hurriedly felt behind her eldest daughter's ears. She quickly undid Dolly's braids and fluffed the hair around her face. No one seemed to notice and Edith masked her worry with a smile.

Onboard at last, Amy clutched the ship's railing; her head swiveled first one way and then another as she watched activity on the wharf. Workmen pushed and pulled wheeled carts loaded high with baggage needing to be stored on board. Horses hitched to heavy wagons bearing supplies moved back and forth on the dock. She looked up at her mother and received a reassuring smile before turning her attention back to shore.

Father held Annie on one arm and shaded his eyes with the other hand as he watched the comings and goings. His small sons held to his pant-legs and tried to see. Reg lifted one little brother, and Cecil lifted another.

Amy's painful memory now kept her from trying to boost Leslie. She'd been warned not to pick up her little brother, but at five-years-old, Amy had felt confident she could manage as well as Mother. When Leslie toppled over her shoulder and landed on his head screaming, the adults had come running. Thinking she'd killed him, Amy fled, and hid in the hedgerow for hours. When Father returned home and placed the horse's bridle on the shrubs in front of her, she imagined it to be the means to hang her. Much later, upon discovering her hiding place, everyone felt she'd been punished enough.

Two short blasts from the ship's whistle alerted passengers they were soon to get underway. The Watts family moved a little closer together and Father smiled at his offspring and circled an arm around Mother's shoulders. "Well, children, you can tell old England goodbye; we'll be leaving directly."

Mother closed her eyes and bowed her head. Amy thought she heard her whisper, "God, go with us," but she couldn't be sure when her mother sniffed and blew her nose. The big ship began to glide through the water. At first Amy didn't know they were moving, but she caught on when objects on the dock seemed farther away. The family breathed in the fresh salt air and stayed on deck during the three mile journey down the Mersey River. They continued watching until the ship cleared the harbor and land became a speck in the distance.

When even the speck could no longer be imagined, Mother lifted her chin, and squared her shoulders. She sighed and said, "Come children, we need to go below and find our room."

CHAPTER 2

F ather removed his hat and hung it on one of three hooks provided at the end of the wardrobe. He ran a hand through his wavy dark hair and brushed at his mustache as he scrutinized the room. "It'll do, it'll do."

A small adjoining room complete with cushioned, wooden sofa, two matching wicker chairs and a small table, would serve as a parlour when needed during their long voyage.

Amy squeezed in amongst her sisters and brothers on the lowest bunk; perched like fledglings on a tree limb they waited to see what happened next. Mother unbuttoned her black coat and placed it in the wardrobe. She dropped to her knees and searched beneath the bunk for their personal belongings shoved there out of the way earlier. Satisfied things needed short-term were available, she rose to her feet and tried to smile.

Four large trunks remained below in the baggage room. Accessible only at limited times for the duration of their voyage. "I hope I won't need anything from the trunks while we're at sea," said Edith. One trunk, with the help of her dear mother, and mother-in-law, she'd crammed to almost bursting with bedding. Another trunk held their clothes. A third trunk held kitchen utensils, dishes, limited household furnishings, towels, dishtowels, tablecloths, and a few precious mementoes such as her mother's Bible.

Most of their things had been sold or given to family members. Edith's treasured piano sold for a good price. Fred allowed they'd buy what they needed when they reached Canada. The fourth trunk contained Fred's professional photography equipment: cameras, tripods, chemicals, trays, enlarger, filmpacs, and much more, lay carefully wrapped within.

Noting the pleasant look on her father's face, Amy piped up. "May I sleep in the top bunk tonight? Please?"

"Nuh-uh. We want to, "chorused her little brothers, Percy, Eric, and Leslie. "And we can climb better'n any ol' girls."

Father winked at their mother. "We'll see," he said. "If this ship starts rolling around you may not wish to be up there."

Six bunks (three on each side) for a family of eight children and two adults, meant they would be doubling up. Her younger brothers could easily fit into one bunk-bed; all but the two oldest boys, Reg and Cecil, viewed it as a lark. Amy certainly didn't mind sharing a bed with her two sisters, especially if she could sleep on the very top bunk. Dolly, looking pale, viewed the uppermost bed with apprehension.

Father removed his pocket watch, secured on a long chain, from a vest pocket and checked the time. "It's almost the dinner hour. We'd best make our way to the dining room."

Unable to conceal her fear any longer, Edith turned and surveyed her family with solemn eyes. "My dears, I'm afraid our Dorothy Mae has the mumps." She appealed to Fred. "They surely won't turn around and put us off now will they?" She held her breath. "Can they do that?"

Father's face reddened and his eyebrows lifted. "Well, I don't think so, but she does need to be in the infirmary so she doesn't expose others on board. I'll take her, explain we didn't know, she just popped out with them. I'm sure they'll understand." Fred stroked his mustache. "Dolly, do you feel bad?"

"No, Father. It just feels funny when I swallow."

"Edith, take the children on to the dinning room; I'll join you there as soon as I can."

Mother hugged and kissed her eldest daughter. "It'll be all right," she whispered. "I'll come see you soon. Go with your father now."

Edith smoothed her hair and straightened her stylish hat. The day remained sunny and reasonably warm. She and the children wouldn't need their coats for the short trek to the dining room.

Waiters, clad in white coats, set steaming bowls of hearty fish chowder in front of them. Crusty loaves of fresh light bread followed, complete with small crocks of butter. Two pots of tea were placed on the table, one at each end. Cream and sugar in serviceable containers were added.

More hungry than usual, Amy silently urged her father to hurry. Fred arrived a little late, slipped into his chair, looked to see if heads were bowed, and quickly returned thanks. "Oh God, our Father, we thank thee for this food. Bless us and keep us safe. In your name we pray. Amen."

After the noon meal Edith excused herself and hurried away to visit and reassure Dolly. Fred strolled the decks with his children while they familiarized themselves with the ship. He spoke mostly for the benefit of his older sons, Reginald and Cecil. "Boys, this is a modern up-to-date vessel we're on. She's the first merchant ship to be fitted with apparatus for permanent wireless telegraph. If there's another disaster, such as the devastating earthquake last month in America, we'll know about it almost as soon as it happens."

"We talked about the San Francisco quake and fire in school," Cecil said. "My teacher read to us people are living in tents now. And it will be a long time before they can rebuild the city. Some officials think there will be another earthquake to follow this one. Preachers are saying it is a sign of the end-times."

Conversation halted as they watched their mother approach. Edith smiled. "Dolly's fine. She's sleeping now." She placed a hand on Fred's arm to halt him before some empty deck chairs. "Do you suppose I might retrieve my yarn from our room, and the girls and I could sit here in the sunshine while I knit? We'll all need heavier stockings if what I hear of Canadian winters is true."

Growing increasingly restless himself, Fred gave his sons permission to further explore the ship.

"Reg, Cecil, keep an eye on your little brothers, and don't go poking around restricted areas."

With a promise to not be gone long, Fred strode away to the smoking room. He never used tobacco himself, but he wouldn't mind having maybe one drink. Helpful information could oft be garnered over a social glass or two. Perhaps he might be lucky enough to engage in conversation a fellow traveler already familiar with Manitoba, the area where he hoped to settle.

Fred hadn't spoken of it while in the dining room, for he couldn't be sure, but there'd been something oddly familiar about the man sitting with his family at a table near the end of the room. On two instances he'd caught the fellow staring at him before he looked away. If it was someone with whom he'd served in the Boer War, he couldn't place him. If he was an ex-soldier, the man had put on a lot of weight, and his hair almost reached his collar in back.

Fred gave a casual look around the gentleman's hazy smoke-filled room and put aside his hope of seeing the man from the dining room.

Most of the men already here were caught up in groups of three or four and intent on their conversations. A few card games were underway. Only one man remained apart and he seemed content to puff on his pipe and observe from a distance.

Fred ordered a glass of ale and watched him from the corner of his eye. He didn't appear unapproachable so much as amused by his fellow travelers. Taking his glass with him, Fred sauntered over and sat down. Instead of speaking to the stranger right away, he pretended to have an aloof interest in the men playing cards.

Without turning his head, the man spoke. "You a family man?"

"What? Why, yes ... yes, I am."

"Thought so. Most of the men in here are. Come in here to drink and get away from there wives. Gonna be a long voyage."

"And you, I assume, are single?"

"That's right. And I like it that way." He stuck out his hand. "Name's William. William Shipley."

"Fredrick Watts. I have nine children, but I didn't come in here to get away from my beautiful wife."

"So where you headed, Mr. Watts? You planning to homestead in Canada? Or are you a city man?"

"I do hope to homestead. But I figure I can do well with my photography too."

"Photography, eh? Then you're not the run-a-the-mill bloke that generally comes to Canada." He straightened and surveyed the man beside him. "You got the grit for blisters on your hands? A back that aches every night? Carvin' a home out of the wilderness can be tough goin.'"

"What about you, Mr. Shipley? Where you headed?"

"Home, my good fellow. Back to Paddle River, Alberta. Got me a nice chunk a ground all staked out. My brother's there waitin.' Not too many folks around yet, but those who are pull together. We're neighborly."

"Paddle River, eh? Alberta. That's a little farther west than I figure on going. Got my sights on Manitoba, maybe around Melita."

"Uh-huh. You could do worse. They raise some good grain up there. Lotsa birds and wildlife, too. You oughta get some good pictures, if you're into that sorta thing." He puffed on his pipe and blew a smoke ring. "Doesn't have the lure for me Paddle River does, though. There's a future in Paddle River. We'll be on the map someday."

Fred swallowed the last of his ale and stood up to leave. "Nice talking to you. See you around again, I reckon." Paddle River. Never heard of it. "Too remote," he muttered. "I'll settle in Manitoba."

When he left the smoking room, he was surprised to find the weather had changed. Fred hurried along to find his family. It had started to sprinkle, and the breeze off the ocean no longer seemed gentle.

Amy saw her father first and hurried the short distance to meet him. "Father, I'm glad you're here. Mother says we have to go in now; it's getting too cold, and she wants to put Annie down for a nap."

"Ah, and you don't need a nap, too?" he teased.

"Father! I'm too big," she sputtered as she looked up at him. "Even Leslie thinks he's too big. And he's only three."

"Speaking of which, where are your rascally brothers? Don't tell me they're still poking into crannies on this ship."

Before Amy could form an answer, Edith gathered her things and rose from the deck chair to face her husband. "The boys came back and I gave them permission to go to the ship's library. Maybe we should go after them. This wind seems to be picking up. The waves are much higher than a few minutes ago."

Edith lifted little Annie and handed her to Fred before gripping his arm. "If we're going to have a storm," she said. "I want my children where I can see them."

CHAPTER 3

Fred shepherded his family to the dining room for the evening meal. He smiled and tried to appear jovial, while simultaneously attempting to hurry them along. Little doubt remained they were in for a storm. Fred had been to sea before, and he knew what to expect. He'd try to get them back to the cabin before the ocean became too rough.

They were served some of the best salmon steaks he'd ever eaten. His older sons cleaned their plates faster than usual. Fred sighed with relief. He didn't want to unduly frighten his family, but they needed to get back to the cabin before the storm broke. Amy finished her salmon, and ate the portion her brother, Percy, left marooned on his plate.

Edith's eyes turned to the window frequently as she moved food around on her dish and tried to shove bits of salmon in Annie's mouth. The child waved her spoon and beat a happy cadence on her wooden high-chair. If Edith worried about the approaching storm, her small daughter remained blissfully unaware.

"Take that spoon away from her," Fred commanded.

Relieved of her utensil, Annie turned her attention to the salmon in her dish. She displayed a toothy grin, and mangled her fish with both hands. The little boys did better, but they too, left food on their plates.

Unwilling to push the issue, Fred signaled for waiters to clear away their dishes and serve dessert, a creamy custard they quickly devoured. Still, they were nearly last to leave the dining room.

Waiters scurried about clearing tables.

"All right children," Father said. "Stay close to your mother and me. Hang on." Fred lifted Annie, and Edith took his arm. The children grouped around them. "You older boys take your younger siblings by the hand. Brace yourselves. Any minute now, this ship is going to start rolling and pitching like a horse gone berserk."

They made it back to their cabin without incident. Edith quickly prepared Annie for bed; Fred assigned bunks. He and the older boys would take beds on one side of the room, mother, girls, and little boys on the other.

To her delight, Amy and four-year-old Eric got the top bunk. They would sleep one at each end. Eric shinnied up faster than a squirrel climbs a tree, and smirked down on his siblings. For now, Leslie had the middle bunk to himself; he'd share with Dolly when she returned from the infirmary. Mother and Annie took the lowest berth.

On the boys' side, Reg took top bunk, Cecil and Percy the middle, and Father the lowest. Curtains one could pull across allowed for privacy.

Minutes later the fury of the storm broke. Wind drove sheets of rain sideways against the ship. If passengers bothered to look, they couldn't tell where sea left off and sky began. Most didn't care. Folks were busy trying to maintain their equilibrium.

Fred suspected what was coming. He procured buckets, extra washcloths, towels, and a jug of water from the purser and carried them back to the cabin where he distributed them around the room. Then he left.

Mother became ill first and grabbed for a bucket. After that everyone seemed intent on being sick at the same time. Amy remained the only one unaffected. She slid from the top bunk and helped Eric down and held him while he retched over a pail.

Little Annie screamed and threw up all over her nightgown. It wasn't a pretty sight. Edith tried to help, but she had turned a bilious shade of green and retched again and again over the bucket. Amy wet a washcloth and bathed her mother's face. She got the nightgown off Annie and wrapped her in a large towel.

The boys too, were sick. Reg heaved, groaned, and collapsed on the lowest bunk. Amy wet another washcloth and sponged his face.

"Pompous little popinjay," Reg hissed. " Left… he coulda helped … shoulda helped."

"Shhh, don't let Momma hear you. She'll wash your mouth out with soap."

Under the circumstances that seemed funny. He wanted to laugh, but he was too sick.

Amy did her best to help her family, and in her child's simplicity begged God to make the storm go away. She bathed her mother's face yet again and heard her whisper. "Amy, you're our little angel. What would we do without you?"

ॐ

Fred sat alone in the gentleman's saloon, brooded and nursed his drink. He'd looked back and seen the contempt on the face of his son when he left their cabin. How could he explain that he could ride out a storm but couldn't endure watching his family be sick? If he'd stayed, he'd have been the sickest of the lot.

The room remained almost empty. Men were either sick themselves or tending those who were. The bartender stood with legs spread and feet braced. He wiped an already clean bar, sometimes clutching it to steady himself as the ship rolled. Glasses were carefully lifted, one at a time, from the rack for an extra polish. Fred looked up with casual interest when the door opened to admit one more gentleman.

Fred watched as the man squared his shoulders, strode to the bar and ordered a drink. He'd be willing to bet the fellow had been in the military. The way he quickly downed his whiskey and ordered another, piqued Fred's curiosity. He hadn't long to wait. With the second shot-glass in hand the man turned, noticed him sitting alone and marched over to his table.

"Pardon me, sir. But aren't you Sergeant Watts? Served in the Boer War?"

"The same. But it's just plain Fred Watts now." Fred motioned for him to sit down. "And you're PFC Bill Clark, I'm thinking. Thought I might know you when I saw you in the dining room. Couldn't be sure."

"Yes, sir. That's me. And I'm plain ole Bill Clark now." He grinned. "Imagine meeting again here on a ship bound for Canada. Makes the world seem rather small doesn't it?"

"That it does." Fred fingered his empty glass.

"Here, let me buy you another round." He signaled the bartender. "Where you headed when you reach Canada, if I may ask?"

"I figure to take my family on to Manitoba. Perhaps settle around Melita."

The bartender carefully handed Fred his glass of ale; which he gripped in both hands and quickly swigged before it had time to slosh. Tables and chairs were secured to the floor, but glasses could go flying off the table.

"And you, Mr. Clark? Where in Canada do you plan to settle?"

"Well, sir, I think I might go on to Edmonton and look around. I'm a fair carpenter and brick mason, but I'd like to homestead. Maybe in Paddle River, Alberta. Talked to a man made it sound pretty enticing."

"And would that man happen to be Mr. Shipley?"

"Yes, sir. You know him?"

"Met him yesterday. In here. He talks a pretty good sell for Paddle River all right. Sounds pretty wild though. I don't believe I'll go that far."

Fred lingered, nursing his ale long after Mr. Clark took his leave. He was in no hurry to face his room. *Paddle River indeed. Too remote. Though I'm sure I could handle an ax and saw with the best of men. I could put my boys to work. Take some of the sass out of them.* The thought brought a smile to his lips.

The inevitable couldn't be delayed forever. Fred sighed, rose from the table, handed his glass to the bartender, nodded, and made his way back to the cabin.

He drew a clean white handkerchief from his pocket and clapped it to his nose. The smell in the room nearly turned his stomach. As quickly as he could he gathered buckets, dirty washcloths, towels, and thrust them out the door for the steward.

He drew the blanket more securely over his wife and little daughter. His family lay sprawled haphazardly across the lower bunks. They looked like so much flotsam tossed there by the sea. No one seemed to notice his presence, though he did hear a few moans. Apparently all slept. Except Amy.

He didn't see Amy anywhere. *Surely she didn't leave the cabin.* Fred hastened to check the small parlour and found his next-to-oldest daughter curled in a tight ball on the wooden settee. She had dragged a blanket from one of the bunks with which to cover herself, but it now lay on the floor. Fred picked it up and tucked it around the sleeping girl.

The odor in the parlour was decidedly better, though both rooms could stand a good airing. Fred would like to have gone on deck and breathed fresh air, but he wasn't that foolhardy. The storm grew less severe, but it could still deal some wicked punches. He settled himself in a chair, and after what seemed like endless time, fell asleep.

With daybreak the wind calmed and spirits lifted, though the mere mention of food earned Fred looks from his family strong enough to start another storm. He did convince them to drink some of the hot tea the steward brought at his request. Fred knew ale could settle seasick stomachs as well, but he knew even better he'd never convince his wife or children.

Rain pelted the windows half-heartedly as Amy took her father's hand and they made their way to the dining room. Tables were mostly empty this morning, testimony to the storm and seasickness. Attendants lingered to visit after serving them a hearty breakfast of ham, eggs, potatoes, toast, and lots of tea with cream and sugar.

"We'll be out of this storm, I think, in a couple more hours," said the waiter. "You'll be able to get your family out in the sunshine. That should make everyone feel better."

Fred exchanged looks with the waiter. He'd wager the man thought as he did. They'd be lucky indeed if they didn't encounter more storms before they reached the shores of Canada.

CHAPTER 4

Used to giving orders and having them obeyed without question, Fred expected no less of his boys. "Reginald! Cecil! You're not going to die. Get dressed! And help your little brothers into their clothes." He turned back at the door. "I'm going for water and soda crackers. You'd better be out of this cabin when I get back."

He softened his voice a bit before addressing his wife. "You and the girls need to get out of this cabin, too. The fresh air and sunshine will make you feel better."

Edith stifled a groan. She looked as bedraggled and miserable as a storm-drenched cat. Her children, with the exception of Amy, didn't look much better. *How long can seasickness last?* The storm seemed to be over, but no one had informed her stomach.

"Children, your father is right. We do need to get outdoors in the fresh air."

"Mother, I can get Annie dressed," said Amy. "And I'll help Eric. He can't find his shoes."

"Thank you, child." Edith sat on the edge of the bunk, smoothed her dark skirt, and tried to overcome dizziness as she attempted to make order of her hair. "I never thought to say this; I miss my little Norah so much, but I'm glad she isn't here to suffer this awful seasickness."

Fred visited Dolly in the six-bed infirmary. Seasickness complicated by the mumps left her pale, weak, and grumpy. She barely acknowledged her father's greeting. The nurse assured him his daughter was on the mend and by evening she'd feel better.

By dusk the Watts' family was able to smile again, sunshine and fresh air the tonic. If not a hundred percent recovered, at least they no longer turned green over the mention of food. Because of Fred's urging, backed by advice from the steward, all made their way to the dining room for supper. Aware many passengers had been seasick, the chef prepared clam chowder for those who wanted a lighter meal, and all the ginger tea one could drink.

After eating a hearty meal of roast beef, Fred folded his napkin, laid it aside, and stroked his mustache. "We'll go to the concert tonight. They cancelled it yesterday because of the storm, but generally there'll be one each evening. Passengers can take part."

"That sounds nice," Edith said. "I'm sorry we didn't bring Reg's accordion." She smiled at her son. "He might have entertained everyone with his lively polkas."

Reg flashed his mother a quick smile before shaking his head. "I'm sure there are those aboard who play much better than I do. My accordion deserved to be left behind. If I had to earn my supper with my playing, I'd starve."

"But you played real good," said Amy. "I wish I could play the accordion."

"Mother will give you piano lessons when we get settled in Canada," Father said. "Piano is much more suitable for you girls."

ॐ

Amy grinned at Reg and Cecil as she took a seat between them. "I really want to sing," said Amy. "I hope they play something we know."

Reg frowned and tugged the legs of his trousers lower. His scuffed, high-top shoes needed polishing. "I wanta sing, too. But I won't if we're the only ones."

Annie snuggled on her father's lap while he and Edith sat close together and held hands. Edith looked around at her family and smiled. The children had been encouraged to sing from the time they were toddlers.

The little boys sat Indian-style on the floor up front, elbows propped on knees, chin in hands. Eyes wide, they missed little as they watched the musicians.

A man stepped forward. "Welcome folks, to our concert. We hope to play some of your favorites. In awhile we'll take requests, and we hope you'll sing along." He smiled. "We're a little hampered tonight, our piano player is ill. If anyone here feels like filling in, we'd be most happy to have you join us."

Fred looked at Edith. "Would you feel like playing my dear?"

"Oh, I don't think so. They may play songs I don't know."

"Well, lets see how things go. But I think you could do very well."

A band consisting of saxophone, drums, fiddle, and trombone players, struck up a lively rendition of "When

You and I were Young, Maggie." Edith relaxed, and hummed softly to herself. By the time they'd played a few numbers familiar to her, she slipped out of her seat and quietly made her way to the piano.

The men in the band beamed and invited her to take the lead. She nodded, announced a number, and began to play, "Rock of Ages." When she finished people clapped and began to call out requests. They sang along as she played hymns interspersed with popular songs. Most numbers she knew from memory. But if she didn't, and the orchestra played a bar or two, she could pick it up and join them.

Near the end of the program the group played, "Froggie Went a Courtin,'" a fun song for the many youngsters in the audience. Edith could pick out her own children's voices, they knew all the lyrics and loved the silly song.

The entertainment for the evening ended with, "Blessed Assurance," a hymn written by the blind American poet, Fanny Crosby.

Amy poked her brother, Cecil. "I like singing hymns here. I don't have to sit so still, like in church."

"True. But I wish Mother had let us sing all of, "Froggie Went a Courtin.'"

"Not me, we'd a been singing all by ourselves."

Life aboard ship settled into routine: children became restless, adults forgot what day it was, and everyone yearned for the journey to end. Folks were often heard to utter, "Thanks be to God." If disparaging remarks were made, they were mostly ignored. Certainly Fred's offspring knew better than to fuss.

The SS *Lake Champlain* plowed through two more less-severe storms. This time the family fared better,

Edith and Dolly (now over the mumps) were the only ones to be seasick. Calm seas and sunshine were cause for rejoicing.

The sighting of another ship brought excitement and speculation among passengers, especially with the children. Adults turned it into a game and awarded a small prize to the first child to sight another vessel.

As the days wore on, Edith, Dolly, and Amy completed six pair of wool stockings for the family. The boys wandered the ship's hallways, searched the library for entertaining books, and read in out-of-the-way alcoves. Reg and Cecil found tales to read to their little brothers. Fred spent more and more time in the gentleman's smoking room.

A camaraderie, aided by a few drinks, developed between Fred, Mr. Shipley, and Mr. Clark. Sooner or later, talk of Paddle River, Alberta, cropped up in every conversation. Fred grew a bit weary of it, but he didn't say so. On the other hand, Mr. Clark seemed most interested, and kept the conversation fueled with pertinent questions.

"I should think, Mr. Watts, Paddle River would be of greater interest to you." Mr. Shipley leaned back in his chair and studied him. "Your boys should be of great benefit in establishing a homestead and getting a farm going. Plenty of land to be had for their future, too. And don't forget the university in Edmonton. Provide a good education for your sons."

Fred smiled and drained his glass, but he didn't reply.

"Well, if you get curious and want to know more, you can always write me. Mr. William Shipley, Paddle River, Alberta. It'll find me."

The captain announced they would reach Quebec Province in a few more hours. Passengers gathered on deck and clung to the rails, eager for a sight of land. Families huddled together and pulled their coats closer around them. They tried to ignore the cold wind, while their teeth chattered, shivers shook them, and their eyes watered.

A shout went up, "Look! Look!" The sight of seagulls and shore birds brought cheers.

"Please. Can't we go in?" Edith shivered and sneezed. "We'll all catch our death standing here in this wintry blast."

Fred put an arm around her. "We'll go to the dining room and ask for hot tea and biscuits. We can watch from there. Time enough for standing on deck when we get closer to port."

Edith breathed a sigh of relief. Fourteen long days on the ocean was about to end. Another four days on the river and they'd reach Montreal. The SS *Lake Champlain*, at 13 knots, wasn't the fastest ship to cross the Atlantic. A small smile played about her lips as she recalled her eldest child, Reg's, remark (said in jest) about this old tub sinking. Silently she directed a prayer of thanksgiving heavenward.

As the ship drew near the mouth of the Saint Lawrence River, passengers spotted an iceberg. The boys clamored to go back on deck and get a better look at this phenomenon they'd never seen before.

"May we go too, Father?" Amy said. "Please? I want to see the iceberg."

"What's an iceberg?" said Leslie.

"Button up your coats." Fred lifted Annie in his arms, and pulled the bonnet closer around her ears.

"We'll all go out on deck where we can get a better look."

A subtle change took place as the ship entered the river. The vessel slowed and rolled more gently. Chunks of blue-colored ice, too small to be called an iceberg, floated in the water.

Seagulls, more numerous now, dipped, turned, dived, and lifted to ride the air currents overhead. Their shrill screeches welcomed or scolded, depending on if people fed them, or ignored them.

Some passengers did throw bits of bread their way. Fred hadn't the money for such foolishness. If he bought bread, it would be for the mouths of his family.

Gradually the river began to narrow, and land appeared in the distance. Rolling hills became visible, green with grass, and in places, colorful with wildflowers. Trees dotted the landscape, and far beyond them, snowcapped mountains glistened. Clear aqua-colored water mirrored a cloudless blue sky. Islands emerged in the midst of the channel.

Wide-eyed, Amy Gladys tried to take it all in.

Everyone appeared to be on deck watching as the big ship eased in to a berth beside the waterfront. As in Liverpool, workmen, clad in overalls, shouted instructions, and scurried along the dock. Drivers with large draft horses hitched to wagons waited to receive cargo from the ship.

Fred grinned and winked at Edith. "I know you're sorry to leave this old tub behind, but we're in Canada. "With a bit of luck, tonight we'll all sleep in a real bed."

CHAPTER 5

A fter fourteen days on the Atlantic Ocean, and four more steaming up the Saint Lawrence River, it felt strange to walk on surfaces that didn't list to one side or the other. And even more astonishing to find their gait resembled that of a sailor too long at sea. They entered the terminus building and quailed at the sight of the long line of immigrants waiting to get through customs. After what seemed an eternity, Fred hurried away to make sure their trunks were sent to the train depot.

Edith bent, hugged Eric, and straightened his tunic. He had a hole in the knee of one stocking, and his short pants needed to be handed down to Leslie. Her children were growing right out of their clothes. She bit her lip and sighed, her thoughts ran to the future, of the need to sew as soon as they got settled. She hoped material wouldn't be too expensive.

Percy pushed the shaggy brown hair out of his eyes. All her boys needed haircuts. Edith reached out to smooth locks, so much like her own, back from Reg's forehead before she settled amongst her children on the hard wooden bench.

The needs of her daughters were a little less evident, but they too would require new clothes before the start of the next school term. And shoes. How are we to keep them all in shoes?

Edith looked up and smiled as she watched her handsome husband stride toward them, a newspaper tucked under one arm. It might be a struggle to keep their lively brood fed and clothed, but Edith loved being a mother, and she thanked God every day for their healthy children.

"Well, my dears. Shall we become landlubbers again, and see what the city has to offer? I've scanned the *Montreal Star* and made some inquiries. I believe if we walk a block or two—"

Edith halted his flow of words. "We have to wait for Amy Gladys, she'll be back in a moment or two."

Amy had never been in a toilet such as this in her entire life. She puzzled over it as long as she could— necessity won out and matters were taken care of. But what was that large brown box on the wall? And why did it have a chain hanging down? Curiosity got the better of her and she pulled the chain. She couldn't believe her ears and eyes. Gravity lost its hold. She flew from the room, shrieking as only a terrified seven-year-old can, "It's going to flood! It's going to flood!"

A red-faced Edith tried to shush her daughter as the panicky child grabbed her around the waist. She spoke quietly and smoothed damp curly hair from Amy's forehead. "Shhh—shhh. It's all right! It's not going to flood."

Folks tried to hide their smiles, but amusement overcame some and a few snickers were heard. Fred, himself, wanted to laugh. The sight of his daughter erupting from the water closet, coat-tail billowing behind her, was just too funny.

A warning look from Edith sobered him and he kept a straight face as he bent and placed his lips close to Amy's ear. "It's all right, little one. You did nothing wrong. That's the way things work in Canada."

Amy released her mother and looked at her father with round solemn eyes. "Well, all right then."

Fred pulled a watch from his vest pocket and checked the time. "We may be able to catch a trolley. Montreal is the largest city in all the provinces. We won't be here long enough to see much, but we'll visit some of the sights."

Edith shivered and pulled her coat tighter around her. The sun shone, but the air felt cold and snow lay in patches on the ground. Dolly and Amy huddled close for warmth.

"I'll see to getting us rooms; I've marked a few inns advertised in the *Star*. We'll soon be warm and cozy enough," Fred said.

With little Norah back in England, two-year-old Annie once more became the baby of the family. Her father reached for her, but she pushed his hand away. "No! Annie walk."

Fred laughed. "Ah, so you're now a big girl? Very well, you shall walk."

Keeping an eye on her offspring, while in a strange city, and especially one so large, challenged Edith. But the older children looked out for their younger siblings, and all knew to obey their father without question.

"All right, you older boys, grab a satchel. Reg, you, Cecil, and Percy take the lead, but not too fast. Make sure we're all following you. Dolly, you and Amy walk behind your brothers; take Eric and Leslie by the hand. And boys, mind your manners." Fred and Edith brought up the rear, holding tightly to Annie's hands; their steps shortened to accommodate their young daughter.

The streets closest to the waterfront were narrow and teeming with horse-drawn lorries and men intent on business. Most of the buildings lining the streets were modern, made of gray limestone mined from a nearby quarry. But now and then an older structure appeared.

"Oh, look!" said Edith.

"Children, stop," Fred ordered. "This is history. I dare say you won't see this again."

A quaint old domicile made of small boulders cemented together with an abundance of mortar stood as testimony to the ingenuity of Montreal's forebears. The stones were of different colors, giving the structure a mottled appearance, not seen in any other style of architecture.

Cecil ran his fingers over the rocks. "Reg, how thick do you suppose these walls are?"

"Maybe three feet?"

"Plaque here says the walls are three feet thick and it was built in the 1600's," said Dolly.

"I wish we could go inside," said Amy.

"Not me," said Cecil. "What if this pile a rocks decided to crumble? You'd be smashed flatter'n a fritter. Anyway, it says no admittance."

They walked on, farther than Fred had intended, his children chattering, giggling, and exclaiming over the sights. A tired Annie submitted to being carried, and dozed on her father's shoulder.

Edith smiled as she strolled beside her husband. She didn't mind walking as long as it was away from the waterfront with its wilderness of masts and spars, freight sheds, huge cranes, grain elevators, and other strange-looking facilities for handling cargoes in the shortest amount of time possible. She longed for the familiar. "I know there's much to see and do here, but it's all so daunting. I'm glad we're only visiting this big city."

Fred dug in his pocket and extracted coins for their ride on the trolley bus. Another first for his family.

"Oh, Fred, look! That lovely old church."

"That's the great cathedral of Notre Dame ," the driver called out. "On the other side of the street, that big building is the Bank of Montreal." Parks, called squares, dotted the city, all of them lovely with trees, flowers, monuments, and numerous paths.

Fred exited first and helped his family down the steps of the streetcar. Edith carried Annie, and Fred managed two satchels. Reg took a third as they made their way up the block to a modest inn.

A buxom proprietress welcomed them, introduced herself as Mrs. Harris, and led the way upstairs to their rooms. "Water closet is at the end of the hall there. Plenty of hot water. Don't think you'll have to share." She smiled. "One other couple staying; honeymooners. They're out seeing the sights, won't be back 'til late." She chuckled before turning and gliding back along the hallway, long skirts dusting the floor. "Enjoy your stay," she called.

The well-appointed bedrooms reminded Edith of home. Home in England. What's my little Norah doing right now? Does she miss her momma? Or has she forgotten me? She walked to the window and pretended to look out as she struggled to swallow the lump in her throat.

Hand-pieced quilts in bright calicos topped the ruffle-skirted beds. Crisp white dimity curtains decorated the small-paned windows. A miniature writing desk nestled between two high-backed cane-bottomed chairs.

Fred removed his hat and coat and hung them in the wardrobe. "Well, children, you'll have a modicum of privacy tonight. Your mother and I will share this room. Annie can sleep here in the crib." He glanced at Edith, who had turned back to face the room. "Dolly, you and Amy will take the room next to ours. And boys, the third bedroom with two double beds will be yours. Arrange to sleep however you want."

Edith removed her hat, looked in the mirror above the tall dresser, and smoothed her hair. She fingered the crocheted scarf atop the bureau and admired the pineapple design. Her stomach gave a disgusting rumble, reminding her they hadn't eaten. *If only we didn't have to go out in the cold again. This room is nice and warm, and I'm so weary...But hungry children must be...*

A knock on the door interrupted her thoughts.

"Don't mean to intrude," said Mrs. Harris. "But I wondered if you might like to come down to my kitchen for supper? I've a big pot of corn chowder. It's thick and rich; I put cheddar cheese in it."

Edith moved beside Fred and placed a hand on his arm. "Mrs. Harris that would be lovely, but we don't want to put you out." *Is she planning to charge us? Paper didn't say anything about meals.*

" 'Tis no trouble. It'll go to waste if you don't eat it; I expected my niece and her family, but got word they're not coming." She lifted a hand to tuck a stray wisp of hair behind her ear. "It's snowing again, and I thought maybe ... with your young 'ns ... an all ... you'd, well, be my guests."

"Mrs. Harris, that's very generous of you, ma'am." Fred gave her his winning smile. "We're most happy to accept."

"Yes, thank you," Edith added.

"Good, then. Come down when you're ready. Turn right at the bottom of the stairs and follow the hallway all the way to the back. Just give the door a push and come on into the kitchen."

℘

Edith never ate better tasting chowder. Her children liked it as well, if their empty bowls were testimony. Most finished second and even third helpings. Mrs. Harris made sure each one had generous slices of baked bread slathered with pear jam. She placed on the table pots of tea, brewed to English perfection. Fred stirred thick cream and spoons of sugar into his third cup.

As a last gesture, Mrs. Harris gave each child a peppermint stick.

The Watts' children sounded like a well-rehearsed litany as one thank you after another echoed along the table. Not to be outdone, Annie added a toothy grin, waved her chubby fist in the air and promptly popped one end of the candy in her mouth.

"Thank you, Mrs. Harris, that was a wonderful meal." Edith began helping clear the table, assisted by her girls. Fred and the boys expressed their thanks once more and excused themselves.

℘

Edith sank into the warm water in the bathtub and closed her eyes. All her children had bathed, most with her assistance, and were now in bed. She had helped her girls shampoo their long hair. Leslie and Eric had complained she scrubbed their heads too hard.

She hadn't been able to resist washing her own hair, though she knew it likely wouldn't dry before morning. Refreshed and clean-smelling, she rubbed her long tresses vigorously with the towel; then wove her hair loosely in a braid, letting it hang down her back.

Dressed in a clean nightgown, she knelt and washed the tub. Satisfied all was in order and thankful the worst of the journey lay behind them, Edith breathed a prayer of thanksgiving and hurried down the hallway. Her husband, also freshly bathed, awaited her.

Chapter 6

Amy rubbed the sleep from her eyes and slid from the warm bed she shared with Dolly. Hands outstretched, feeling her way in the dark, she padded barefoot across the room, opened the door a crack and peered out. A naked light bulb hung from the ceiling above the hallway, casting a dim glow on the linoleum below. She made her way to the water closet, shivering, and walking on tiptoes.

Before she could return to her room, she met her mother in the passageway. Without uttering a sound, Amy wrapped her small arms around her mother's middle and squeezed. Edith hugged her daughter and smoothed the hair back from her temples as Amy gazed up at her.

"My precious little Amy," Edith whispered.

"Mama, are we going on the train today?"

"Yes, love. And you must wake your sister. We need to be up and dressed before your father wants to shave."

"Mama? When will Father go after Baby Norah?"

Edith's eyes filled and she hugged Amy a little tighter. "God willing, it will be soon. But you mustn't trouble your father by asking him. Do you understand, my daughter?"

Amy nodded, cheek against her mother's breast.

Back in the bedroom, Amy turned on a lamp and shook Dolly awake. "Get up! Mother says."

The girls hurried to dress. "Button my pinafore, then I'll button you," said Dolly.

"I think my pinnie's dirty," said Amy. "But I'll keep my coat on, no one will see."

"Mine's dirty too. But we can't trouble Mother." Dolly heaved an exaggerated sigh. "I wish we'd hurry up and get there. Wherever *there* is."

The girls chattered and twittered like robins in the springtime, until Amy sobered and squeezed her sister's arm. "Dolly, do you think we'll have to wait long before Father goes to get baby Norah? I asked Mother, and she said not to bother him with that question."

Dolly studied her shoes. When she looked back at Amy her eyes were teary. "I think our father spent all his money getting *us* here. I heard him tell Mother he's almost broke, and that it's a good thing train tickets were included with ship's passage. I think he has to earn enough money first, and, Amy Gladys, I don't think you should ask Mother either. It makes her sad."

Amy hung her head. "I won't ask her no more. Dolly, do you think we'll ever go back to England?"

"Not me! I'm not crossin' that old ocean again. I'll run away first."

"But don't you want to see our grandparents again?"

"Not if I have to cross the ocean. Grandmother Rampling and Grandmother Watts both said they'd meet us in heaven if we don't meet on earth. I reckon that's where I'll see them."

"But that'll be forever and ever. Oh, Dolly, I wish we hadn't left England."

"Don't cry! If you cry, I'll cry and Father will be upset...."

A light knock sounded, and their mother pushed open the bedroom door. "Girls, go downstairs and wait in the lobby when you're ready," she whispered. "Go quietly—others may be sleeping. I'll tell the boys to meet us there as well. Your father and I will be down directly."

ॐ

Amy and Dolly fished the funnies from the *Montreal Star* and scarcely looked up when their brothers entered the room. Reg and Cecil grabbed sections of the paper before sitting on the couch. Eric, Leslie, and Percy settled on the floor and urged their sisters to finish with the funny paper.

They all looked up when their parents entered the room. Amy thought her father seemed especially happy this morning. He wore a wide grin as he handled all their luggage as if it contained feathers. Edith followed in his wake, holding Annie by the hand as they descended the stairway one step at a time.

Reg and Cecil stood, ready to assume responsibility for some of the baggage. Amy and Dolly rose and waited for their mother to lead the way.

"Where's Eric?" said Edith.

"Eric? He was here a minute ago," said Reg.

Fred scanned the room. "Well, he's not here now. Why weren't you watching? If we're late..."

Edith laid a hand on Fred's arm. "Maybe he's gone back upstairs."

"I'll run upstairs and fetch him," said Reg as he raced away.

"If we're late for the train," Fred fumed. "I've a notion to whip the lot of you."

Amy and Dolly paled, Leslie began to cry, Cecil looked stubborn, and Percy chewed his lip and sidled closer to his brother. Edith started to speak when a red-faced Reg pounded down the stairs.

"He's not up there. I looked in the toilet and all the bedrooms. I can't find him."

Edith put a hand to her heart. "Surely he wouldn't venture outdoors," she said. "Where could he be? We have to find him."

Fred's face looked like a thundercloud about to rupture when an unaware Eric traipsed down the hallway from the kitchen followed by a smiling Mrs. Harris. "Oh, you folks are ready to leave aren't you? Well, this young man came to tell me goodbye. He thanked me again for the meal yesterday. Such a little gentleman! You've trained your children well." She beamed on the parents. "I've fixed a few biscuits for you to take on your journey. If you get to Montreal again, I hope you'll come see me."

Edith recovered herself enough to smile at Mrs. Harris and cast a warning glance at Fred. "That's very kind of you ma'am. I'm sure our children will enjoy the treat."

Not wanting to appear a boor, Fred switched expressions faster than an actor on stage and in a pleasant tone said, "Yes, thank you, Mrs. Harris. You are most generous."

Reg grabbed up two satchels, and Cecil quickly hefted the remaining bag. Dolly reached for Leslie, and Amy gripped Eric by the hand. Edith carried Annie; Fred tipped his hat to Mrs. Harris and ushered his family out the door.

An orange glow in the east promised a nice day. A light dusting of fresh snow lay on the ground and a chilly breeze had the family shivering and pulling their coats closer around them.

As soon as they were on the sidewalk, Eric yanked his hand from Amy's grasp. "Ouch! Amy Gladys, don't squeeze so hard! That hurts!"

About to give his children the lambasting he thought they deserved, Fred hesitated when he looked up the street. A matching pair of bays clip-clopped their way up the avenue, pulling a cab. He signaled, and the driver guided the team to the curb.

"We want to go to the Canadian Pacific train depot; but if you can stop at a market on the way, I'd like to run in for a minute and purchase a few things."

"Certainly, sir. There's a grocery in the next block. I can stop there, sir. Not a bit out of our way."

They rode in utter silence as the horses pulled the conveyance along the nearly deserted streets. Annie popped a thumb in her mouth and clung to her mother. Snow lay in patches along the route; early morning sunlight glinted off the shiny surface. They met a milk wagon, pulled along by a swaybacked old nag. The driver waved and called a cheery greeting as the vehicles passed. A short while later the cab driver stopped the horses in front of the emporium.

The children watched in wide-eyed wonder as Father entered the market and returned with a large sack, but no one dared ask him what he had purchased, fearing to further anger him. Even little Annie remained unusually quiet.

When they approached a magnificent old cathedral, Edith broke the silence. "Oh, what a beautiful edifice. Do you suppose it's Anglican? Or maybe it's Roman Catholic. Wouldn't it be wonderful to go inside?

Fred glowered. "Well, my dear, if you'd married a rich man perhaps you could do that."

Edith touched his hand, and smiled into his eyes. "But, my husband, I chose you."

"Ah, Edith, you're one in a million." Fred took her small hand and tucked it in the crook of his arm. "I do wish we had the time to take in more of the sights. I'd love to take you and our children out to Mount Royal Park; it's the largest and grandest park in all of Montreal. Did you know, the city is named for the snowcapped mountain in the background?"

Fred drew her even closer and whispered in her ear, "Someday, we'll come back to this island; just you and me—for the honeymoon we didn't have." Edith blushed.

The horses drew the carriage up in front of the train depot and halted as the driver pulled on the lines and called a distinctive, "Whoa." The man hopped down from the high seat and hurried around to help his passengers. Fred exited first and offered his hand to Edith.

"Children, stay close to your mother and me. And Eric, if you wander off again without permission from your mother or me, you'll get a whipping. This journey isn't over, and I haven't time to waste looking for you." Fred pulled out his watch and checked the time. "We've half an hour before departure time. You'd better be glad you didn't cause us to be late."

The big black engine belched steam as the locomotive sat on the tracks. The conductor took tickets and helped each person to board. He retrieved the small stool used for boarding, clung to the hand rail and waved his free arm up and down. The engineer blew the whistle, a warning the train was ready to depart. Slowly, but steadily the train began to chug forward.

Amy squeezed in between her mother and the window with her nose almost touching the glass. She watched wide-eyed as the city slid past in colors more vibrant than Grandmother Rampling's picture post-cards on the stereopticon. "Look at that big house," Amy said. "There's red lamps in all the windows."

The Watts' family occupied three seats close together: Father held Leslie on his lap and sat facing Amy. Dolly took the seat next to Father; Percy filled the remaining space. Mother held Annie on her lap, and a subdued Eric leaned against her. Reginald and Cecil took the seat across the aisle. Later they'd change. Everyone wanted to look out the window.

All the seats in the parlor car were filled. A very wrinkled, white-haired old lady beamed at them; while the gentleman seated beside her kept his nose buried in the newspaper and ignored everyone around him. Other passengers gave a friendly nod and returned to their own musings. A tiny baby and two nearly grown children were the only other youngsters in the car.

The train started across a high bridge spanning a wide river. "Mother, look! That boat down there looks smaller than the one Father carved for Leslie."

"Oh, does it?"

Amy tugged on her sleeve, but Mother steadfastly looked across the aisle. "Reginald, would you like to trade places with me, and sit here beside Amy?"

Reg settled beside his sister and peered over her shoulder at the water far below. "Amy Gladys, can you see the bucket on that boat in the middle of the river?"

"What?" She stared for a moment before she realized he joshed. "No, but I can see the fish swimming in the water," she came back at him.

Amy forgot they hadn't eaten breakfast until her stomach rumbled. Maybe Father heard, or more likely his own hunger reminded him. He reached for the sack between his feet and doled out cheese and bread to his family. A juicy red apple topped the menu. Amy thought she'd never tasted anything so good as she bit into the tart sweetness.

CHAPTER 7

The train rattled and clattered over the rails; the engine belched black smoke like some fire-eating behemoth with indigestion. Fred relaxed in his seat beside the open window, unmindful of the cinders drifting his way. He liked what he saw: prairie with verdant spring grass and wildflowers rippling in the light wind. Even more satisfying were the farms spread out over acres of rich ground.

The only trees seen on the prairie were grouped around farmhouses or the willows and cottonwoods that grew naturally along the banks of streams and rivers. Tall planted poplars swayed in the breeze and acted as a windbreak for farmers and their animals.

Large barns, silos, and two-story farm houses dotted the landscape. Fred's children loved seeing the animals: horses, oxen, cattle, chickens, pigs, sheep, and goats. Especially the goats. Fred reached and pulled Annie onto his lap; she giggled when he pointed out the kid goats romping around a barn lot.

The engineer blew a long blast on the whistle. "What a mournful sound," said Edith.

Fred disagreed, but he didn't say so. To him the whistle meant progress. It was music to his ears as the train took them closer and closer to their destination.

They reached another crossing, and a loaded farm wagon pulled by a matched team of Percherons waited patiently for the train to pass. The driver, seated on the high wooden seat, waved to passengers.

Shadows lengthened as the train pulled into the depot of yet another prairie hamlet. "Don't leave the train," Fred cautioned his children. "But you can walk around a bit and stretch your limbs."

Reg stood and stretched, arms over his head. "We're in Ontario province aren't we? How much longer before we reach Winnipeg?" At thirteen, going on fourteen, Reg was almost as tall as his father. "How long before we reach this place where we're going? Mileta, is it?"

Fred shook his head and answered with one non-committal word. "Depends." It could depend on a lot of things. In truth he didn't know how long it would take, three or four days anyway. Longer than any of them wanted to be on this dirty old train. He saw the weariness on the face of his wife, and knew himself to be a fortunate man, blessed by God with an uncomplaining mate.

The train hissed and shivered as wheels began to turn accompanied by the chug-chug-chug, as it gained momentum. Four Indians, dressed in brown buckskins, rode up on their ponies and sat watching the train pull away from the depot.

"Are those real Indians?" said Leslie.

"Yes, son. Those are real Indians. They're people just like you and me."

Fred changed seats and sat beside Edith. She smiled up at him and took his hand. After nine children, she still had the looks to turn him to mush.

Their children shuffled around and rearranged the order of seating. They too, looked tired, but at least stomachs remained on an even keel, and appetites hadn't suffered. The bread, cheese, and apples were gone. So was the bag of peanuts Fred bought from a vendor. Nothing remained but a sack-full of empty shells.

The sun became an orange glow in the west, and soon after darkness settled over the land. After taking turns in the necessary, located in the far corner of the railcar, a compartment not much wider than a bread box, they began to settle for the night.

The porter came through and stoked the fire in the small stove at the front of the car. He passed out small pillows and blankets, one to a seat. The pillows didn't help much, but the blankets gave a measure of comfort. Annie curled up with her head resting in her mother's lap. Leslie took advantage of one pillow and his father's leg. The older children scrunched together beneath a blanket, and leaned against one another. Edith rested her head on Fred's shoulder. Fred stretched his legs full length and disciplined his mind for sleep. Worn out from constant travel, by midnight, each member of the Watts' family had fallen into a fitful slumber.

Long before morning, Fred woke to rain pounding on the roof of the railway car. Every joint in his body felt stiff as an iron poker. With care, he repositioned Edith and eased to his feet. In exaggerated slowness, he stretched and looked around at his sleeping family.

Surprised to find they now had the entire car to themselves, Fred bent to add more coal to the fire. Sometime during the time he dozed, the two couples sharing their parlor car had left the train or retired to a berth.

Leslie and Annie had found their own means of comfort, reasonable to them. They now lay on a seat Fred hadn't paid for, beneath a blanket not theirs. Annie lay knees bent, rump stuck in the air, and a thumb in her mouth. Leslie had managed to confiscate two pillows; he now slept full length on the bench, with both cushions tucked beneath his head.

Fred grinned. His children were nothing if not resourceful. Instead of sitting stiffly upright, like so many sticks of kindling, they had found a way to lie down. Cecil's head peaked from one end of a bench; Reg's curly brown hair stuck out beneath the blanket on the opposite corner. Closer inspection revealed Eric wedged in beside Cecil. Feet had to be close to faces, but his sons didn't seem to mind.

On the bench across from them, Dolly and Amy snuggled spoon fashion beneath their blanket. Percy occupied the other end of the seat, his half of the blanket pulled high.

"Fred?" Edith whispered his name. "You can't sleep?"

He turned at the sound of his name and closed the distance to again sit beside his wife. Taking her hand in his, he gently caressed the back with his thumb. "I'm sorry you're having to endure these deplorable sleeping conditions. You deserve better. Someday … I'll … "

Edith placed two fingers across his lips. "Shhhh … We'll be just fine."

છ

Fred couldn't remember spending a longer night, not even while in the army. If only he had access to a bar, this trip would be more tolerable. He brushed his trousers, squared his shoulders, and ushered his family to the dining car. A simple breakfast shouldn't be too expensive. Hot tea and a little food in the belly should brighten everyone's outlook.

"Good morning, sir, madam." The waiter placed menus before them. "I trust you had a good night."

Fred scanned the menu and frowned, prices were higher than he imagined. A fried egg for each of them, toast, milk for the children, and a pot of tea came to twenty five cents. He'd have to see about buying provisions from the vendors. Perhaps at the next scheduled stop, he could buy something for a reasonable price.

The waiter withdrew after placing the food before them. Edith sat with hands in her lap and waited. All but Annie followed her example. Annie chortled and reached for her spoon, which Percy, sitting next to her, quickly shoved out of reach.

Fred lowered his head; his muttered words sounded more like an apology than a prayer. "Father-bless-this-food-in-your-name-we-pray. Amen."

Edith smiled, unfolded her napkin and laid it in her lap. She spooned a bite of egg and offered it to Annie.

"Take your time," Fred admonished. "Eat slowly, this is the only time you'll get to have a meal here." He looked pointedly at each child. "Today will mean more sitting. More riding. Just like yesterday. We've got a couple more days on this train, then—with a bit of luck—we'll be on the home stretch. No more traveling."

Passengers straggled in and the dining room filled. Fred cleared his throat. "I suppose we'd better give up our table."

The porter came through the parlor with more coal for the fire. "Good morning. Looks like we're in for a bit of rain. Always makes things seem a bit gloomy, eh?" He gathered pillows and neatly folded blankets. "I'll see if I can't find a newspaper and some magazines for you to look at." He smiled. "And perhaps something for the bairns. I have six of me own—it can be tough travelin.'"

The engineer sounded a long blast on the whistle as the train approached a hamlet and rolled on through without stopping.

By mid-afternoon the rain ceased; clouds broke apart and the sun came out. Finally, after passing through two more villages, the train stopped beside a sizeable loading dock. The porter walked through and called out, "North Bay, North Bay, Ontario. We'll be here forty minutes."

Fred turned to Edith. "Let's get off here and stretch our legs. Judging by the station house, I'd say this is a sizeable town. Maybe there's a market nearby, stuff has to be cheaper than on this train."

His brood following in close procession, Fred checked the time on the big wall clock, and led the way through the station house and to the street beyond. Reg lifted Annie, and Fred swung Leslie into his arms; Eric and Amy trotted to keep up with their father, mother, and older siblings.

Back on the train once more, Fred sighed in satisfaction. He'd purchased enough food to last them until they reached Winnipeg: jerky, a brick of cheese, a box of soda crackers, raisins, a bottle of milk, and last but not least, long ropes of licorice for his children.

Fred took out his knife and cut chunks of jerky and cheese to hand to each child. *I can't do much about the hard benches,* he thought. *But no one will be hungry tonight. And maybe I can persuade the porter to give us an extra blanket or two.*

CHAPTER 8

Amy Gladys followed her mother off the train. Next came Dolly, trailed in close succession by her brothers; Reg, entrusted with part of their luggage, brought up the rear. Fred wore an expansive grin as he watched the last of his family alight on the station platform.

He gave Annie a light squeeze and handed her to Edith. "Well, here we are. Winnipeg! The wheat capitol of all Canada. Rail center as well—all the trains come in here." He cleared his throat. "And I've got to see about getting us on one for Melita. Doubt that's going to happen today. Maybe not even tomorrow. Well, the sooner I ask, the sooner we'll know."

Reg and Cecil took charge of their little brothers; Amy and Dolly held hands. All walked briskly to keep up with their father. "Wait here." Fred motioned to a bench. "This should only take a few minutes. I'll make sure our trunks are tagged to go with us on the train to our final destination."

Fred marched up to the ticket master and inquired, "How soon can I get reservations for my wife and me and our eight children for Melita? And I have four trunks needing to go as well."

"And your name would be?"

"Watts. Fredrick Watts. We just came in on the train from Montreal."

"Well, Mr. Watts, there's a train leaving for Melita at six in the morning. Do you wish to purchase fares now?"

The ticket master took the money, and shoved tickets across the counter. "Four trunks, you say?" He handed Fred four tags. "Go through that door over there. Trunks'll be in there if you came in on the train from Montreal. Give the tags to the handler; he'll fasten them on for you and your trunks will go to Melita."

"Thank you."

The baggage room appeared nearly filled with trunks, suitcases, crates, and an odd assortment of luggage. Things to be loaded on the train, ready to leave, were stacked on one side of the room, and things most recently taken off and waiting to be picked up were on the other half. A wide painted stripe down the middle presumably kept them separated.

Claim checks in hand, Fred approached a baggage handler. "I have four trunks in here somewhere that I want to go on to Melita on tomorrow's train."

"Uh, huh. Okay." He took the checks from Fred. "Do you see 'em anywhere?"

"That looks like three of my trunks over there underneath that high window."

The man wove his way over to the trunks. "Says Fredrick Watts for Winnipeg right enough. You say you want these tagged to go to Melita?

"Yes, sir. I have the tags right here. But there's a fourth trunk somewhere. I'd a thought it would be with the three, but I don't see it."

"Is that it over there in the corner?" said the handler as he walked over to look. "Nope, name says Bates." He looked around. People were claiming their baggage, workers moved trunks onto hand-carts and pushed them out the double doors. The room emptied fast. Still he hadn't located the Watts' fourth trunk.

"I'm sorry, Mr. Watts. It doesn't seem to be here. You'll need to see the ticket master and file a missing baggage claim." He grimaced and scanned the room again. "Do you know what was in the missing trunk?"

Fred felt his face getting hot. "Not without checking the three trunks that are here. The trunks all look alike."

"Well, sir, come on over here and lets see what's what."

Fred unlocked the near trunk and lifted the lid. "Clothes." The handler watched as he opened the second trunk. "Looks like bedding. You got anything really valuable in any of these trunks?"

"My cameras and equipment. I'm a professional photographer."

The employee gave him a sharp look. "Well, lets hope all that's in the next one you open."

Fred took a deep breath, twisted the key in the padlock, and heaved the lid upward. Dishes, and kitchen necessities.

"I'm sorry, sir. But we'll track it down. May take a few days to get it to you, but I've never known of anything to be permanently lost." He attached tags to the three trunks and directed a handler to move them to the proper location for transport to Melita.

Reg met his father coming from the baggage room. "Is anything wrong, Father? It seems like we've been waiting a long time."

"Yes! Plenty is wrong!" Fred snapped. "And there'll be more wrong if you don't get back there with your mother and help watch your brothers and sisters."

Reg turned red, but made no reply as he turned on his heel and retreated back to his mother.

"Did you find your father? Did he say what's taking so long?" inquired Edith.

"I'm sorry, Mother. He didn't say. But I think there's some kind of trouble."

"Trouble? Oh, dear." She circled her arms around the children nearest her and drew them closer. Silently, Edith asked God for help.

Fred, face and ears red as wind-blasted embers, eyes ablaze, strode up to his family. "Well! The railroad has lost the trunk with my photography equipment. My cameras. Everything! Now what am I supposed to do? How am I supposed to keep the wolf from the door if I can't take pictures? *How?* I ask you!"

Edith paled and plopped Annie on Amy's lap. She rose to stand before her husband. "Oh, Fred! I'm sorry. This is terrible!" She placed a hand on his chest. "But surely they'll find it, and get it to you. Won't they?"

"That's what they say. But when? If, in fact, they can even find it." He scowled. "How can they lose one big trunk? Our trunks were all together. Maybe some sticky-fingered railroad employee decided to help himself to some very fine equipment. *My* equipment."

"Father, did you have it insured?" said Reg.

"Of course, I had it insured. Do you think I'm a complete imbecile?"

"Well, then … won't they … "

"Yes— If it isn't recovered—they'll replace the cameras. But that can take weeks! Maybe months. What do you suggest I do in the meantime? Take pictures with an old box camera?"

Tears brimmed in Amy's eyes; Father's anger scared her. She hugged her little sister tighter and whispered in her ear, "Don't cry, Annie. I love you! Please don't cry. Father isn't mad at you."

Annie twisted around, encircled Amy's neck in a bear-hug and planted a noisy kiss on her cheek. "No cry, A-mee. I wuv you."

"Fred, I think they'll find it. You know all four trunks were at the depot in Montreal." Edith gripped his arm, her eyes solemn as they met his. "Maybe they've already discovered their error and even now the trunk is on its way to Winnipeg."

"Edith! My eternal optimist." He took a deep breath and let it out in a rush. "I hope you're right—I really need those cameras. I have a letter of promise from the Commissioner of Immigration to buy all the pictures I can take in and around Melita."

Fred stroked his chin. "Well, it won't help to stand here jawin' about it, will it?" Fred inspected his children and motioned for his older boys to muster the hand-baggage. He reached for Annie, swung her high, and settled her on his arm.

"While talking to the ticket master, I learned another little morsel of good news! The city transit system is on strike. The hacks are taking advantage and charging exorbitant prices. We'll be walking. If we're lucky, there'll be an affordable inn nearby."

"My dear, perhaps what we all need is a hot cup of tea?" Edith smiled at her husband, her eyes warm and compelling. "Mother always said everything looks better over a good cup of tea."

Leslie and Eric crowded close to their mother, one on each side of her. Edith bent to hug them, and nodded approval when they grabbed a fistful of her skirt as Fred started the family's promenade up Main Street.

It was the middle of May, and the sun shone warm. People didn't appear in a hurry; they smiled and nodded as they met others on the street. Amy and Dolly held hands as they walked along behind Father. Amy smiled shyly when she met a little girl her size.

Fred stopped in front of a teahouse and lowered Annie to the sidewalk. He held his small daughter by the hand as he opened the door for Edith and the remainder of his brood to enter first.

The proprietor greeted them and quickly arranged two tables to accommodate his customers. A wooden highchair and boxes to boost the small fry appeared almost as if pulled from thin air.

"We'll have tea, please," said Fred.... He tugged at his mustache, glanced at Edith, and then added in a rush, " Three mugs of milk for the younger children, and a plate of chocolate biscuits too, please."

Amy and Dolly laced their tea with milk and spoons of sugar. Mother added a scant amount of sugar and milk to her tea, as did Reg, Cecil, and Percy. There were biscuits to go around and Amy savored the taste of chocolate melting on her tongue. Father added spoons of sugar to his tea, but divided his sweet cake between Annie and Leslie.

Amy thought her grandmother Rambling a wise woman. Things did seem better after a hot cup of tea. And the milk and biscuits helped, too.

Father lost his angry scowl, and even smiled as Reginald quickly gathered the baggage without being asked. Percy volunteered to carry one satchel. Cecil lifted Annie from the highchair and settled her on his hip. Father's hands were unencumbered.

Back on the sidewalk, Fred took Edith's hand and tucked it through his arm. No need to belabor the point, Fred thought, but how am I to provide for my family if I can't take pictures? Tomorrow would be another arduous day of train travel. Fred had made previous arrangements for his family when he visited Melita the year before, but after months of absence, who knew what awaited them in the small village?

CHAPTER 9

Edith stood as if rooted to the station platform; her face paled and for a moment she forgot herself and simply stared. Melita. Could this small rural community—in the midst of endless prairie—be the place her husband had chosen for them? The town she'd crossed an ocean and half a continent to make her home? Heart already sore from leaving behind Baby Norah, she swallowed the lump in her throat and plastered a brave smile on her face.

Amy gripped Dolly's hand, and the two girls moved closer to their mother. The boys stood together in a tight knot and waited for their father to issue orders. Annie twisted in Fred's arms and removed her thumb from her mouth long enough to utter one word.

"Doggy."

A black and white, shorthaired mongrel crossed the train tracks, trotted full-length of the loading platform, nose to ground, tail wagging furiously, and disappeared behind the station house. Leslie and Eric watched as though they'd never seen a dog before, until their father barked.

"Well! That dog knows how to move and we need to do the same. Unless I'm greatly mistaken we have a house waiting for us." Fred expanded his chest and handed Annie to Edith. "Reg, you and Cecil come with me. We'll go to the livery, hire a horse and wagon and move these trunks to our new home."

Snow blanketed the ground, though it wasn't deep, and in places it had melted and refrozen. Horses and oxen left their hoof prints and droppings, and wagon wheels had churned up the snowfall revealing a hard-packed dirt road leading to the livery. Men's boot tracks added to the mixture, and smaller shoe prints, along with animal's paw marks, dotted the less than pristine snow.

The boys tried hard to step in their father's footprints, but their shoes were getting wet and their feet cold. Reginald trudged along, careful where he stepped. He grinned when Cecil looked back over his shoulder, grimaced and winked at him. The brothers knew what the other was thinking. If only they had a pair of boots.

"Afternoon, sir. You have need of horse, wagon, buggy, perhaps?"

"That I do," said Fred. "Name's Fredrick Watts, these are my boys, Reginald and Cecil. We just came in on the train from Winnipeg. My wife and six more children are waiting at the station, and I have three large trunks as well. I have a house waiting on the edge of town."

"Welcome, I be Ivan Gorsky. The liveryman reached forth a paw the size of a small ham and shook hands with Fred and his boys. "I have coupla bays here, Babe and Ruth, they'll do the job for you. I'll get 'em hitched up to a wagon."

Ivan ran fingers through shaggy blond hair before replacing a black cap on his head and leading a sizeable mare from a box stall.

⁓

Leslie, Eric, and Percy sat perched like crows atop the Watts' three trunks left on the loading dock. The boys kept their eyes busy and their necks swiveling as they waited for their father. They were most curious and not a little in awe of the two blanket-wrapped Indians standing stoically beside the station house. Both braves puffed on cigarillos and sent impressive clouds of smoke spiraling upward.

Leslie, first to spot his father and brothers coming with the team and wagon, shouted, and squealed, "Here they come! Here they come!"

Percy, one eye on the Indians, tried to shush his little brother, but Leslie, coat tail flapping, jumped down and raced to the end of the platform.

To the wide-eyed astonishment of the children, as soon as Fred and Reginald loaded one trunk into the wagon, the Indians hefted another and placed it beside the first. Fred, though an ex-officer used to giving orders, didn't know about Indians. How to treat them? Should he pay them? Thank them? Before he could decide, the braves simply turned and walked away.

⁓

With as much dignity as she could manage, Edith boarded the wagon and sat beside her husband. A quick glance behind her assured the young mother her children were settled and ready for the last leg of the journey to their new home. As usual the older siblings kept an eye on the younger.

Fred took up the lines, and clucked to the team. The horses leaned into their harness and began to pull. The wagon creaked and groaned as the wheels began to slowly turn, easing the load forward.

The trip to their new abode didn't take long, but the family remained silent when Fred pulled up in front of a white two-storied box-like house. Would Mother like it? It certainly didn't compare to their home in England.

"Well, my dear, I'm afraid this is it. What do you think?"

"Why, Fred, it's charming." If her voice quavered, she hoped no one noticed. "It certainly looks adequate to house our growing family, and that big oak tree in the yard is a plus." She smiled. "If you'll help me down, I can't wait to get started making it our home."

Fred took a key from his pocket, unlocked the front door and bid his wife enter. The house felt cold and damp and held a musty odor. Edith swallowed and tried not to let her dismay show. The parlor, though large, held no furniture and the wallpaper, now faded, consisted of huge red roses. The formal dining room offered a little more hope with an elegant mirror flanked by candle sconces. The wallpaper in this room appeared less faded and in better taste with stripes running up and down. But it too, lacked furniture, and the linoleum on all the floors lay worn and cracked.

Edith noticed the look of apprehension on her husband's face and spoke quickly to reassure him. "Fred, don't worry, I'm sure you've done your best. With some furniture and bright curtains for the windows, we can make the house quite cozy."

Amy didn't think she'd go so far as to call the house charming—but it did look big enough to hold lots of beds. The two bedrooms upstairs were large, and Amy knew her mother would soon have rag rugs on the bare wooden floors. Maybe she could have her very own cot. But then if it were cold, she'd surely miss snuggling with her sisters.

In no time Father and the boys had the wagon unloaded. The trunks sat in the middle of the parlour like familiar friends from a far country, ignored for now, while mother bustled about getting a fire started in the kitchen range. Thankfully, the former tenants had left a bit of coal and some wood chips in the shed behind the house, enough for two days if they were careful.

Amy knew her mother wouldn't rest until she had heated water, found her homemade lye soap, and scrubbed the entire kitchen. She'd pay particular attention to the Hoosier cabinet with its bins for flour and sugar. The kitchen table, benches, and pantry shelves would receive an equal scouring. The floors could possibly wait until tomorrow, at which time the girls would be expected to help their mother scrub the entire house. For now the children were free to investigate, and they lost no time racing about, upstairs and down.

If doors banged and the children were a bit too rambunctious, the parents said nothing. Fred still seethed over his missing trunk—but there were more immediate needs. The kitchen range, a potbellied heater in the parlour, a small table, three benches, and one double bed completed the furnishings. He'd paid for a furnished house, and this decidedly fell short. The old lady who rented him the house could expect a visit within the hour.

Fred had no intention of sharing a bed with his wife plus eight children, even if his brood did snicker over a writing they found on the wall of a bedroom. *When Father turns, we all turn.* Had the former tenants made do with only one bed?

Amy stopped her giggling when Father invited her and Dolly to go along with him in the wagon. "You two young ladies will make a better case for needing more beds than all your brothers combined," Fred explained.

Mrs. Fillmore answered Fred's knock on the door, smiled and invited them in. But her smile soon turned to a frown when her tenant began to explain their needs.

"Bess, you want old Bess? But I don't have the old mare anymore, I sold her, you know, when I moved here."

"*Beds!* Mrs. Fillmore. Beds!" Fred's face turned red and his voice rose. "We need more beds!"

"Well, you don't need to shout! I'm not deaf, you know. But I've told you, old Bess is gone."

Dolly saved the day, and her father's sanity, when she thought to place her hands together, pillow her head, and close her eyes as though in sleep.

"Oh, you want more *beds*? Well, why didn't you say so?" She placed hands on hips and sighed. "I have feather beds stored in my spare room here. I've set traps all around, so do be careful when I take you up to get them." She beckoned them forward. "Don't want the mice chewing them up, you know. Make a terrible mess, you know."

ℛ

The last vestiges of daylight were slipping beyond the horizon as Father guided Babe and Ruth to pull the wagon close to the front door. Amy jumped from the wagon and ran to the house, eager to tell her mother of their find.

"Mother, we have three more feather beds. Mrs. Fillmore is nice, but she's deaf as a lamp post. She thought we wanted a horse."

Edith smiled and lit a lantern for the boys to light the way up the stairs. A lamp already cast a cheery glow in the kitchen. Amy noted the trunk containing her mother's household supplies had been shoved against the wall nearest the pantry.

Her mother's hands were red, evidence of the scrubbing she'd done in their absence. A bright blue gingham cloth covered the table, and a teakettle whistled on the back of the stove.

"What can we do to help?" Dolly inquired.

Their mother looked tired beyond belief, but she dredged up another smile. "Nothing for now, my dears. Tomorrow we'll get busy. As soon as Father and the boys carry in the beds and set them up, we'll have tea. And then it's off to bed with you."

Amy climbed in the soft featherbed with her two sisters. Annie, safe in the middle, reached over and kissed her on the cheek. Then she kissed Dolly. "I wuv you," she whispered.

"We love you, too, little sister," they answered.

Amy decided she didn't want a bed all to herself after all.

CHAPTER 10

Amy woke up when the sun streamed through the east window and shone on her face. She eased from the bed, careful to not wake her sisters. Eager to begin the day and learn more about their new home, she dressed quickly and crept down the stairs.

By the time she reached the kitchen, the urge to scratch her arms and legs became a need she could no longer ignore. Mother, seated at the table with a cup of tea—looked at her daughter and groaned.

"Oh no! Not you too. Fred—we have to do something!"

Fred's face loomed darker than an approaching thunderstorm as he rose from the table and scrutinized Amy's arms. "Bedbugs," he roared. "Don't scratch—it'll only make the bites worse!"

Tears formed in Amy's eyes and she looked to her mother for reassurance. *Why is Father so angry? What have I done?*

Edith placed an arm around her daughter and pulled her close. "Don't cry. Your father and I have bites too." She shuddered. "I think these awful vermin were here waiting for us. We'll be rid of them before tonight—or we'll be staying elsewhere."

Fred caught himself scratching, and squared his shoulders. It wasn't often Edith asserted herself, but when she did, Fred knew she meant business. She'd not stay in a place infested with bedbugs. And she'd expect him to do something to rid the house of the pests.

When Leslie entered the kitchen, followed in close succession by his brothers, Fred knew none of his family had escaped the unwelcome night invaders. Eric rubbed sleep from his eyes with one balled up fist and scratched his neck with the other hand. Red welts appeared on all the children. In a stern voice, Fred warned them not to scratch. But he might as well have told the wind not to blow during a storm. Especially when he could scarcely refrain from scratching his own bites.

Fred finished his tea with a gulp. "Don't worry—the little devils are cowards. They only come out at night. They won't bother you during the day." He lifted an eyebrow as he donned his hat and coat. "What we need are a few cockroaches to eat their sorry hides."

Edith looked as if she might be sick until Fred grinned to let her know he teased. His hand already on the knob, he quickly opened the door and closed it behind him. He strode from the house with purpose and covered the distance to the center of town in record time. The walk helped to cool his anger, and with the cold his bites itched less. He knocked on Mrs. Fillmore's door before he remembered he hadn't eaten breakfast. The enticing aroma wafting from her kitchen made his stomach growl.

ॐ

Reg picked up the nearly empty bucket and brought more coal from the shed behind the house. Edith smiled her thanks, and added a few more briquettes to the fire. Amy and Dolly set more cups on the table. Mother sliced the last of the bread and divided two apples into thin pieces. She poured tea for her children. If breakfast seemed skimpy, no one complained. If Edith had doubts about this new beginning, she kept them to herself.

With a smile on her face, Edith directed her children to join hands as they circled the small kitchen table. Reg lifted Annie and Leslie and stood them on the benches. With the added height they were now almost as tall as their big brother. This made them grin. Mother bowed her head and uttered a quick prayer of thanksgiving for their simple fare and their new home.

They barely had time to clear the table, wash the dishes, and tidy the kitchen and themselves before Fred returned with a team and wagon.

"Get your coats and hats on," Fred boomed. "I'm taking you to the hotel for breakfast."

"Fred, whatever... can we...?"

"Oh—it's courtesy of Mrs. Fillmore, my dear. And that auspicious lady has invited us to her house for supper this evening."

"But what about the bedbugs? And what is that package you have under your arm?" Edith inquired.

"Ah, the package. Brimstone, my dear. Brimstone! As soon as you're all in the wagon I'll light this in pans throughout the house and we'll soon be rid of the little devils. They'll bedevil us no more."

The Watts family spent the day becoming acquainted with the village of Melita. Warmed by the friendliness of people they met along the way, and with full tummies after they'd dined on ham and eggs at the hotel, Amy voiced an opinion shared by her siblings.

"This is fun!"

Fun it might be, thought Edith as her mind raced ahead, *but how are we to sleep in a house that smells like sulfur? And how am I to rid the house of the odor?*

In the end Mrs. Fillmore solved the dilemma for them. She didn't have enough beds for everyone, but she did have lots of quilts and blankets. If the children didn't mind sleeping on the floor, they were welcome to spend the night at her house.

The next morning after a hearty breakfast of pancakes, prepared by Mrs. Fillmore, the Watts family helped with cleanup and then took their leave. Amy whispered to Dolly as they climbed into the back of the wagon. "Mrs. Fillmore is nice, but she still thinks Father wants to buy her old horse."

"I know," said Dolly. "She's really quite deaf—I think she tries to read lips—but Father's mustache gets in the way and she doesn't know what he's said. But she did tell Father she'd send a wagonload of furniture before the day is over."

"I'm not so sure she's doing it for Father." Amy kept her voice low, but she couldn't help snickering. "I think Mrs. Fillmore took a shine to our mother. Mother doesn't raise her voice, and she makes sure she faces Mrs. Fillmore when she speaks."

"What are you girls giggling about back there?" said Edith.

"Nothing, Mother."

"Well, enjoy the ride. We've work to do when we get home."

And work they did. Mother quickly opened every window in the house that could possibly be opened. Still the stench of sulfur nearly took their breath away. Father built a roaring fire in the kitchen range, and from somewhere he located a copper boiler. Reginald and Cecil took turns at the pitcher pump on the porch just off the kitchen, and soon had the boiler filled with water and heating on the stove.

Amy and Dolly, aided by their brothers, stripped the beds and carried the bedding to their mother in the kitchen. Only Annie and Leslie were spared. They went with their father in the wagon to purchase more supplies.

True to her word, toward evening Mrs. Fillmore sent a wagonload of furniture. Fred and the older boys carried each piece into the house as if it were a gift from God. The furniture was not new, but it didn't matter. They had a large dining room table, and chairs, enough for their whole family. A rocking chair, straight-backed chairs, a small table and sofa graced the parlor. A chest of drawers sat in each bedroom.

Before nightfall every inch of the floors in the house had been scrubbed with hot soapy water. Mother had washed all the bedding, except for a few heavier blankets, and most had blown dry on the clothesline behind the house. What she couldn't wash, she pinned to the lines to air in the wind.

Tired almost to the point of exhaustion, Mother declared it time for tea. And they must have it seated at their new dining room table. Not to be outdone, Leslie and Annie clamored to be allowed to carry the cups to the dining room. Fred handed them one cup at a time and they proudly placed them on the table.

Father seated Mother beside his own chair at the head of the table and poured the tea himself. Fresh biscuits, purchased that day from the General Store, were passed around. Too tired for banter—almost too tired to drink their tea—the children murmured a polite thank you and ate their treats in silence.

From some inner source Mother summoned the energy to prepare a simple supper of potato soup. Father had purchased a large sack of potatoes, as well as a side of bacon, onions, and bottles of milk. He had purchased other staples as well, and they would be used later.

After supper beds were made up with clean sheets that smelled like fresh air and sunshine. Mother declared only one thing remained to be done before they could retire. They must all have baths. The boys had been kept busy most of the day pumping water to heat in the boiler on the stove. Now with one or two more buckets of cold to cool down the hot water, they'd have the benefit of a warm bath.

The girls bathed first in the galvanized tub beside the kitchen range. When they finished and went off to bed in fresh nighties, the boys were called in for their turn.

Reg and Cecil emptied the tub for what seemed like the umpteenth time that day and refilled it with clean hot water from the boiler. After testing the water with a finger, Reg told Leslie he could be first.

Leslie made a face, but there was no escaping. Mother was sure to check behind his ears.

In bed, Amy pulled the sheet over her nose and inhaled the fresh scent, thankful she no longer detected the smell of brimstone. Mother said they should leave their window open an inch or two. The air from outdoors, though cold, smelled good too.

"Good night, Dolly. Good night, Annie," v mumbled.

They didn't answer. Her sisters were already asleep.

CHAPTER II

After almost three weeks in Melita, Mother declared, "Fred, I think it's time we all went to church."

On their excursion around the village, the family had seen Christ Church Anglican. Amy and her sisters agreed; the little white church sitting on a rise at the edge of town looked inviting. A bell tower rose above the roof at the front of the building. There'd been some good natured bantering over which boy could do the best job of ringing the bell should they be allowed to pull the long rope.

Ten pairs of shoes, including Mother's and Father's, sat lined in a row behind the kitchen stove. Each pair had been polished the day before until they shone like a newly minted penny. Mother had baked seven loaves of bread Saturday, plus a huge beef roast in preparation for today.

Awake early this Sunday morning, excited over the prospect of meeting potential playmates at church, Amy tiptoed down the stairs. Dolly followed close behind, and together the sisters dashed to the necessary behind the house.

Glad for the convenience of a two-holer, Amy wondered why Dolly scowled.

"Amy, did you see Mother's face? She's white as milk. And I think I heard her throwing up when we came down the stairs."

"Oh no! Mother can't be sick. I wanta go to church! What do you suppose is wrong? Do you think we'll have to stay home?"

"I think we'd better hurry to the kitchen and get breakfast on the table," said Dolly. "Father didn't seem worried, but he won't like it if we dally. He'll expect us to help."

The girls raced back to their room, and dressed in record time in their Sunday best, unwilling to believe they might not be going to church. A sleepy Annie crawled from bed. "I has to go potty."

"Use the chamber," said Dolly. "Hurry, we have to help Mother." Together they helped Annie dress. Dolly brushed her little sister's hair and pinned a large red bow in back.

Father turned and nodded approval as they entered the kitchen. He was busy making what the children thought of as his special eggnog. He made it for Mother whenever she had an upset stomach. Eggs beaten together with rich whole milk and added to hot tea usually had the desired effect of settling the tummy.

Mush bubbled in a pot on the back of the range. The girls reclaimed their shoes from behind the stove and quickly tied the laces. Amy helped Annie with her footwear, while Dolly washed her hands and began setting the table in the dining room.

The boys arrived on the scene in time to help with the finishing touches for breakfast. "Good morning Mother, good morning Father, sisters." Reginald placed a kiss on Mother's pale cheek. Edith smiled her

thanks when he held a chair for her to be seated at the end of the table.

Mother ate little breakfast, excused herself and went to her bedroom. The boys helped clear the table of cups and bowls. Dolly washed the dishes; Amy dried them and put them away. Fred whistled as he poured hot water into an enamel basin and stropped his razor.

Reginald inspected Eric and Leslie. "Stand still, you two scallywags, or I'll stick your head under the pump." He slicked their hair down with water and combed it into submission.

Amy guessed her fears were unfounded, for Mother reappeared looking regal and beautiful in her long black dress and stylish black hat. Father held her dark coat while she slipped her arms into the sleeves. Thankful the snow had nearly melted—the Watts marched off to church—stepping carefully to protect their shoes.

Feeling a bit shy to be a newcomer entering a strange church—Amy stayed close to Dolly and kept an eye on her mother. After receiving a nod from a man at the back of the church, Edith led the way to a seat near the door and their family filled the entire bench.

A small choir took their places in the loft and the service began with a familiar hymn, "When I Survey The Wondrous Cross." The choir sang a cappella. A piano sat off to one side in front of the room, but no one played it.

Father raised an eyebrow and looked at Mother. Mother could certainly play the piano for the service, but Amy saw her shake her head ever so slightly.

The robed minister took his place behind the tall lectern. He gave a few announcements, prayed for the service by asking God to bless His word, and launched into his sermon. A tall man, of medium girth, he sported a full head of thick hair, white as a summer cloud against a sky of blue.

Amy soon forgot her desire to look around, and dutifully kept her eyes straight ahead. The twinkle in the pastor's eyes and his easy manner captivated her. Unlike the austere preacher in England, Reverend John Smith talked as though he were telling a story beside a cozy fire in someone's parlour.

In no time the sermon ended and they stood for the benediction. The Reverend Mr. Smith hurried to the door. Detained by members of the congregation, Father shook hands with each one and acknowledged their welcome. Two little girls smiled shyly at Amy and her sisters.

The pastor shook hands with each parishioner and murmured a few words as they exited the building. To Annie he said, "You have a pretty hair ribbon, little Miss."

Annie ducked her head, stuck a thumb in her mouth and clung to Mother's coat. Edith picked Annie up and held her before shaking hands with the minister and moving on. Last of the family to shake the pastor's hand, Fred lingered a moment.

"I notice you have a lovely piano. Is there no one to play it then?"

"Regrettably, no. The dear lady who played for us passed away last month."

"Well, sir, my wife plays quite well. I'm sure she'd be glad to help out if that would please you."

"Mr. Watts, I believe my prayers have just been answered. Please tell your Mrs. we'd be delighted to have her play for us."

Fred waited until they all sat down to Sunday dinner before he cleared his throat and announced. "My dear, the good Reverend John Smith has requested that you play the piano for all the services. He said you are the answer to his prayers."

All eyes turned to Mother. Edith put down her fork and smiled. "Fred, I believe you must have alerted him, but I do thank you." She sipped her tea, and beamed on her family. "I do love to play, and it seems a shame to not use such a beautiful piano. Perhaps I can even give lessons to some of the children. If so, my prayers will be answered too."

Amy knew there was no use wishing for a piano of their own. They were far too expensive, and Reg said Father had spent most of his money on the trip across the ocean.

In England, Sunday had been declared a day of rest. Amy knew it would be no different in Melita. She and Dolly could dawdle over the dishes. They would never dare to say so, but for them most Sunday afternoons were boring.

Mother and Father took long naps in their bedroom. Annie and Leslie passed much of the afternoon sleeping as well. The older boys fared a little better. They could climb trees and do all sorts of boy things. They might play mumblety-peg with their jackknives, or have spitting contests, or maybe just sit in the woodshed and whittle.

Amy thought she could climb a tree as well as Eric—maybe better—but if she tore her dress she was bound to get a good scolding. Father might even whip her.

They could always read, or write a letter to grandmother. Amy loved to read, but there were no new books. *I know,* Amy thought. *I'll look in the Bible and see if I can find that story the Pastor talked about. Something about Queen Esther saving her people.*

The rest of the week, Amy had no time to be bored. On Monday Mother washed clothes, scrubbing them on a washboard; the older children were kept busy pumping water, stoking the fire to heat the water, emptying and refilling tubs. Father even got into the act, helping to wring moisture from some of the heavier pieces.

Mother ironed on Tuesday, heating the four sad-irons on the kitchen range. As soon as one cooled, she switched the handle and picked up another. She ironed all their shirts and dresses. Edith sighed as she poured herself a cup of tea and sat at the small kitchen table.

"All right, Dolly dear. It's your turn. You can iron your pinafores." Mother smiled. "And then my sweet Amy, you can iron all our handkerchiefs."

Amy used two hands to lift the heavy iron from the stove. She carefully placed the hankie on the board and smoothed out the wrinkles. Fold and press again, the way she'd seen Mother do. Wanting to help too, little Annie took the growing stack from the end of the ironing board and placed them on the table in front of Mother.

"Oh! I'm sorry, Mother. I've scorched this one." Amy's face reddened. She hadn't learned the knack of testing with a wet finger the way Mother did.

"It's all right," Edith said. "It'll wipe a nose just the same.

ଔଃ

Amy watched Mother continue to be sick in the mornings. Father persisted in fixing her tea with egg, but he didn't seem overly concerned with their mother's illness. From what Amy could tell, she and Dolly were the only ones who worried.

Reginald and Cecil, with their paper routes, were out of bed and gone before daylight. They didn't see Mother when she was so sick. Amy thought of asking Father what ailed their mother, but only for a moment. If he thought she should know, he'd tell her. These days, Father was crankier than an old badger with a sore tooth. She dared not trouble him. Worried over the loss of his photography equipment, Father wrote letters to the railroad authorities and continued to hound Melita depot each day.

Late Friday afternoon things improved. Father came home whistling, his face wreathed in a big smile. The trunk bearing his equipment had just been unloaded at the Melita depot. It would be delivered to the house shortly. The stationmaster had apologized again for the delay. He issued Fred a small check as consolation for the inconvenience.

No explanation had been forthcoming to Fred's questions of why or where. Now that he had his trunk back, with all his equipment intact, it didn't seem to matter. He could set about taking pictures and earn some much needed money.

That very day Mother sat down and made out an order to be sent to Hudson Bay in Winnipeg. She ordered materials to be made up into clothes for her ever growing family. Before they started school again in the fall, the children would need new shoes, but she'd wait to order those. The boys mostly went barefoot in the summer.

Edith dipped the pen in the inkwell and wrote down yarn—heavy serviceable yarn for knitting stockings and softer yarn for little sweaters, booties and caps. Yards of white flannel were added to the list.

Amy watched as her mother carefully addressed an envelope, folded the paper and tucked it neatly inside.

"I'm going to the newspaper office," Father said. "I'll take the letter and mail it for you on my way."

"Thank you, Fred, but I believe the children and I need an outing." Mother smiled. "It's a beautiful sunny day, and I just may have enough change to buy us all a treat. We'll stop by the Emporium. Mrs. Fillmore told me they have delicious pickles in a barrel. Of course we don't need a whole barrel full, but three or four to share might taste good."

CHAPTER 12

Summer arrived overnight, or so it seemed to the Watts family. With the snowmelt came hordes of mosquitoes. There were clouds of the daggered little bloodsuckers that seemed more threatening than the thunder clouds building over the prairie. Every mosquito appeared to want in the house.

"Be quick, Amy, shut the door!" Father roared. "This house must be sitting on a marsh," Fred grumbled. "I'll start a smudge pot going; the smoke will soon discourage them."

Fred rounded up a couple old lard buckets and sent Eric to the woodshed to gather dry woodchips and bits of coal.

"Cecil, you and Percy get busy and gather up a lot of green fireweed down toward the river. Reg, you go the other way. We'll need as much as you can carry. Fireweed 'll make a smokescreen fit to dissuade an army."

Finished with his task, Eric hitched up his pants and ran barefooted after his brothers. Not wanting to be left behind, Leslie raced after him, his short legs pumping like pistons on a steam donkey.

An hour later, a bucket belching thick white smoke sat in front of each door. It did help to dissuade the winged insects, although a few still managed to find their way indoors. Edith declared her own war on these. She handed rolled-up newspapers to her girls. Together they swatted all that came within range.

Tired of watching his wife and daughters swat mosquitoes, Fred slung his leather equipment bag over his shoulder and slapped his hat on his head. He kissed Edith on the cheek. "Don't worry if I'm late, Dearie. Business may take me out of town." He hoped the local newspaper might have an assignment for him. He'd about exhausted the possibilities in Melita and the surrounding countryside. Nothing new or exciting challenged his abilities. Fred felt his interest waning, and with it the all-too-familiar wanderlust settled over him like fog off the ocean.

He needed a drink. Glad the tavern was nearly empty, Fred sat at the end of the bar and nursed a glass of ale. His camera bag rested on the floor at his feet. He preferred to be left alone, but the bartender wanted to talk.

"Ain't you that photographer guy been takin' pictures for the paper? Seen your bird pictures in the *Manitoba Free Press*." He refilled Fred's glass. "Pretty good, I'd say. Liked your write-up in our local paper too. Picture looks like ya."

Fred took a long swallow and set the glass down. He held out his hand. "Fred Watts, and yes, I'm the photographer."

"Thought so." He poured Fred another drink. "This one's on me, Mr. Watts. Glad to have a man of your caliber in our town. Drop in anytime. We try to live up to the town's motto—Peace and Plenty." He wiped another glass. "Town's a right nice haven after the Boer *War*."

Fred nodded and kept his thoughts to himself.

The bartender hurried away to wait on another customer. Fred downed his drink, picked up his pack, and left. Back on the board sidewalk, he blinked against the daylight. He reckoned he'd better hasten home. The darkening sky warned of a storm brewing in the distance.

›‹

Edith set a large bowl of mashed potatoes on the table. She glanced again at the clock on the shelf. Fred should have been home long before now. *Should the children and I eat without him?* A worried frown creased her forehead. *I can put his supper in the warming oven, but will he be upset if I don't wait?*

Dolly gave another stir to the gravy and began pouring it into the gravy boat. Amy carried glasses of milk to the dining room. Annie and Leslie were already sitting at their places beside the table. The older boys finished washing up and hurried to take their seats.

Reg carried a platter of fried pork to the table, then pulled out a chair to seat his mother. Edith's oldest frowned. He uttered a couple words, "Should I..." Before he could finish the front door flew open and banged against the wall. Fred strode in and stopped just short of bumping the dining room table.

"Well, looks like you're waiting—like one hog waits for another." His eyes roamed the table and came to rest on Reginald. "What's your big hurry? Did you work hard today or something?"

Reginald laid his fork aside and kept his eyes on his plate.

"Please, Fred." Edith faced him. "We've just now sat down. The children were hungry and you are later than usual." She let out a careful sigh. "I haven't eaten a bite yet, Fred. Won't you please sit down and join us before the food gets cold?"

"Humph! Don't know as you need me." Fred stomped off to the porch muttering something unintelligible.

The children turned questioning eyes to their mother. Edith tried to smile even as tears threatened. She shook her head ever so slightly as they listened to the up and down squeal of the pump handle. Only Annie dared put food in her mouth.

No one spoke as Fred launched himself into his chair at the head of the table and began to load his plate with food. After a quick glance, Amy kept her eyes averted and pushed meat around with her fork. She jumped when Dolly poked her and handed her a bowl to pass down to Father. The scowl on his face frightened her.

Edith ate little. She didn't fear her husband, but his moodiness and stern demeanor upset her. She had hoped things might be different in this new land.

Fred ate in silence for a few minutes; then he laid aside his fork and looked at Edith. "Now, Dearie, I don't want you to cry, but I'm going to be gone for awhile. Maybe a month."

Edith turned white. She could scarcely breathe. "But, Fred," she stammered.

"I've exhausted the possibilities for pictures here— and I've a great longing to see what's out west. I'll take a look at British Columbia. Maybe take some pictures of the railroad through the mountains. "

The children stared at him. Reginald's face turned red. He transferred his attention back to his mother and their eyes connected.

Edith spoke with a slight tremble to her voice. "Children, you may be excused if you've finished your supper."

As though echoing her distress, lightening chose that moment to flash across the sky. A deafening clap of thunder followed in seconds and loosed the floodgates for a torrential downpour.

Three days later Fred boarded the train for Winnepeg; the first leg of his journey to British Columbia. Edith saw him off and waved until the train departed the station. Heeding her husband's admonition to not cry—she kept a stiff upper lip until she could no longer see the train in the distance.

Once back home, her children gathered around her. Edith sat at the kitchen table and bowed her head. *What am I to do? I have only myself and my children to rely on. Thank God my parents won't know Fred's left yet again. They can't say, I told you so!* Slowly the tears ran down her face and dripped onto her lap. If Fred said he'd be gone a month—it would more likely stretch to two or even three.

Amy hugged her mother. Dolly handed her a handkerchief. Annie crawled up on Edith's lap. "I wuv you," she murmured, while patting her mother's wet cheek, trying to stop the tears.

Leslie and Eric crowded close, unsure what they might do to help. Cecil built up the fire in the kitchen range. Percy filled the water bucket and put the kettle on for tea. But it was Reginald who offered the greatest amount of comfort.

"Mother, please don't fret. We'll be fine. I have a new job at the brick yard. They'll pay me a dollar a day as soon as I've proved myself. Seventy five cents for now. Percy can take over my route and deliver papers."

"A dollar a day? Why son—that's more than some grown men make."

Edith brightened and beamed on her family as she took down the fixings for tea. In her mind, she named each child in turn to God—asking a special blessing on that one. Tears threatened again when she came to precious little Norah. She choked them back and aloud said, "We'll be just fine, but we must pray for your father—that God will keep him safe and return him to us."

છ

The weeks wore on with all of them busier than ants in a disturbed nest. Edith gave music lessons on the church's piano to three students. The older boys spaded a spot for a garden beside the house. All the children helped Mother plant vegetables, carrots, beans, tomatoes, and corn, to name a few. A neighbor gave her enough starts for a whole row of raspberries.

Cecil and Percy continued with paper routes. Reg worked six days a week at the brickyard. Dolly and Amy helped Edith with housework. Occasionally Dolly had babysitting jobs for neighbors or friends from church. All the children willingly gave their earned money to their mother.

When not otherwise occupied, Edith, Dolly, and Amy made the knitting needles fly. Mother made no mention, but Dolly whispered to Amy in the privacy of their bedroom, "I think we are going to have a new little brother or sister."

Amy's eyes grew big as horse apples. "I want another little sister."

The children knew how to work, but there was time for play too. The boys swam in the lazy Souris River nearly every evening. Eric learned quickly when he fell in. Knowing it was sink or swim, he swam.

Amy followed her brothers one day hoping she too could swim, or maybe wade. Her brothers saw her, turned and shouted, "No, Amy. Go home!"

She stuck out her lip and complained to Dolly.

"You goose," Dolly said. "You can't go. They're skinny-dipping."

Amy figured she'd get even when she caught her brothers smoking homemade cigarettes behind the pigpen. She promised not to tell Mother, on the condition that they'd let her try too. The "tobacco" was nothing but bark pulled from posts of the pigpen and rolled tight to resemble a real cigarette. The matches were snitched from the kitchen.

Amy got hers lit and tried to imitate puffing like her brothers were doing. The bark smoldered and gave off a stench. She made a face and dropped it to the ground. "You, my dear brothers, are crackers," said Amy. "But don't worry, I won't tell Mother."

CHAPTER 13

Eric and Leslie hopped and danced around the kitchen. Their excitement made it impossible to stand still or stay out of the way. Mother smiled and shoved them aside as she opened the oven door. A large crock of baked beans simmered in the oven. The aroma of blackstrap molasses and brown sugar, mixed with onion and bacon, wafted throughout the house.

Amy and Dolly were no less excited as they sliced tomatoes and peeled cucumbers from their garden. Annie stood on a chair and watched her sisters. Dolly slipped her a slice of cucumber which she promptly stuck in her mouth.

Annie chewed and chattered. "Is we for sure gonna have ice cream?"

"Yes, Annie. We'll have ice cream at the picnic," Mother answered with more patience than she felt. She had answered the same question at least a dozen times.

Thankful, friends had insisted on coming for them with their wagon, Edith laid aside her apron and smoothed her hair. She washed her hands yet again and inspected her children. Eager for the picnic, even Leslie and Annie had stayed clean.

"They're here! They're here!" shouted Eric.

Edith lifted the beans from the oven and carefully wrapped newspapers around the pot. She folded a dish-towel and placed the hot beans in the center, bringing the ends of the towel up and knotting them on top for a handle with which to carry the dish.

Another towel protected a bowl of tomatoes and cucumbers her girls had prepared. On cue, Reg appeared at her side, lifted the heavy bean pot, and placed it in a basket. Another basket, prepared earlier, contained cups, tin plates, cutlery, and a red-checkered tablecloth for their picnic. Into this container Dolly placed the sliced tomatoes and cucumbers. Edith took Annie's hand and ushered her children to the waiting wagon.

Amy clambered into the back of the wagon and quickly sat down beside her best friend, Maggie Wilson. Maggie beckoned Dolly forward, then scooted over to make room for Annie on the blanket. Annie giggled and wiggled her bottom to make more room for herself between the girls.

The wagon rapidly filled with children and baskets of food. Reg knew he could ride too. His siblings would squeeze and make room, but he'd rather walk.

"Come on, Cecil, Percy," he challenged. "Bet we can beat 'em if we hustle." The boys laughed and strode off after their big brother.

The adults sat up front on the high wagon seat. Mr. Wilson took up the reins. "All right, children; here we go. Sit still now, don't wanta lose any of ya."

Edith and Mrs. Wilson looked back to make sure their children were indeed sitting still as directed. Mr. Wilson clucked to the team and the horses leaned in to the harness and began to pull the wagon forward.

The sun shone warm on Edith's face, but she thought she could smell fall in the air. She relaxed and let a small sigh escape her lips. *I wish Fred was here,* she thought. He does like picnics. Aloud she said, "I so appreciate you giving us a ride, Mr. Wilson. This is a perfect day for the Sunday school picnic, but it would have been a far walk carrying heavy baskets."

"No problem at all," said that gentleman. "Had to come this way anyhow."

"We're glad to have you and the younguns along," said Mrs. Wilson. "My little Maggie wants to play with your Amy." She smiled. "I'm glad they'll be starting school together. Margaret Anne's a bit shy and frightened of starting in a new school."

Mr. Wilson guided the team and wagon to a spot under the trees well away from the picnic tables. Other wagons were already there. The horses were unhitched and tethered. Some picked at grass, most dozed, and stomped now and again to dislodge a pesky fly.

Each year the churches sponsored a picnic. The entire community was invited and most came. The Souris River wound lazily around Melita; the park along its banks provided a beautiful spot for people to gather.

Swings, teeter-totters, and a merry-go-round kept children running from one to another. Their happy squeals and laughter carried to their parents. Some of the men engaged in a game of horseshoes; others gathered in small knots to discuss farming and the price of grain.

The ladies smiled and chatted as they spread tablecloths on the rough plank tables and set bowls and plates of food out. Platters of fried chicken, still warm from the frying pan, fluffy baking powder bisquits, and crocks of sweet-cream butter lined the table.

Ladies brought their home-canned pickles, preserves, and fresh produce from their gardens. More than one watermelon resided in a tub of melting ice. Pies and cakes were set out. Mrs. Fillmore brought a three-layered chocolate cake that had folks' mouths watering.

Pastor Smith stepped up onto a bench and called for everyone's attention. Folks, let's pray and ask God's blessing; then we'll partake of this bountiful food."

Railroad executives came to the picnic and brought four large cream cans of icy lemonade. Amy thought she'd never tasted anything so good. She wanted more, but Mother said they had to share, and there might not be enough.

After everyone had eaten about all they could hold, the ladies and older girls helped clear the tables. Leftover food was covered and returned to their rightful baskets. Plates and silverware were gathered and whisked away.

Only then did the men bring out the ice cream freezers. Children gathered around to watch, and some begged for a chance to crank the handle. At first turning the handle was easy—but as the mixture of cream, eggs, sugar, and vanilla thickened—it took a strong arm to keep the paddle rotating.

Amy watched. Surely it's ready, she thought. But no, Reg shook his head and kept on turning that handle. Amy smiled, her big brother was almost as strong as their father. She noticed some of the older girls were watching him too, but Reg didn't seem to see them.

At last paddles were lifted from the freezers and frozen cream clung to the blades. Reg grinned and handed his to three little boys to share. Children and adults lined up with cups and bowls for their part of the rich treat.

Amy and Maggie took their cups and went to sit on the banks of the Souris River to eat their ice cream. To their surprise three canoes came gliding down the river. Indians looked their way, then turned the dugouts and headed for the bank where the girls sat.

Should they run or sit still? Amy didn't know. She turned her head to search for her mother, but it was her brother Reg who came to sit beside her. "Don't act like you're afraid of them," he whispered.

Three braves, dressed in brown buckskins and moccasins, climbed the bank and trod single file to the picnic area. They passed within three feet of the children. Amy forgot to breathe. She also forgot her manners and stared. If the Indians saw her, she couldn't tell. They kept their eyes straight ahead and marched stoically to the tables.

The tallest of the braves uttered one word. "Food?" For barter, he offered a brown eel taken from the river. Pastor Smith accepted it—his expression as unreadable as the Indian's. The ladies standing closest turned quickly away, trying hard to mask their revulsion at something that looked like a snake.

Edith hid a smile, and told no one she'd eaten eels in England. They were quite good.

There wasn't much food left, but the womenfolk gathered what they could. The men handed each brave a cloth sack of provisions. The Indians returned as they had come, and only as they pulled away did Amy notice dark-skinned little children in the canoes. She saw a small boy chewing on what looked like a chicken leg. *They're cute,* she thought. *But I'm still afraid of the big ones.*

Shadows lengthened as they started for home. Annie and the little boys fell asleep, lulled by the clip-clop of the horses and the sway of the wagon. Amy, too, could barely hold her eyes open. She and Maggie might have slept if Dolly hadn't poked them when they sagged against her.

The older boys appeared tired as well. Reg willingly climbed into the back of the wagon to ride home. Even the adults had little to say as they journeyed along. It had been a fun but tiring day.

Mr. Wilson guided the team and wagon close to the Wattses front walk. "Whoa, there." The horses stopped. Glad for the chance to rest a few minutes, they lowered their heads and shook themselves, making the harnesses rattle. The absence of motion, coupled with jangling harnesses, woke the children.

Reg hopped to the ground and quickly helped his mother down from the front seat. Edith stifled a yawn; together she and the older boys gathered up the baskets, blankets, and helped the younger children from the wagon.

"Thank you so much, Mr. and Mrs. Wilson," Edith called and waved as the wagon pulled away.

ॐ

Weary to the bone, Edith sat at the kitchen table, head in her hands. The picnic things were washed and put away and the children were in bed. *I miss Fred.* She hadn't heard from him in over two weeks. I wish he would come home. My Reg is such a help, but he's barely fourteen. I can't burden him with my problems.

With another baby coming, things would be tight. How were they to manage? With winter coming on, they needed meat in the smokehouse. Should I buy and raise a couple weiner pigs? I know nothing about raisings hogs.

The tears came unbidden and ran down her cheeks. Only God knew of her distress.

CHAPTER 14

Amy awakened early; a robin sang in the tree outside her window. She pulled the curtain aside and smiled. Baby birds twittered in the nest, waiting for their parents to come with a juicy morsel.

Edith pulled a cake from the oven; the aroma filled the kitchen with the scent of vanilla. She turned and smiled as her daughter entered the room.

"Well, here's my birthday girl. Happy birthday, Amy. You're up early." Edith hugged her. With Fred away, and so many children to care for, there wouldn't be money for anything but the necessities. Still, she'd do what she could to make her daughter's eighth birthday special.

"It smells good in here. Mother, is that my cake?"

"Yes, my dear." Edith set the pan on the table and covered it lightly with a dishtowel. "And you get to choose what we'll have for supper."

"Chicken?" Amy's eyes, so like her mother's, sparkled. "May we have fried chicken?"

"I think we can manage that." Edith laid aside her apron. "Do you want to walk with me to the Miller's farm? I know Mrs. Miller has some young fryers. I'm sure she'll sell me some; especially if I tell her it's your birthday."

Edith wrote Dolly a note and propped it on the kitchen table where she'd see it when she woke and came downstairs. She instructed her to watch the younger children while they were gone.

To be allowed to go with Mother—just the two of them—made her birthday special. Amy giggled. It wasn't often she spent time alone with her mother.

"We'll go now, before it gets hot," Edith said. "It's a long walk out there."

"Father says walking is good for us. And I can walk a long ways,"Amy declared.

℘

Edith selected three young fryers. Mrs. Miller positioned each chicken's neck against the chopping block and chopped its head off with an ax. She quickly released the bird and Amy watched it flop about the yard. When the chickens no longer moved—Mrs. Miller picked them up and put them in a bulap sack.

Amy didn't much like the killing part, but she loved chicken fried the way Mother did it.

"Today's my birthday," she told Mrs. Miller. "I'm eight years old."

"Well, then. You're a big girl." She chuckled. "You can help your momma carry the chickens. Ja. Leave the sack there on the grass and come in," she invited. "We'll have tea and strudel before you start your trek back."

The scent of spice and cooked apples greeted them as soon as they entered the kitchen. A teakettle whistled on the back of the stove. Mrs. Miller poured tea and set generous slices of apple strudel on the table in front of her guests.

This kitchen is big, thought Amy, *our kitchen at home isn't half this large. This table is big too.*

Mrs. Miller read her mind when she said, "This is our country kitchen. Big table. Ja? Not so big when our ten children gathered round. Now it's yust Wilhelm and me. No formal dining room, we have."

Sun streamed in an east-facing window, making the kitchen a light cheery place. Dust motes danced in the sunbeam, but the wooden table, floor, and stove gleamed. Amy wondered if Mrs. Miller scrubbed her floor on her hands and knees, the way Mother did each Saturday.

"I have something for you before you go. A birthday present, maybe. Ja?"

Amy watched, wide-eyed, as Mrs. Miller filled a small jar with thick fresh cream. She tightened the lid and placed it in a larger jar, which she then filled with skim milk. With a smile, she handed the big jar to Edith.

"It'll be our little secret. Ja?"

"Thank you so very much." Edith said. "This is most generous. And the tea and your strudel were delicious." She smiled, and rose from the table. "But now we really must go. Come, Amy."

Back on the dusty road, Amy shouldered the sack with the chickens, and trudged along beside her mother. Edith carried the jar of milk under her left arm, her right hand underneath the bottle to balance the weight.

"Mother, why did Mrs. Miller put the jar of cream inside this bigger jug?"

"I'm not sure; perhaps it's to keep the cream cool." More likely to keep anyone from knowing she gave us the cream, especially the stern and practical Wilhelm, Edith thought, but she kept her opinions to herself.

The farther they walked, the heavier the sack with the chickens became. Amy didn't complain, even though her steps lagged, and chatter became nonexistent. Mother carried the heavy jar of milk.

As if in answer to an unspoken wish—or maybe a silent prayer—a team and wagon came lumbering along the road behind them. The woman driver called out, "Whoa, there, you daft beasts. Hold up!" She tugged back on the lines, the muscles in her arms stretching the fabric of her sleeves tight.

When the mules stopped, she straightened her bonnet and called out, "Mornin.' Looks to be you and the youngun are totin' a load there. Climb on up here and ride with me. You can put your burdens in the back there." She laughed, and reached for a can at her feet, into which she spit a great gob of tobacco juice.

"Name's Ida Mae." She stuck out a less than clean hand.

"Thank you! I'm… Edith." She shook Ida Mae's hand. "This is my daughter, Amy."

"Glad to meetcha. Ya live in town then?"

Edith nodded.

"Friday. First of the month. My time to go to town. Get supplies. Need a barrel of flour. Sack a sugar. Hope the price ain't gone up none." She laughed again, and pulled on the skirt of her calico dress as she released the brake on the wagon.

"Git up there, you longeared critters. You think we got all day?" She slapped the reins against their backs.

As long as Mother carried the jar of milk under her arm the cream had more-or-less stayed in place. Now—sitting on the floor of the wagon—it rattled and clanged against the glass with each jolt of the wheels. Amy tried to steady it with her hands, but it didn't help much.

Edith glanced nervously at the driver. *What will she think? Will this woman assume we've stolen something and are trying to hide it?*

Ida Mae paid no more attention to the clinking sound than to the pesky flies landing periodically on her face and hands. She merely brushed them off and continued talking.

"Let me guess. Ya'all from England?"

"Yes. Yes we are. From Ipswich. We arrived here in May."

"Thought so." She laughed. "I'm a North Carolina Tar Heel myself. Never thought I'd git this far north." Ida Mae laughed again. "Husband is a Canuck, you know. Came lookin' for a Southern Belle." She really hooted now, as though she'd made a huge joke.

The mules halted in front of the General Store. Edith thanked Ida Mae again and climbed down from the wagon. She helped Amy over the side, and they reclaimed their burdens."

As soon as they were out of hearing, Amy blurted, "She talks funny. And she chews tobacco. Nasty!" She made a face, then fearing Mother might scold her, she hastened to add, "But it was nice of Mrs. Ida Mae to give us a ride."

Mother smiled. "Yes, it was kind of her to let us ride. And remember, my dear daughter, she thinks we talk funny."

When they reached home, Dolly had a large kettle of water steaming on the stove. Hot enough to scald chickens.

Leslie and Annie pushed little wooden cars across the floor in the parlor. Eric lined up tin soldiers and pretended to shoot them down.

Amy looked out the window. Cecil hoed a row of beans in the garden. Percy sat at the end of the row, squishing dirt between his toes.

"You have things well in hand, Dolly. I do thank you," Mother said. "I'm glad you thought to heat water. I'll change my dress and scald the chickens. You girls can help pick the feathers. But first I need to put this milk and cream down in the well."

"I'll do it," said Dolly. On the back porch, she set the jar in a basket attached to a long rope. She lifted a square board from over the well and carefully began to lower the container. Her hands, one after the other, fed the rope down into the water far below. She wound the rope around the base of the pump and hooked it the way Father had shown her.

Mother slipped an apron over her head and tied it at the waist. She poured the kettle of hot water into a bucket and carried the bucket to the woodshed. One by one, she removed the fryers from the sack and dunked them in the scalding water.

The smell made Edith nauseous. She turned her face away and gulped a breath of fresh air. "Wait till they cool, so you don't burn your fingers," she warned her girls. She laid the birds on newspapers to keep them clean.

Dolly did pretty well, but Amy had only half the feathers off her bird. The feathers stuck to her fingers, and when she tried to shake them off, they made her sneeze. Mother quickly finished the one she worked on.

"I'll take this one to the kitchen, singe the pin feathers, and remove the entrails. By that time, you girls will have finished plucking yours.

That evening, the table was set for supper with Mother's prettiest dishes. Dolly lit the candles. Annie placed the birthday card she and Dolly made together, on Amy's plate. Reg carried in a platter of fried chicken and placed it right in front of Amy.

"You get to take the first piece," Mother said. "You're the birthday girl."

Everyone ate his or her fill; then Dolly carried in the cake. Mother had covered it with red ripe raspberries from their garden. She had whipped the sweet cream given to them by Mrs. Miller. It stood in peaks atop the raspberries.

Amy opened her handmade card and beamed. "This is just the best birthday ever."

CHAPTER 15

Aday later, Fred arrived home in a jovial mood. He kissed his wife—lifted her off the floor and swung her around twice—before letting her feet again touch solid kitchen linoleum. He smiled at his children and made the little ones giggle when he jumped flat-footed, back and forth, over a kitchen chair.

"Sorry I didn't make it home in time for your birthday, Amy." Father shrugged and pulled a package from the pack he'd dropped on the floor. "There's enough here for everybody, but you get to choose the very first piece."

Amy's eyes grew large as teacups as she looked at the box of chocolates her father placed on the table. Her mouth watered as she tried to select a piece. Never had she seen so many shapes and sizes. Are they hard or soft? If only everyone wasn't watching her—she might poke a piece or two before she made her selection.

"Hard to choose just one among so many, eh?" Father chuckled, his brown eyes twinkled with amusement.

With a maturity far beyond her years, Amy lifted the box of candy and offered it first to her mother. Edith smiled, selected a piece and quietly gave it to an eager Annie. Like a peddler offering his wares, Amy held the box in both hands and watched the chocolates disappear as her siblings all grabbed a piece.

Amy offered the box to her father. Only three pieces remained in the top layer, one for him, one for her, and one for Reg when he returned home from the brickyard.

Fred picked the largest remaining piece. He smiled and winked at his young daughter as he held the sweet to her lips. Surprised, Amy opened her mouth and accepted the treat.

"You get one more piece, Amy," Father said, "for I just gave you mine."

Fred stooped and pulled one more surprise from his bag. He handed Edith a small package wrapped in flowery paper and tied with a red ribbon. The children crowded around—eager to see as their mother carefully undid the wrapping—smoothing the wrinkles from the paper, as she removed it.

"I wanna see, I wanna see," begged Annie as she struggled to peer over the table. Father picked her up and held her. Annie draped one small arm across his neck and peered down at the parcel her mother held. Edith opened the tiny black box and gazed in wonder at the contents.

"Oh, Fred! This is lovely!" She lifted the delicate brooch from the velvet and held it in the palm of her hand. "But isn't this terribly extravagant? Can we…"

Fred frowned, but quickly replaced his scowl with a smile. "Ah, but I've taken many pictures. They'll bring a good price." Fred's chest swelled. "British Columbia is beautiful, but I don't believe our future lies there. I have some stories to tell you; we'll talk later. Saturday,

I know, is a busy day for you. When you're ready, I'll pump water for our baths and get it on the stove."

Amy and her siblings thanked their father again and dispersed. Some needed to finish tasks; the younger children ran outdoors to play. Their imaginations provided what they might lack in material things.

"I've finished most of my chores, but I do need to scrub this floor." Edith smiled at her husband. "I'll not be long; then perhaps we can talk. I'm eager to hear all about your trip."

Edith had let the fire go out right after breakfast; the house stayed cooler without the heat from the kitchen range. She and the children were satisfied with cold cucumber sandwiches, onions from the garden, and tall glasses of milk for lunch.

"Ahhh, Edith my love—let the floor go—this once. It doesn't look dirty to me." He pulled at his dark mustache. "Come here and sit on my lap. I've missed you, you know." Fred patted his knee. "You're a beautiful woman, as pretty as the day I married you."

ço

The remaining days of summer flew by faster than geese headed south. School would start in less than a week. Mother finished hemming the second dress she'd made for Amy. Dolly struggled to hem her own new dress. In and out, she pushed the needle through the gingham with her little thimble.

Amy longed to try—but when she saw tears in her sister's eyes—she knew it couldn't be easy.

"Mother, my stitches wobble worse than baby bird tracks." Dolly sniffed and held the dress up for her mother's inspection. "They're all uneven," she moaned.

"You're doing much better than I did with my first dress," said Edith. "It takes practice, my dear, to make your stitches uniform. Perhaps if you don't try to make your stitches quite so small, they'll be more even." Edith smiled and took the dress in hand. "You may make us some tea, Dolly. I'll see what I can do with this."

In no time, Mother's busy fingers had the dress hemmed. She did let Dolly hem one of her pinafores. Amy also tried and found she could do a credible job hemming one of her own pinnies.

With two new dresses apiece, four crisp white pinafores, and a brand new pair of shoes, the girls were ready to start school. Cecil had new clothes and shoes as well. Little Percy clamored to go to school with his sisters and brother, but he wouldn't be six until the end of October.

"Well, Percy!" Father chuckled. "We'll get you all spit-polished up and see if they won't let a big boy like you go to school."

The day school started Father took Percy in hand. He hadn't been "spit-polished" but Mother had scrubbed him until his face shown like a summer sunset. He wore new knee britches, and a white shirt made by their mother. Father combed his hair into submission and the cowlicks he generally sported lay flatter than a new page from a pencil-tablet.

Amy turned slowly for her mother's inspection. Her blue-checked dress matched Dolly's, and she thought her sister looked nice indeed. Mother pinned matching bows in their hair and kissed each departing child on the cheek.

"Remember," said Mother, "pretty is as pretty does. See that you mind your teacher. And learn your lessons well."

Cecil, Dolly, Amy, and Percy each carried a small lard bucket with a tight-fitting lid, their dinner pail. Mother had filled each one with thick slices of bread and butter, carrots, a small tomato from their garden, and a chocolate biscuit.

The older children walked ahead. Along with lunch buckets, they carried a tablet and two pencils. The early morning air felt brisk and they quickened their steps. Amy watched other children making their way to school. Some walked, and others rode horses. Still more arrived at school in buggies and wagons.

Father kept Percy's hand tucked in his as he went to talk to the principal. Amy and her siblings followed—like baby ducks being led to water for their first encounter—they stayed close. This was no small schoolhouse; Amy wondered how she'd find her room. Would she and Dolly be together? Amy reached for her sister's hand.

"Hello, I'm Fredrick Watts." Fred shook the principal's hand. "These are my children: Fredrick Cecil, Dorothy May, Amy Gladys, and Percy Claude. Cecil will be in your eighth grade, Dolly starts fifth grade, Amy in the third. And Percy here isn't quite six, but he'd very much like to be in first grade." Percy squared his shoulders and tried to be taller.

"Percy knows the alphabet. What with older brothers and sisters, he gets plenty teachin.'"

Mr. Adams smiled at them. Amy released her grip on Dolly's fingers.

"Well, sir, I believe we can accommodate the young gentleman. Not sure how many first-graders we will have this year. Our total enrollment fluctuates, last year we had 230. The year before that, our students numbered 254. I'm sure it'll be higher this year. It's been increasing over the last seven years, and just last year Johnston and Pope added four new rooms to our schoolhouse at a cost of $6,300. We now have eight classrooms plus my little office here." He turned to look out the window.

"We have a larger playground now and new shed for those who ride horses. Three years ago, the district bought more property from C.P.R. (Canadian Pacific Railroad) for $150.00.

He looked at Cecil and explained. "I'm not in my office during school hours. I teach eighth grade. But I'm here at seven in the morning and I don't leave before five in the afternoon."

Father left after telling Percy he'd be there at 2:30 to walk home with him this first day. Indians were about: they were friendly, but that didn't keep Percy from being frightened of them.

Mr. Adams walked each of the children to their classrooms. Amy felt pride in going to such a new brick schoolhouse, a school with eight rooms! Even her school in England hadn't been this big. She felt a little sad that she and Dolly wouldn't be in the same room, but they'd walk home together after school.

Amy felt better when her teacher, Miss Lewis, smiled at her. Miss Lewis wore the prettiest pink lawn blouse with a delicate cameo fastened at the high neck.

Highly polished black shoes peeked from the hem of her dark skirt. She wore her brown hair piled atop her head; a pencil peered from behind her ear. Her blue eyes twinkled.

She's almost as pretty as my mother, thought Amy. *I wish Mother could wear pretty blouses like that.* There was no use wishing though, for Mother generally had a baby spitting up on her shoulder. Not that Mother ever complained. She seemed to love them all equally.

୧୨

Edith placed a hand on her stomach—did she feel a flutter? *Probably it's just a gas bubble,* she told herself. *It's months before the baby is due. My husband is home now, and I must stop worrying about our future. He's in such good spirits; surely everything will be all right. I do wish, however, he'd tell me how much money he has, what we have to live on.* Edith did her best to push doubt below the surface. Fred wouldn't like it if she questioned him. He'd view it as criticism of his ability to provide for their family.

CHAPTER 16

Fred continued to take pictures in and around Melita. His reputation as a photographer grew; people stopped him on the street now and inquired if he could take their portrait. Couples about to marry wanted a wedding picture. Would he come to the church or the bride's home?

Young families, like his own, wanted a photograph of their children, especially when a new baby arrived to bless the family. For the most part, Fred complied without complaint. He'd set up his camera on a tripod—slide in a glass plate—drape the black cloth over his head and hope for a good picture. The results rarely completely satisfied him. His customers, however, praised him.

Where he could, Fred devised the method of taking portraits through a window. He found the subjects became more relaxed and squinted less if they sat inside. Children were the better candidates, as they tended to forget themselves and act more natural.

Making posed portraits of people put butter on the bread, but Fred much preferred a more natural setting. Birds and wild animals challenged him, as did the men who worked in the fields.

He would set up his equipment and try to catch the essence of the scenes as he saw them, be it of man or beast. The dust-coated faces of the men at harvest—shouting to one another as they paused to wipe their eyes with a red bandana—this made a captivating picture. Horses—dark with sweat—straining to pull the combines—chaff, caught in updrafts, swirling around them—these scenes caused Fred to smile. And today he'd take Edith with him.

Fred touched Edith's hand and halted her busyness as she wiped crumbs from the table. "Dearie, I want you to go with me today." He grinned at her. "I'll go to the livery, rent us a horse and buckboard. We'll drive out in the country, and watch the farmers harvest wheat. Make an occasion of it, take a lunch."

"Why, Fred, a picnic sounds lovely, but what about the children? I'd want to be here when Percy gets home from school. He's too little to stay alone. He'd be frightened if I'm not here. Would we be back in time?"

"Ah, my little mother," Fred chuckled. "No need to worry. I've taken care of that already—Percy will stay at school and come home with Cecil and his sisters. Eric, Leslie, and Annie will go with us, of course."

Eric heard his name and piped up, his voice squeaky with excitement. "Can we Mother? Please? Can we go?"

"May we go, Eric? It's may we go." Edith smiled. "And yes, we'll go."

Eric ran from the room to find his shoes. In moments, he raced back, a shoe in each hand. He plopped his bottom on the floor and began pulling the scuffed brogans onto his feet. "Father, can I go with you to get the horse? Please? Huh, can I?" Eric sucked in a breath and let it out in a rush. "I mean—may I?"

Edith hid a smile as she turned to slice bread for their picnic.

Fred laughed and tousled Eric's hair. "I don't know half-pint, think you can keep up?"

"I'm big now," Eric crowed. "I'm five." He held up his hand, fingers spread like candles on the birthday cake Mother had made him less than a week before.

Eric held fast to his father's hand, and trotted double-time trying his best to match Fred's stride. His little-boy chatter kept time with his pounding feet. When both slowed, Fred swung him up on his shoulders. Eric giggled, and tried not to bounce when his father trotted with him.

The most fun was yet to come. Fred held Eric on his lap and let him take the reins as the gentle mare, Duchess, pulled the shiny new buckboard down the hard-packed road.

Leslie and Annie wriggled their way behind Mother's lace curtains, and stood with noses almost touching the glass. They waited and watched for their father and brother to return.

Edith smiled as she positioned her hat on her head and picked up her gloves. She strolled down the walkway to the front gate, the picnic basket over her arm. Leslie and Annie raced ahead—making the short cross-boards rattle under their feet.

Fred set the brake and wrapped the lines around the stake. He hopped down in one smooth motion and assisted Edith up the step into the buckboard. She sat on the right side of the front seat and smoothed her long black skirt over her knees.

"Thank you," said Edith. "If you could just hand Annie up, I think she might sit here between us." Eric had already scrambled to the back. Fred boosted Leslie up and he plunked down beside his brother.

Leslie poked Eric. "Did you really get to drive the horse?"

Eric swelled with pride and showed off his muscle for his little brother. "Yep," he said.

Fred took up the lines and released the brake. "All right men, we're rollin.' Sit still now, no monkey shines back there," Fred, admonished his sons. "Old Duchess here might not like that." He grinned down at Annie and winked at Edith.

The picnic basket sat on the floor by their feet. Two water jugs, encased in soaked burlap, hung from the sides of the buckboard. Edith smiled at her husband and touched him lightly on the arm with a gloved hand. "How far is this farm where we're going today?"

"Hmmm, not sure. A far piece? Long buggy ride?" He kept a straight face and ran a finger across his mustache, but there was a note of tease in his voice. "An hour on a fast horse? Longer?"

"Fred! How far?"

He tipped his head back and laughed. "You tired of my company already?"

Edith ignored him and reached for the parasol she'd tucked unnoticed beneath her seat. She opened it and pink frills unfolded like a rose opening it's petals to the sun. Her father had given it to her for her sixteenth birthday. He'd laughed then and said a bumbershoot would be more practical. Edith had loved her gift, though her more austere mother had frowned at the extravagance.

The parasol looked almost new. She smiled down at her daughter and noted the wonder in Annie's eyes.

"Annie, when you're older—perhaps you'll have one too."

Fred pulled his hat lower over his eyes. He held the reins in one hand and reached for Edith with the other. A gentle squeeze on the shoulder brought a smile to her lips. Blue sky spread like a warm blanket overhead—a few white clouds billowed in the east. Sun warmed their backs, but the air felt muggy, a day when one could perspire with little exertion.

Edith looked back at Eric and Leslie. She'd heard a few snickers, when the horse did what horses do, with accompanying sound. "You boys are awfully quiet back there. Is everything all right?"

"We're playin' pretend. I'm lettin' Leslie play with my new wooden truck."

The horse's hooves made a steady clop clop along the narrow dirt road. Duchess twitched her ears from time to time and swished her tail at pesky flies. Houses were few and far between. The farm they came to now had a large barn and several outbuildings. The small white house hunkered down amidst a grove of trees.

A brown and white mongrel dog ran to the edge of the road and barked at them.

A lady stood in the barnyard; she grasped a long white apron in one hand and scattered grain to a flock of Rhode Island Reds with the other. A rooster crowed and strutted amongst the hens.

The woman waved and called a cheery, "Good Mornin' to ya! The dog's all bark and no bite. Don't be a worryin' about him. Get back here Rover," she shouted. She shaded her eyes with her hand and watched them drive on past.

Fred tipped his hat. Edith and the children waved, though it's doubtful the lady saw Annie, her short frame wedged between her mother and father. That didn't keep Annie from waving until they were out of sight.

The sun grew warmer—Edith dabbed at perspiration on her forehead with a white lace hankie. She had about decided her husband intended to drive across the entire province—when they came to a grove of trees on a small rise. Fred drove the horse and buckboard up the hill and into the shade.

The boys didn't wait for help, but scrambled over the side of the conveyance and dropped to the ground, agile as cats. With Fred's help, Edith and little Annie made a more dignified exit.

"Oh, Fred—I forgot to bring a blanket!" Edith apologized.

"Not to worry, we'll just sit on that big limb over there."

Lightning had struck one of the oak trees sometime during an electric storm, and a sizeable branch now lay on the ground. The boys were already walking its length—arms outstretched for balance.

Fred poured cups of water for everyone while Edith handed wedges of cheese, slices of buttered bread, and an apple to each child. They were munching on juicy summer apples when a lone rider came thundering down the road. He pulled his horse to a halt and called out to them. "Better not stay too long in that grove. Storm's a comin.' I gotta feelin' in my bones could be a bad un." The man tipped his hat and urged the gray stallion on down the road.

Edith looked at Fred—they both scanned the sky. Why hadn't they noticed the increasing clouds before? They were now more numerous than sheets flapping on clotheslines on a Monday morning. The gray clouds were getting blacker by the minute. "Jumping Jehosophat!" Fred scowled and leaped to action. Before Edith and the children had time to question—they were in the buggy and headed back down the road toward town.

"Get up there—you old nag—move those feet!" Fred stood, bracing his legs apart, and slapped the reins down hard on the horse's rump. The mare lunged and broke into a run.

"Get on the floor back there. Now!" Fred shouted at his boys. "And hang on tight. How far is it back yonder to that farm we passed on the road? Reckon we'll make it before the heavens rip apart? Before we drown or lightening fries us?"

Edith blanched, flinging one arm across Annie to brace her, and hung on as best she could while praying they wouldn't be thrown from the buggy. She hoped Fred didn't expect an answer. Fear had stolen her voice.

CHAPTER 17

Lightning flashed across the sky. Thunder boomed—obliterating the sound of pounding hooves as Duchess raced down the road. Edith gasped; sure they'd fly from the buckboard if the horse didn't slow.

In a desperate move, Edith yanked on Fred's trousers. "Slow down!" she shouted in a voice she did not recognize as her own.

Fred allowed the mare to slow to a fast trot; whether in response to her pleading or the horse beginning to tire, she didn't know. Edith continued to grip the sides of the buckboard, but she did chance a look behind her to check on her sons. They lay splayed on their bellies, hands clutching the seat supports in front of them.

She was unaware she held her breath until the air escaped in a whoosh and jangled her nerves even more. Edith bit her lip, and tried to form a comprehensive prayer in her mind. Her brain refused to cooperate. She couldn't think beyond help us—help us—help us. Please God! Help us!

Fred sat on the edge of the seat, shoulders hunched forward, reins gripped tight in his hands, as if by his will alone he could get them to safety. He urged the horse to greater effort; his voice was confident and soothing.

Lightning continued to illuminate the sky with jagged bolts that reached the ground. Edith flinched each time thunder rumbled across the skies like a drum roll on heaven's parade ground. Against the clouds, she saw what looked like the farmhouse they had passed earlier, but how could that be? Did Fred see it too?

Annie pointed. "Mother, look! A house in the sky."

Well, at least I'm not crazy, Edith thought. *Annie sees it too.* But what kind of phenomenon is this? Is it a reflection? Or is it one of those mirages I've heard about, something folks in Melita say can happen during a thunderstorm?

Fred stood and slowed the horse for the turn in to the yard. This house was no mirage. They had made it! As quickly as he could, Fred drove under cover of the open-ended section of the farmer's barn. No chickens scratched in the grass now—the darkened sky had sent them to roost.

As soon as the buckboard stopped rolling, the boys jumped up and scrambled to the front. They crowded as close to their mother as room permitted. Edith barely had time to release her strangle hold on the sides of the seat when lightning struck a tree in the yard. Thunder followed in seconds with a blast that left them temporarily deaf.

The two little boys hurled themselves onto Edith's lap. Annie wailed and buried her face under her mother's arm. Fred leaped from the buggy and hurried to the horse's head. The mare's eyes showed fright, and she tried to rear. Fred kept a grip on the bridle and spoke to Duchess in soothing tones while he stroked her neck.

The last thunderclap ruptured the clouds, and rain fell in torrents. Thankful they had made it to cover in

time, Edith hugged her children close. Rain changed
to hail and beat against the shake roof with a racket
loud enough to send any mice still lurking in the barn
to their hidey-holes.

After what seemed an eternity the hail stopped. The
sky grew lighter and the storm appeared to be moving
on. Rain now fell in a halfhearted effort. Fred watched
a man stride across the barn lot; his boots sent up a
geyser of water with each step.

"Afternoon, looks like you folks found shelter just in
time." He cleared his throat. "Missus says come to the
house. She'll put the kettle on. Make tea." He hooked
thumbs behind red braces, and harrumphed again.
"Name's Peter Russell."

"I'm much obliged to you, Mr. Russell, for the use
of your barn." Fred shook his hand. "I'm Fred Watts
and this is my wife, Edith. I surely thank you for the
offer of tea, but I 'spect we better be gettin' on home.
Don't know yet what has happened in town. We have
children that will be frightened if they get home from
school and no one is there."

"Mr. Russell, please forgive our rudeness, and thank
Mrs. Russell for her gracious offer." Edith smiled and
spoke from her seat in the buckboard.

"Not a'tall. Perhaps you'll stop in again if you're out
this way."

"We surely will, Mr. Russell. We surely will," Fred
affirmed.

೮೦

Amy saw the flashes of lightning through the schoolhouse windows. Thunder crashed louder than anything

she'd ever heard. She'd crawl beneath her desk and cover her head with her arms, but she didn't want her little brother to think she was a scaredy-cat. Percy huddled on the seat beside her. When another thunderclap seemed to shake the very building, Percy grabbed Amy's hand and squeezed hard.

"Ouch! That hurts," Amy squealed. She pried his fingers loose and put her arm around his shoulders. Her lip quivered and two big tears rolled down her cheeks.

Miss Lewis lit the coal oil lamps and stood in front of the class. "Children, I know the storm is frightening, but I think it will be over soon. Perhaps we could sing a song while we are waiting."

The teacher led with a chorus of "Froggy Went a Courtin.'" Amy loved the silly song, and she loved to sing, too. But today her throat felt like a wool sock stuffed with cotton. A look around the room told Amy her classmates didn't feel like singing either.

Miss Lewis didn't seem to notice. She kept right on singing as she walked up and down the aisles. She smiled, when lightning lit the room. When thunder boomed, she sang a little louder.

Gradually a few children's voices joined the teacher's. Percy peered at Amy; together they began to sing the silly lyrics. Amy knew at least fifteen verses, and she and her siblings often made up more.

Amy hoped Father might come to walk home with them. It was past their usual dismissal time, but the principal had said they should all stay indoors until the storm moved on. That didn't seem to be happening very fast. The clouds were black as Mother's coal bucket, and thunderclaps continued to make her jump.

After they had exhausted the frog song, Miss Lewis started the class on a round of "London Bridge." The bridge had fallen at least a dozen times when Mr. Adams came to the room and said he thought the children could go home. "Don't dally along the way," warned the principal. "Get home as quickly as you can. This storm may not be completely over."

The Watts' children formed a tight nucleus and ran most of the way home, walking only when they needed to catch their breath. Cecil boosted Percy onto his back and gave him the fastest "horsey" ride he'd ever had. Amy and Dolly carried the lunch pails and raced along behind Cecil and Percy.

Thunder continued to rumble in the distance like an army of warhorses tramping across a bridge. Suddenly Amy stopped and stared. Cecil slid Percy to the ground. Dolly grabbed for Amy's hand. They all saw it. But what was it? The children put their arms around each other and gaped at this wonder in the sky. Was it a judgment from God? Could this be the City Foursquare they had heard about? An entire village appeared in the heavens, a town not unlike Melita. Amy and her siblings stared in awe, temporarily rendered speechless.

Cecil spoke first, his voice squeaky. "Come on—let's go! We gotta get home. I don't know about you jackanapes, but I'm not telling anyone about this. They'll think we're off our trolley." He grabbed Percy by the hand and started to run. "Cities don't just appear in the sky."

Amy thought she might tell her mother what they had seen, but no one answered when she called out, "We're home!"

The girls were quiet as they climbed the stairs to change out of their school clothes. Amy bit her lip; she didn't want Dolly to know how close she was to tears. Dolly buttoned Amy's pinafore, then turned so her sister could fasten hers. Together they made their way to the kitchen.

Cecil struck a match to the paper beneath the kindling he'd laid in the cook stove. He waited, impatient, for the wood to catch and burn. When the flame had consumed the *Morning Free Press* and most of the kindling, he added more wood and shut the door to the firebox.

On the back porch, Percy did his best to fill a teakettle with water. He pushed and pulled the long handle, up and down, up and down. Water gushed with each pull, but his arms felt weak as Mother's homemade noodles. This was going to take awhile. If he could swing on the handle, it might be faster. Of course, Father had warned him never to do that. He'd get a licking for sure, if caught.

Cecil gently pushed him aside, and with a few strong pumps of the handle, he finished filling the teakettle, and then the water pail. Not to be outdone, Percy ran to fill the coal bucket. In no time, they had hot water for tea.

Amy stood on a stool, and with both hands took down cups and saucers from the cupboard, careful not to drop them. Dolly went to get milk and cream from the well. "Mother says things go better with a good cup of tea," said Dolly, as she struggled to pour hot water over the leaves and let them steep in the china pot just the way Mother would.

The children sat around the kitchen table and sipped their tea, listening for the sound of their parents' arrival home.

"I'm hungry," said Percy. "Can't we have a biscuit with our tea?"

Before anyone could answer, Mother entered the kitchen. She hugged and kissed each of her children where they sat around the kitchen table. Annie copied her mother, before she climbed up and settled herself in Dolly's lap. Eric and Leslie crowded in close and peered longingly at the tea.

"I'll have supper ready presently, but you may all have a piece of bread and butter now to go with your tea." Their mother smiled and tied an apron around her waist.

Fred and Reginald arrived home together, Fred from retuning the horse and buckboard to the livery. Reg returned from his day of labor at the brick factory.

"This has been quite a day." Edith sighed. "Thank God we're all back together safe and sound. We'll have supper soon, and then I think tonight it's off to bed early for all of us. I know we have stories to tell, but they will wait until morning."

Later, Amy burrowed into the feather bed beside her sisters. Rain on the roof soon lulled her to sleep. What would Mother say if tomorrow she told what she had seen?

CHAPTER 18

Dolly pulled the covers back and gently shook Amy's shoulder. "Get up, sister," she whispered. "It's Saturday, we have a lot to do today, and we don't want Father up here rousing us out of bed."

Amy touched her feet to the floor and wiped the sleep from her eyes with two balled up fists. She dressed hurriedly in faded dress and worn pinafore and followed Dolly down the stairs. Annie, snug in the middle of the feather bed, didn't awaken.

Mother turned from stirring a large kettle of porridge on the back of the stove and smiled. "Good morning, my dears, early to bed and early to rise makes Dolly and Amy healthy and wise."

Amy and Dolly giggled and spoke in unison. "Mother, you left out wealthy."

"Harumph!" Father glanced up from the paper and continued stiring cream into his tea. He uncrossed his legs, moved forward, and smoothed the newsprint across the table in front of him. "Listen to this story, Mother, girls, it made the front page." Fred read the article aloud.

"Residents of Melita saw a phenomenon in the heavens yesterday during a severe thunderstorm. Upper air disturbances caused a mirage, the nearby town of

Napinka shown against the sky in vivid detail. The grain elevator appeared in bold relief. Some folks said they could read the name Napinka on the side. Others thought they saw people walking on the street."

"Is there a picture in the paper?" asked Edith.

"No, no picture." Fred sighed. "If I'd been here maybe I could have gotten one. Probably wasn't much time though."

"Father, we saw that town in the sky on our way home from school," said Amy. "It was pretty strange; we didn't know what to think."

"I guess we weren't crackers after all if they wrote about it in the *Manitoba Free Press,*" said Dolly.

Fred folded the paper and looked at his daughters. "Well, I'll declare," he said. "You children all saw that—the boys, too?"

"Yes, Father, we did," said Amy.

Mother looked at her girls as if they had just announced they'd seen the King of England. "Well— I'm sure you children won't soon forget it. It can't be that common an occurrence." Quickly Mother placed bowls of hot oatmeal on the table. "Certainly, I've never heard of it before—though we did have our own wonderment yesterday." She hugged Amy and Dolly in turn and kissed each one on the forehead. "But, I'll let Annie and your little brothers tell you about it. I'm sure they'll be bursting with the story when they wake."

The kitchen smelled warm and yeasty; seven loaves of bread sat on the cabinet rising beneath a dampened dishtowel. Mother scooped more flour into a bowl and broke an egg into a well she made in the flour. She began to mix the dough for noodles.

Amy took her empty bowl and dropped it into sudsy water in the enameled dishpan. *I wish this were my day to help Mother in the kitchen; I'd love to pat the dough out for noodles and hang them on the rack to dry after Mother cuts them.*

But fair was fair, and today was Dolly's turn to help their mother in the kitchen. Amy had other tasks to see to this Saturday. If she found them unpleasant, she'd nevertheless better do a good job the first time. Mother always caught a sloppily done task and sent the errant child back to do it over again.

Amy emptied the chamber pots down the hole in the outhouse, but not before she checked to see if any lizards or snakes lurked about. She and Dolly had both screamed the time a snake reared its ugly head just as they opened the door to the privy. Mother had said the snake was harmless, but Amy wanted nothing to do with them. She suspected her little brothers caught the snake and put it there, then waited to hear her shriek.

Careful to not spill hot soapy water on herself, Amy carried the bucket to the back of the outhouse. She poured water into each pot, and with an old broom, saved for that purpose, swished the water round and round until the chamber pots were scrubbed clean. She tipped the pots at an angle, and placed them out of sight behind the necessary, where sunshine would complete the job. Later, Amy would discretely put them back in their proper rooms.

She dumped a can of lime down each hole, and used the remainder of hot water to scrub out the toilet. A spider or two raced for cover. Amy giggled when she remembered her mother said spiders were in king's palaces.

Her outside chores completed, Amy raced back to the house. Father paced in the parlour, impatient for Cecil to arrive with a horse and buggy. Amy thought her father had never looked more handsome; he wore his best dark suit and vest over a white shirt with a blue striped silk tie. His hat sat on his head at a jaunty angle. A leather bag with his camera equipment lay on the floor by the front door.

Edith brought Fred another cup of tea to sip while he waited. "You'll not be late, husband. I'm sure Cecil will be back with horse and buggy in plenty of time for you to arrive at the church early." She placed a gentle hand on his arm in an effort to stop his pacing.

"Humph! My old man always said if you want something done right, do it yourself. I should have gone to the livery myself; I told Cecil I don't want some old nag, but chances are Mr. Gorsky will shove some old bag of bones off on him. And that boy doesn't know how to assert himself. If I have to go myself I will be…"

Eric dropped from a limb of the tree in the front yard and ran to the house shouting, "He's coming, Father. He's coming, Cecil's coming!" Bursting with his news, Eric gulped a breath of air and boasted. "I can see the horse and buggy down the street. He got a real fancy rig. And that horse sure is a high-stepper. Looks like Cecil brushed and combed him, too. Just like you said he should."

"You look dapper," said Amy, but her father paid her no mind as he rushed out the door. *Maybe he didn't hear me,* she thought.

Cecil came to the house looking glum. "I did what Father asked me to do, and rented the best horse Mr. Gorsky had. I paid the liveryman a little extra out of my earnings, Mother. I did not tell Father; I hope he won't be angry with me. Father didn't say anything a'tall about my efforts; he just took the horse and buggy and left."

"Son, you did a fine job." Edith smiled at him. "The horse and buggy are spanking. I'm sure your father is pleased; he's just anxious about doing the wedding portraits. He wants everything to be perfect. These are very important people. The bride's parents are wealthy land owners and pillars of the community. They will expect perfection."

A small sigh escaped Edith's lips. "Come, children, let's be busy. Idle hands are the devil's workshop. Amy, you're upstairs chambermaid today. Take the dust-mop with you, and don't forget to shake out the rugs." Mother smiled and brushed a hand across Amy's curls.

"If Dolly has finished churning the butter, she can help you change the sheets and make up the beds. If not, I'll be up to help you," said Mother.

Leslie and Annie picked up their toys after a reminder from Mother, and then ran outdoors to play in the sunshine. Eric dogged big brother Cecil, jabbering faster than a horse trots. "How big do I haveta be before I can drive a horse the way you do?"

"Well, half-pint, you'll haveta be nearly tall as that cornstalk." Cecil dug another carrot from the garden and handed it to Eric. "Here, squirt, take this and wash it off under the pump. Ask Mother or Dolly for a basket." Cecil shouted after him, "I need something to hold all these carrots, potatoes, and onions."

છ૭

Fred held the reins loosely in a firm hand. This horse needed no encouragement to step lively. *I didn't know old Ivan Gorsky had such a steed in his stable. If only I had the money to buy this horse and rig.* He shrugged. *Fred, old chap, while you're at it, why don't you just wish for the moon?* His thoughts mocked him. *Give me a toehold, and I'll not always be poor,* Fred promised himself.

The horse trotted past the tavern; the temptation to pull up and stop for a drink drew Fred like a bride to flowers. But he didn't dare arrive at the church with liquor on his breath. If he intended to get good pictures, he needed a steady hand. *Maybe later,* the thought lurked in his mind like the promise of a well-developed picture.

໒ຈ

Amy opened the bedroom window wide to air the room the way her mother had said to do. She pulled and tugged on the sheets to get them off the bed. When the last corner loosened from the mattress, she almost fell on her bottom. She stuffed the sheets in the hamper at the end of the hallway, and resolutely began to push the dustmop under the bed.

Mother stepped into the room with an armload of fresh sheets. Dolly followed with hand-embroidered pillowcases edged in crocheted lace. Amy and Dolly had worked on the pillowcases under Mother's careful direction.

Dolly and Mother stretched the bottom sheet tight over the feather mattress. Mother smiled, and offered this sage advice. "Be careful girls, how you make your bed, for you will have to sleep in it."

Amy started to giggle, but something zoomed past her head and her laughter turned into a shriek.

"Quick! Shut the door!" Mother gasped. She blanched, a protective hand flying to her stomach.

Dolly slammed the door and ducked as the winged creature sailed past her head. "It's a robin," said Dolly. "He's scared. Maybe we can shoo him back out the window."

Amy took the dustmop and eased the bird from the corner where he beat his wings against the wallpaper. After circling the room more times than they could count, the robin found the open window and flew to safety.

Mother collapsed on the end of the bed and held her hands to her fast-beating heart. Amy cuddled close on one side of her mother and Dolly squeezed in on the other side. The girls didn't credit the old superstion, but they knew their mother believed it and Grandmother Rampling had certainly thought it true: a robin flying through an open window or repeatedly pecking on a window meant a death would occur in the family.

CHAPTER 19

Edith removed her foot from the treadle, and pushed back her chair. She'd been sewing for over an hour at the old machine. Fred had purchased it secondhand from an elderly woman who claimed she had no further use for it. Large now, and feeling heavy and awkward, Edith placed a hand on her lower back. As she stood she tried to ease the strain of burdened muscles.

She pushed aside the curtain on the front window and watched snowflakes drift down willy-nilly to join the accumulation already on the walk. A melancholy settled over Edith, not unlike the snow gripping fenceposts outside. In less than two weeks, she must be ready for Christmas. This year there would be no grandparents to participate in the festivities. She couldn't count on help from her mother or father, as she might have while in England.

Christmas wouldn't be the same without them, but in ways, Edith felt relieved to be out from under their scrutiny. Her parents had never entirely forgiven her for sliding down the drainpipe and running away with her handsome Fred. Her mother had barely spoken to her for a month afterward. When she did speak to her, it was to declare a sage proverb. "Marry in haste, repent in leisure."

Her thoughts on little Norah, Edith wiped at the tears trickling down her cheeks. How she missed her baby girl. Fred rarely mentioned her now. In all fairness, she knew her husband wished to spare her the pain of constant remembrance. Norah would be walking now, talking some, and wide-eyed over Father Christmas and presents he might bring her. Gifts would be supplied by her auntie and uncle—not her parents. *How that hurts.* A tremulous sigh escaped Edith's lips as she gathered the garments she worked on, and tucked them away out of sight. *I'll sew more tonight after the children are all in bed.*

Edith pulled the Mother Hubbard away from her bulging abdomen; she'd welcome a new baby, but no child could ever take the place of the one left behind in England. "God, if you're listening," Edith whispered, "please help me through this sacred season of remembering your birth. Help me make it a joyful time for my children."

Eric trooped down the stairs rubbing sleep from his eyes. Naptime passed all too quickly for Edith; she treasured the moments she had to herself. In some ways her workload lightened in winter, in other areas her tasks became more difficult.

The little ones were underfoot more; the cold temperatures kept them indoors. Clothes were more difficult to dry, often making it necessary for the family to live in a moist jungle of clotheslines strung about the house. Water dripped on the floor from the garment she couldn't wring quite dry enough. But winter did put an end to all the canning and preserving she felt compelled to do in the summer months.

Edith stoked the fire in the parlor's potbellied stove, and replenished the coal in the kitchen range. Tending fires in wintertime kept her busy. She poured warm water from the teakettle into the enamel basin and watched as Eric washed his hands and splashed water across his face.

Edith smiled. "You may have tea with me now, or you may wait for Annie and Leslie to awaken. Percy will be home soon, too."

Eric grinned and climbed up on the chair beside his mother. "Now, please, Mother."

Edith laughed, and before he could ask, she handed him a slice of bread and butter lightly sprinkled with sugar. She poured the tea and filled her little son's cup with a generous amount of cream and sugar.

Eric shoved the last of the bread in his mouth—and with eyes grown large and somber—he voiced his worry. "Mother, does Father Chrismas know where we are? Will he find us here in Canada?" He sniffed. "I've been a pretty good boy, haven't I? I won't get a lump of coal in my stocking, will I?"

Edith smoothed the hair back from Eric's forehead. "My dear, Father Christmas will find you, and you can tell your brothers, if they don't stop teasing you, they will find a lump of coal in their stocking."

Eric's face lit up in a grin to make the winter sun blush. His small arms circled her neck and squeezed until she tickled him and they both giggled. In truth, of all her children, Eric remained the most likely to find trouble. He was also the most affectionate of her boys, coming often for a hug or a reassuring touch.

Together, Annie and Leslie popped into the kitchen, holding hands and sleepy-eyed from their naps. No more than sixteen months apart, these two formed an alliance against the world. They had their squabbles, but if a third entered the picture, they quickly became united.

Edith made more bread and butter and sliced winter apples for her hungry children. Before she could turn around, or so it seemed, Percy, clad in coat, cap, and mittens burst into the kitchen, home from school, his nose and cheeks red from the cold.

"I'm hungry, Mother," six-year-old Percy declared. "May I have tea?"

It had stopped snowing, but the temperature dropped well below freezing. No one wanted to be more than three feet away from a stove. Some of the heat did make it upstairs; still the bedrooms were icy cold. Thankful her trunk contained more quilts, Edith determined to add another layer to the beds before nightfall. Fred would welcome the extra warmth if not the weight. No doubt he'd grumble and say he had to get up to turn over.

It started snowing again before nightfall; Edith sent Amy and Dolly outdoors with careful instructions on how to gather clean snow into a bowl. As a special treat, she made snow icecream with sugar, vanilla, and thick cream saved for the occasion.

With everyone in a festive mood, Edith brought out red, white, and green paper she had purchased earlier. She rounded up scissors and mixed a bowl of flour and water paste to set on the kitchen table. The children gathered around, eager to begin the Christmas project.

Reginald and Cecil were in charge of measuring and marking on sheets of colored paper. Amy and Dolly cut the carefully marked paper into strips and stacked the pieces in neat piles. All the children dipped fingers into the paste and smeared it on ends of the strips to fasten the ends together. A few rings needed doing over, but no one complained, and the older children helped Annie, Leslie, and Eric, so they too, felt included.

The bright chain grew; Annie's eyes danced with merriment. Eric and Leslie tried to count the links, but stalled out and mixed their numbers after reaching thirty. The children continued to glue and add more and more circles until no one wished to try counting the number of rings in the long chain.

Fred surprised his children by popping corn over the hot coals in the parlour stove. Edith smiled and allowed her children to stay up past their bedtimes. Eager hands dipped into the bowl of hot buttered and salted popcorn, making it disappear in record time.

Satisfied all her children were warm and snug in their beds and perhaps dreaming of sugar plums, Edith sat down at the sewing machine once more. She must finish the outing flannel nightgowns for her daughters and make nightshirts for her sons in time for Christmas. They were practical gifts she knew her children would welcome. With any flannel left over, she hoped to make nappies.

Fred stoked the fire in the parlour stove, shut off the damper and went to bed. He left their bedroom door ajar for warmth; Edith could hear him snoring in the other room. She had asked him about fillers for the children's stockings and received a grunt for reply. Perhaps tomorrow with his morning tea, she could coax a more satifying answer. Surely, he knew the importance of not disappointing their children. They must have something for Father Christmas to put in the stockings, especially for the youngest of their brood.

Edith placed a hand against her lower back, and straightened her shoulders in an effort to lessen the cramping. She had stayed too long at the sewing machine, but only two nightshirts remained unfinished. Those, she could easily sew while the older children were in school, and the little ones napped.

ഇ

Christmas Eve day arrived, and Edith confessed to herself that most of her worries were for naught. Fred had purchased stocking-stuffers: nuts, candy, and little china-head dolls for the girls, shiny new jackknifes for the older boys, and miniature Stanley Steamer Moxie trucks for Percy, Eric and Leslie. Edith didn't dare ask what those cost.

Decorations, made by the children, transformed the parlor. Red, green, and white paper chains anchored at each corner of the room, draped and came together in the center of the ceiling. Fred fastened a large red bell, fashioned from the finest crepe paper, at the point where the chains met. The bell, folded flat when not in use, had been a stowaway in Edith's treasures from England.

Edith wished she could sit with her family, unnoticed in the back of the church, but no one else knew how to play the piano for the Christmas Eve services at the Anglican Church. She wore her bulky black coat buttoned and hoped she didn't look as large as she felt. Her mother, Edith knew, would never approve of showing herself so immodestly in public. Nevertheless,

Pastor Smith counted on her to play for their Christmas Eve service.

A little before midnight, "Father Christmas" went about filling each child's stocking hanging from the foot of their bed. If the giggles and happy shrieks they heard echoing upstairs Christmas morning, were any indication, the bearded old gent did himself proud.

The first to come downstairs, Amy and Dolly hugged their mother and whispered, "Thank you! We love our nightgowns, and we like our stocking stuffers, too."

The aroma of roasting turkey already filled the kitchen. "Mother, it smells good in here," said Amy. "What can we do to help you?"

Edith smiled. "You girls may set the table in the dining room with the very best china. Mrs. Fillmore will be our guest for dinner today, please set a place for her, too."

A little after one o'clock they sat down to a well-laden table. Mrs. Fillmore delighted everyone with a bag of Florida oranges; Mother placed a bowl of them on the sideboard. Mrs. Fillmore did most of the talking while they ate. Fred seemed unusually quiet. Shortly after the meal, he put on his coat, and hat, then left out the back door without a word.

Edith waited up well after bedtime, but still Fred had not returned. She lay awake, shivering in the cold bedroom. This wasn't the first time he'd left and come home in the wee hours of the morning, but did he have to leave on Christmas day?

CHAPTER 20

On New Year's Day, Edith was up and in the kitchen before daylight. She got a fire going and planned a special breakfast for her family. She set two cast-iron skillets to heat on the back of the stove. With a sharp knife, she sliced thick slabs of ham, and cut previously boiled potatoes for frying. She cracked more than a dozen eggs into the brown crockery bowl and added a generous amount of creamy milk.

Thankful for the quiet, Edith eased her bulk onto a kitchen chair. She held the bowl in her lap and with a wire whisk beat the eggs and milk into a frothy mixture. *A new year is like a brand new slate on which to write*, thought Edith. *Or else a slate washed clean, a chance to start fresh.* Edith sighed, and determined to let go of past grievances; she'd not allow a worm of doubt to chew away at her peace of mind.

Reg surprised her with a kiss on the cheek; she hadn't heard him enter the kitchen. He had today off, the first in many weeks. Edith thought he might sleep in, but rising early for work at the brickyard had become a well-ingrained habit.

"Good morning, Mother. Happy New Year! I thought I might be the first one up, and I'd get a fire going for you." Reg chuckled. "I should have known better; I can never beat you. You're always here tending to our needs."

Edith smiled. "Happy New Year, Son. I thought you might sleep in this morning. You've certainly earned the right; you work so hard."

That brought a laugh, and before his mother could speak further, Reginald grabbed the teakettle and bucket. On the porch, the pump made a protesting squawk as he pushed and pulled the long handle to fill the vessels with fresh water.

In no time, the water heated. Edith watched as Reg fixed tea for them, her heart grateful for this time alone with her son. She loved all her children, but to herself she admitted there would always be a special place in her heart for her firstborn, partly because he was her first, but even more significant, she could rely on him. His help with the younger children, and the money he entrusted to her were invaluable. In her opinion, Stanley Reginald Watts exhibited a maturity far beyond his years. *Someday, Lord willing, my son will make a lucky lady a wonderful husband.*

Reg stirred cream and sugar into the tea he liked strong. "I wonder what changes 1907 will bring to our family. Surely Father won't pull stakes and move us again. I, for one, have had enough travel to last me awhile."

Edith smiled at her son, her hand going unconsciously to her stomach, now hidden behind the table. She tried not to frown as her unborn child gave a healthy kick to her midsection.

Edith rose and stretched; she and Reginald stood before the kitchen window and watched the sky turn pink in the east. The day promised to be sunny but cold.

"Mother, if you have no objections, I thought Cecil and I might take the guns and hunt birds today. If we get some, I'll clean them; you won't have to worry about doing it." Reg's eyes, so like her own, sparkled. "I think I could even fry them up if you gave me a bit of instruction."

Edith laughed a low chuckle pleasant to the ear. She barely had time to encourage her son to take the day for himself before the kitchen overflowed with children eager for breakfast. Keen to start a new year properly, all her brood greeted this new day with big smiles, hugs for their mother, and a chorus of "Happy New Year!"

Fred remained the only one not on the scene this morning. Edith suspected he had already celebrated the arrival of the New Year, perhaps a little too exuberantly. She couldn't be sure of the time he'd flopped into their bed, cold and shivering, but it had to have been after midnight. Well, his breakfast will be in the warming oven when he does greet the day.

ॐ

Amy waited on the steps of the schoolhouse for Dolly. She switched her lunch pail from one mittened hand to the other, and wrapped and rewrapped the wool muffler around her neck. Mother had said she might not be there when they arrived home from school. They were not to be frightened though, she'd said. If Father wasn't home, he would be there shortly.

The sisters held hands as they trudged along the brick walkway, and later the snow-trampled path that led to their home. Their exhaled breaths made puffy little clouds against the frigid air. "This is better than trying to smoke those nasty old cigarettes the boys made behind the pigpen," said Amy. "We can pretend we're smoking, and no one will ever know."

"You're silly," said Dolly. "Everyone looks like they're smoking when it's this cold." She tugged on Amy's hand. "Come on, let's run; I'm freezing."

"Okay, but what if I get a stitch in my side? And what if Mother isn't home when we get there? And what if Father is in one of his grumps? And why would Mother say she might not be home? She's always there when we get home from school."

"Amy, you ask more questions than my teacher. Will you please just hush? And run? I'm freezing, I tell you!"

Faces rosy from the cold, Amy yanked open the back door and the girls burst into the kitchen. The warmth from the kitchen stove enveloped them like a baby's fuzzy blanket. It was comforting, but it couldn't replace their mother's warm greeting, and she wasn't there to welcome them with her smile. Amy plunked her lunch pail on the table. She looked at Dolly, her eyes silent question marks. *Why is the house so quiet? Where is everyone? Is Father home?*

Amy started up the stairs to change her clothes, but halted on the second step when a giggle reached her ears. On investigation, she discovered Annie, Leslie, and Eric in the parlour, grouped around Mrs. Fillmore. The children sat on the floor and watched wide-eyed as this grandmotherly lady wielded scissors on folded newspaper and produced long lines of paper dolls. Some were girl dolls and some were boy dolls. All held hands as they emerged and took shape.

First to notice Amy, Annie jumped up and ran to show her sister the paper dolls.

"That's clever," said Amy. "But where is Mother?" And why is Mrs. Fillmore here?

Alerted by the younger children's actions, Mrs. Fillmore turned to see Amy and Dolly watching her. "Well, hello girls; I didn't hear you come in." She laid aside the scissors, and sat up straighter in the rocking chair. "I suppose you are wondering where your mother and your father are?"

Amy stepped closer and nodded her head. Experience had taught her there wasn't much use verbalizing questions to Mrs. Fillmore. Though kind and gentle, the woman simply did not hear. Trying to make her understand was about as useful as talking to a statue in the park.

Nothing, however, hampered Leslie's hearing; he flew to the door and pulled it open when they heard their father clomping up the front walk. Fred removed his hat and shook off the snow before entering the parlour. A sigh of relief escaped Amy at the same time Dolly stepped forward with a reassuring touch on her shoulder. Father wore a smile worthy of a man told he'd just won a million dollars.

Fred tousled Leslie's hair. He picked Annie up and chucked her under the chin. His smile extended to everyone in the room as they waited for him to say something. "Well, children, you have a new baby brother. Harold David Watts made his entrance into the world about two o'clock this afternoon. One more day and he would have been a valentine baby."

☙

Tired beyond belief, but more thankful than she knew how to express, Edith held her tiny son to her breast. With one finger, she stroked the downy hair on his head. Her labor and delivery had been longer and more difficult than she'd anticipated since Harold was her tenth child.

Fear had hammered at her soul, though she managed to keep the doubts to herself. Fear that God might take this baby from her as punishment for leaving little Norah behind. Fear that this child might be marked from the fright she'd received when the robin flew into the girl's bedroom. But Dr. Nelson assured her the baby was strong and healthy. If his squalls were any indication, this boy was indeed robust.

Dr. Nelson's office was a handy extension of his home. If patients needed hospital care, he assigned them to one of the five bedrooms and Mrs. Nelson, the doctor's wife, acted as nurse. She also functioned as cook and housekeeper. A cheerful petite woman, with snapping brown eyes and graying dark hair, she moved about quietly and with purpose.

"I'll take the little fellow now," said Mrs. Nelson as she lifted Harold from Edith's side. "I expect he needs his nappy changed, but you need only to rest Mrs. Watts. Your time for work will come again all too soon."

Edith smiled even as her eyelids fluttered closed. It felt so good to lie back against the comfortable featherbed. For a few short days she could relinquish her duties, cares, and worries over the future. She'd recommence her duties soon enough. For now, she simply wanted to sleep.

CHAPTER 21

Almost four months old now, Harold cooed and giggled, garnering the attention of his brothers and sisters as his due. When home, Dolly and Amy vied for the chance to hold him. Harold had only to fuss and a big sister rushed to comfort him.

Amy squirmed in her seat. She'd squandered the last half-hour daydreaming about home and her baby brother. Harold was more fun than any old doll, and today should be her day to play with him. She chanced the teacher seeing her, and again glared at the clock ticking away the minutes from its shelf in the corner. Had the hands moved at all?

Not much escaped Miss Lewis. She came silently up behind Amy, and slapped her on the shoulder with a ruler. The teacher frowned and shook her head, before marching to the front of the room.

"Ten more minutes, children, and you may put away your books. Don't forget, your poems are due tomorrow. It may be a poem you've written yourself, or one by your favorite author. I'll expect you to read the poetry in front of the class."

Amy kept her head down and pretended to read, but the words on the page swam before her eyes. She felt badly to have disappointed her teacher. Even worse, if Mother heard of it, she'd be in more trouble than a sneak caught with his hand in the cookie jar.

Miss Lewis dismissed the class for the day. Amy wanted to bolt for the door—not waiting for Dolly— and run all the way home. Instead, she forced herself to walk decorously, an arithmetic book under one arm, lunch bucket in her hand.

Amy stopped just inside the front door and waited for her sister. She hadn't long to linger before Dolly rushed up, eager to get home. Together the girls pushed open the doors and started down the steps of the schoolhouse. As their feet touched the second step, they abruptly halted and stared wide-eyed.... There on the sidewalk stood their father.

"What is he doing here?" Dolly whispered, a hand in front of her mouth. "Father never comes to meet us."

Fred frowned, reached in his vest pocket and withdrew his watch. "School dismissed ten minutes ago; what took you so long to get out here? Do you always dally this way before starting for home?" he grumbled.

Amy and Dolly stared at each other. Neither one knew how to respond. Father didn't seem to expect an answer as he rushed on to explain his presence.

"The bloomin' Indians are about, that's what. They bear watching. Eh? Indeed, one of those bucks might like to capture a blonde-haired squaw." Not quite smiling, Fred flicked a finger across his mustache. "I've got a bit much invested to let that happen—now haven't I? I'll just be walking my girls home today."

Amy reddened and moved closer to Dolly taking her by the hand. Fred chuckled, a sound deep in his throat. The sisters stared at their father. He had been teasing them; nevertheless, that didn't diminish their awe on seeing the Indians.

Indians mounted on horses passed by on the road. Curiosity got the better of Amy; she watched them though she tried hard not to stare. Dressed in buckskins, the Indians' hair hung in long dark braids across their shoulders. Most wore an eagle feather in their hair. If the Indians noticed the girls, they gave no indication—their faces stoic—eyes straight ahead.

To herself, Amy counted eight horses. The last Indian to ride by showed no reticence, but openly watched the palefaces from his cradleboard on the back of his mother. His eyes were nearly dark as the coal Mother shoveled onto the fire in the kitchen range.

"He's cute," Amy whispered to Dolly. "How old do you suppose he is?"

Dolly shrugged. "I don't know, not as old as our Harold."

A few white clouds scudded across an azure sky. Sun shone in golden puddles on spring grass turning green. *No wonder the Indians are about, thought Amy, today is gorgeous.*

Fred slowed his usual fast pace to accommodate his girls. But as soon as their house came into view, he lengthened his stride forcing Amy and Dolly to trot to keep up.

Once the trio entered the front gate, Eric dropped from his perch in the tree. Bursting with his news, he began jabbering even before Father could hook the latch.

"Father, did you see the Indians? Amy, Dolly, did you see them? Did you see those bloomin' Indians? That old squaw took Mother's rug—I saw her! She snatched it right off the fence. She did!" Eric gulped a breath and pulled on his father's sleeve. "If I'd had rocks in my pocket, I could'a beaned one right off her old noodle."

Fred laughed and tousled Eric's hair. "Well sport, if you had, those bucks might have plucked you out of that tree and gave you what for. Best leave the Indians alone."

Eric lost some of his fervor as he recounted for their mother how the squaw made off with her rug. He left out the part about the rocks.

A fleeting frown crossed their mother's face before she placed Harold across her shoulder and gently patted his back. "Well son, I'm glad you stayed quiet and hidden. Perhaps the lady thought we no longer needed the rug if it was on the fence."

No Indians were about the next morning as Amy traipsed off to school with Dolly, Cecil, and Percy. The poem Miss Lewis asked for lay copied and folded neatly inside her tablet. Amy hadn't eaten much breakfast this morning; but the butterflies making a stopover in her tummy didn't seem to notice. *I hope Miss Lewis doesn't call on me first.* Amy tried to swallow and found her mouth had gone drier than a sunbaked mud-hole in August.

The cool wind tugging at Amy's hair had little to do with the shivers running up her backbone, and even less to do with the robin's egg blue sky. Could she read her poem without stumbling over the words?

Miss Lewis took roll call and read a psalm from the Bible. The class sang a couple songs and then the expected moment came. "Amy Gladys you may read your poem next."

Amy, with paper in hand, made her way slowly to the front of the room and stood in front of the teacher's desk. Carefully she unfolded the piece, glanced shyly at her classmates and began to read:

There was an old lady, so I've heard tell,
Who went to market, her eggs for to sell.
She went to market, all on Market's Day,
And fell asleep on the King's Highway.
There came by a peddler; his name was Stout,
Who cut her petticoats all 'round about.
He cut her petticoats up to the knees,
Which made the old lady both shiver and freeze.
When at first this old lady did wake,
She began to shiver and she began to shake.
She began to shiver and she began to cry,
"Lawk-a-mercy, this is none o' I."
"But if it be I, as I hope it will be,
I have a little dog at home—he'll know me.
If it be I, he'll wag his little tail.
If it be not I, he'll loudly bark and wail."
Up got the old woman, all in the dark.
Up got the little dog and he began to bark.
He began to bark and she began to cry,
"Lawwwk-a-mercy, this is none o' I."

A second or two passed before the children burst into loud laughter. Startled, Amy stared at her classmates. Eyes cast down; she raced back to her desk and buried her face in her arms. *Ooooooh, they're laughing at me!* Amy tried to muffle her sobs as her classmates laughed even harder.

"All right, children. That's enough laughter," said Miss Lewis. "I believe Amy thinks we are laughing at her."

Miss Lewis quietly walked back to Amy's desk and laid a gentle hand on her arm. "Amy, your poem is very funny, and your elocution was faultless." The teacher continued in a voice all could hear. "I'll be giving you a good mark for your performance today."

With measured strides the teacher walked back to her desk and called a boy forward for his recitation.

Slowly Amy lifted her tear-stained face and wiped her eyes with the handkerchief she carried tucked in her sleeve. Had her classmates not been laughing at her afterall?

The girl sitting in the desk behind her tapped Amy on the shoulder and whispered, "Amy, your poem is really, really funny! Lawwwk-a-mercy -I liked the part about the little dog. I wish I had a poem like yours."

Amy brightened and whispered a reply while teacher's back was turned. "I know it by heart, I can tell it again at recess if you want."

CHAPTER 22

F red did well with his photography; he worked hard and Edith wouldn't dream of finding fault. Nevertheless, frugal as she tried to be, the money simply didn't go far enough. The older children worked at whatever fell to hand, and they willingly gave their money to their mother. Edith tried her best to put that money aside for her children, but more often than not, their earnings slipped away for day-to-day living.

With trembling fingers, Edith tore open the envelope the postman delivered. She felt her face growing warm as she looked at the bill. *What does the Bible say about pride? Something about going before a fall?* Well, she'd simply have to swallow hers; though it stuck in her throat like too large a chunk of humble pie.

"Dolly, Amy, Cecil, I'm glad you're home. I have an errand I must run. Please do your chores and watch after Annie and your little brothers. I'll take Harold with me." Edith buttoned her long coat and placed her hat atop her head. Taking the baby in her arms, she squared her shoulders and marched out the door.

Seated in a chair—the desk between them—Edith faced the doctor. She licked her lips and tried to slow her racing heart. "Dr. Nelson, I so appreciate your excellent care of me and baby Harold, but I have no money to pay you." Edith thought she might faint, but she refused to take her eyes from the doctor's face. "Is there some way I might work to compensate you?"

Except for the doctor's six-foot height, and twinkling brown eyes there was nothing remarkable about his looks. A man in his mid to late fifties, he had a shiny baldpate, a well-trimmed mustache, and a full dark beard. One had to get to know him, before appreciating his sense of humor and his compassionate nature.

"My dear Mrs. Watts, I know you to be a genteel and educated lady. But, if you don't mind a little blood, puke, and sometimes worse, you may start when you're ready." He smiled. "Work as many hours as you feel comfortable being away from your family."

☎

Wanting to help, Amy raced to get clean nappies from the drawer in the sideboard. She watched as her mother kissed baby Harold's soft cheek and placed him, along with the nappies, in the pram. Edith smiled at her daughter and pulled the small blue and yellow quilt over her son.

Amy strolled along with her mother to the doctor's office. She started to push Harold in his perambulator toward the front door, but Mother reached out a hand to stop her.

"No, no Daughter. I always go in the back way. The fewer people who know I'm working outside my home the better."

Amy nodded her head and proceeded to push the pram close to the back door. Mother bent and placed a kiss on her forehead before lifting Harold, swaddled in his quilt, to her shoulder. "Be sure you help Dolly when you get home," admonished Mother.

Amy nodded again and rushed off to her job of helping a lady who often suffered with sick headaches. To give the ailing mother some quiet time, Amy took charge of the little three-year-old girl and her baby sister. Often she placed the baby in the pram and pushed her around the block numerous times. Always she walked slowly enough for the three-year-old. For this, Amy earned twenty-five cents a week.

To the industrious Watts family, it felt like their summer sped along faster than flotsam rushing down a swollen river.

By far the most important task allotted to Dolly was keeping an eye on her younger siblings. Mother said to her, "My dear, I couldn't work without your help." Father, sounding like a drill sergeant or maybe a bull moose, laid down the law. He threatened the razor strop if they didn't mind and help their sister.

Cecil continued to deliver papers and take on other jobs as well. He whitewashed fences and outbuildings, cut grass, and tended gardens. He learned to milk cows and did so frequently for a farmer who took a liking to him.

Gone from early 'till late, Reginald earned wages at the brickyard. Sometimes he made more in a week than did his father.

Everyone pitched in to help at home, but Edith surely worked the hardest. Up before dawn, it was often after midnight when she tumbled into bed. If Edith sometimes wondered if she were coming or going, who could blame her? With the help of her older children, she managed to can and preserve quantities of fruits and vegetables for the winter that lay ahead of them. Days passed when the only time she sat down was to eat or to nurse baby Harold.

ℬ

Edith sighed and stirred the batter for another cake. Annie had just turned four on February 6 and today they would celebrate Harold's first birthday. What time he wasn't hanging on to her skirt, or plopped on his bottom, the baby tottered on chubby legs after Annie and Leslie. The three were now the only children home in the mornings.

Eric, her mischief maker, had trotted off to school with Percy last September, proud as a bantam rooster amongst a dozen hens, to be starting first grade. Those two would be home from school shortly. Edith's biggest helpers, Cecil, Dolly, and Amy, would come trouping home two hours later. Edith knew from experience her day would go fast; she had no need to watch the clock.

This wasn't true of Amy; stuck in school, she tried hard to keep her attention focused on her work. Not stealing glances at the slow-ticking clock was about as hard as not dipping a finger in the cake batter when Mother turned her back. She wanted to rush home now and help her mother prepare for Harold's birthday party.

ℬ

Amy and Dolly excused themselves and cleared the dirty dishes from the table. Little Harold seemed to know attention focused on him. He laughed, crowed, and slapped his hands on the wooden tray of his high-chair. Ordinarily a reprimand would be forthcoming, but Father was in a jovial mood this evening.

Mother smiled as she set the layered cake for the family on the table. She had baked Harold his own special treat, a tiny cake with chocolate icing. All eyes were on the baby as Edith placed the dessert on the tray in front of him.

An experimental finger touched the frosting. Harold giggled. Encouraged by smiles and chuckles from his family, two little fists grabbed for the cake. Some found its way to his mouth, a lot more covered his face and decorated his hair.

Father laughed and spoke to Edith. "Next Sunday, you can hold our little rapscallion and I'll take your picture." Fred beamed on his family. "When we get home from church, and you have on your Sunday-go-to-meetin' clothes, I'll take everyone's picture. I'll seat you two at a time on a chair, set up my camera outside and focus through the window."

On April 11, Edith baked another birthday cake. This year Dolly's birthday fell on Saturday and Amy helped her mother with all the preparations. Because it was her special day, Dolly could choose what she wanted for supper.

After the cake was safely in the oven, Amy took a deep breath and approached her mother. "Mother, do you think it would be all right if I took a few pennies of my earnings and bought candles for Dolly's cake?"

Edith looked a bit startled and then quickly smiled. "My dear, what a nice thought. I think we can arrange it. And while you are at the store, you may pick up a few things for me. I'll give you a list."

Happy to have twelve little candles to put on Dolly's cake, Amy knew better than to ask for money to buy her a card. Maybe she could scrounge enough paper to make one.

☙

By the time Reginald's sixteenth birthday rolled around in July, the family had been in Melita more than three years. It felt like home. Out of school for the summer, the older children were once again in demand for odd jobs.

No one had been more surprised than Amy and Dolly when at the end of school, Mother declared she again wished to work for Dr. Nelson.

"Dolly," said Mother, "will you mind so terribly watching your little sister and brothers again? You and Amy can share in the housework."

Alone in their bedroom one night after Annie fell asleep, Amy questioned Dolly. "Why do you think Mother is working for the doctor again? I thought she didn't like leaving our home."

"How should I know?" Dolly hissed in a whisper. "I'm knackered from housework, chasing after Harold, and keeping an eye on Annie and Leslie. As for Eric, I just may kill him. He ran off again today."

"I'm sorry. You could tell Father." Amy gently touched her arm. "Maybe we could trade jobs for a bit."

Dolly softened. "You know we can't. And you know I can't tell Father. He'd whip the hide off Eric."

"Maybe you should tell Mother."

"I don't think so," Dolly lamented. "I think she's worried about something. And she's so tired all the time." Dolly sighed. "Maybe I'll ask Reg to talk to Eric."

Amy began to wonder if Mother had forgotten her birthday. This was Saturday, in two more days, August 3, she'd be ten years old. Shouldn't Mother be asking her what she wanted for supper? Maybe Mother planned a surprise. That would be nice. Amy liked surprises.

Amy did receive a surprise, but it didn't pertain to her birthday. A surprise her mother had nothing to do with. Father marched in, took his place at the supper table and announced, "Now—Dearie—don't cry, but I'll be leaving come Wednesday. I've gotten a letter. I'll go to Edmonton and from there to Paddle River. I aim to get us a homestead. And it's pretty clear, that's not going to happen here."

The family ate their supper in stunned silence. Reg excused himself and rose from the table. One by one, the older children begged to be excused and quickly disappeared from the dining room. They'd come back later and help their mother.

True to his word, Fred left on Wednesday. Edith kissed him goodbye, and saw him off at the train station. Once back in the privacy of her home, she allowed herself a good cry. That over, she squared her shoulders, lifted her chin and got on with it.

Trusting her own judgment, Edith bought a lamb and two little piglets. They would need meat for winter, and the larder was nearly empty. The children immediately made a pet of the lamb, even though she warned it would be butchered later.

Edith ended her job with Dr. Nelson at the beginning of September when the children started back to school. Fred had promised to be back home by then, but of course he wasn't.

He finally made it back home the last week of September. Edith breathed a sigh of relief and welcomed him as though he were King Midas with a bag full of gold. Happy her husband would be with her for the birth of their next child, due any day now, Edith thought she could forgive him just about anything. No doubt, his return meant they would soon be moving again, and this time with a tiny baby. Nevertheless, with his arms around her, she felt loved and protected.

CHAPTER 23

Reginald gave two weeks notice and quit his job at the brickyard. His family needed him at home to help get ready for the move. A part of him resented his father for uprooting the family yet again. It had to be doubly hard on his dear mother, now that she had little Evelyn, and she only a few weeks old. Still, if he were honest, he'd have to admit the thought of carving a homestead out of the wilderness appealed to his budding manhood. Swinging an ax, clearing brush, and building their own log house, were all things he secretly longed to do.

It started to spit snow as Reg tucked his lunch pail under his arm and began the trudge home. He pulled his cap down over his ears. This time of year bears began to think of hibernation and families huddled close to their stoves. What would it be like for his family to face an uncertain future with winter on the threshold?

Home at last, Reg quickly closed the kitchen door to conserve heat. Edith looked up and smiled but her eyes telegraphed worry. Baby Evelyn whimpered. Mother lifted the infant to her shoulder and gently patted her back.

Dolly and Amy, under their mother's tutelage, prepared a simple supper of bangers and mash. The kettle for tea simmered on the back of the stove. Percy and

Eric scuttled back and forth with plates and utensils for the table.

"Reginald?" Fred roared from the top of the stairs. "Are you down there? Cecil?" "You boys get up here— now—and help me with these bloody trunks."

Reg stopped preparing tea and raced up the stairs two at a time.

Cecil popped up behind his father and croaked, "I'm here."

"What? ... Where were you?"

"In my room, sir. Studying, sir."

Irritated at having bumped his head while retrieving the trunks from the cramped and dusty closet under the eaves, Fred grunted something best not repeated. Cecil inched his way around his father and hefted one end of a trunk. Reg grabbed the other end. Fred recovered himself and helped his boys get the chests safely down the stairs.

Edith tucked Evelyn in her cradle and glared at the trunks shoved against the parlour wall. By now, she should be adept at preparing to move. In truth, she felt at a loss. Should she start with kitchen utensils, bedding, or clothing? Once on the train, there would be no opening of chests until they arrived at their destination. Things needed while on the trip, must go into the valises.

Immediately after supper, Fred began to carefully wrap his photography equipment and stow it in one of the trunks. It was a task he must do himself. He allowed no one to touch his cameras.

The children gathered around their mother, willing to help in any way they could. Amy searched her mother's face hoping for a clue how she might feel about moving. Not that it mattered—Mother would do what their father wished her to do. They all would.

Harold tugged on his mother's skirt and held up his arms. "Up, up," he begged. Distracted, Edith absently smoothed his hair, but she didn't pick him up. *Poor little tyke, he feels neglected. He's not the baby anymore, and I don't even have time to cuddle him.*

Annie and Leslie pulled Harold away. "Come on, little britches," chirped Leslie. "You can play with my soldiers."

Edith smiled, and smoothed her apron before turning around to cast another disparaging look at the trunks she needed to fill. Could she possibly pack the jars of food she had canned? Did she dare ask Fred to purchase another trunk? Edith's thoughts churned in her mind like cream waiting to solidify into butter. First, she needed to wash the nappies Evelyn had soiled today, and get them dried. Edith feared she'd run out of clean diapers, and there'd be no way to wash or purchase more while on the train.

A few days travel by rail surely didn't compare to the weeks it took to cross an ocean. Edith, nevertheless, dreaded this move with a tiny baby and a toddler not yet two years old. Mentally, she derided herself, but it didn't stop her from feeling like a leaf pushed by the wind as she scurried from kitchen to trunk with carefully wrapped bowls.

Finished loading his chest with camera equipment, Fred took charge. With the force of a drill sergeant, he issued orders to his children. No one doubted what he or she was to do. Amy and Dolly emptied kitchen cupboards and washed shelves. Reginald, Cecil, and

Percy scampered upstairs. The boys trouped down with armload after armload of bedding, linens, and clothing.

Taking Edith by the shoulders, Fred guided her to a kitchen chair and bid her sit down. He poured them both a steaming cup of tea, and laced it heavily with cream and sugar. "Now my dearie, don't you fret, everything's going to be fine. You'll see! A month or two and we'll have a place of our own. No more of this renting; we'll be land owners."

Edith hid her fears behind a smile; her husband's enthusiasm called for a positive response. If she thought of the old axiom, *don't count your chickens before they hatch;* she'd save the proverb for her children.

Comfortable here beside the fire, a warm cup of tea in her hand, Edith frowned when the door burst open letting in another blast of cold air. With nine children and two adults running to the outhouse periodically, they might as well have a swinging door.

"Mother, Harold fell asleep on the bedroom floor and Annie and Leslie are curled up on your bed. Harold didn't even wake up when I got his nightgown on him. He did stir a little when I tucked him in his crib. Shall I wake Annie and Leslie and get them to bed?" questioned Dolly.

"We all need to get to bed early," barked Fred. "You'll be rousted out in the morning before the roosters even think about crowing. Where's Eric? I haven't seen that scamp in awhile."

"I think he's saying a last goodbye to the lamb and the pigs," said Dolly.

"Thank you, my dear, for putting little Harold to bed for me. And yes, please get Annie and Leslie upstairs and tucked in. Your father is right, morning will come sooner than we like."

Edith reached out to hug Eric as he attempted to sneak past her. "Son, were you saying goodbye to your animal friends?" Eric ducked his head and nodded. "That's fine then, but you must get ready for bed now. We'll be leaving very early in the morning."

Thankful she had one less thing to worry about, Edith breathed a sigh of satisfaction. Neighbors had paid her a good price for the animals nearly large enough to butcher. As a kindness to her children, the lamb and pigs would remain where they were until sometime tomorrow.

Baby Evelyn let out a muted howl. Before Edith could rise and go to her, Amy brought the baby to her mother. "I'll go to bed now Mother, Father, if there is nothing more I need to do," said Amy.

Morning did indeed come early. Somewhere nearby an owl called his mournful cry. First out of bed this eventful morning, Fred lit a lantern and built a small fire in the kitchen range. He needed hot water with which to shave.

Fully dressed, her hair neatly combed and arranged in a bun on the back of her head, Edith softly climbed the stairs. She stopped in the boys' room first. "Reg, Cecil, it's time to rise. I know I can count on you two to help your little brothers. Reg, you know to strip the beds and somehow stuff the remaining blankets and quilts in the trunk."

Amy and Dolly were already pulling on long underwear as Edith stepped into their room. Annie stirred in her little nest in the center of the featherbed. Slowly she opened her eyes and stretched like a lazy cat reluctant to leave the warmth.

Edith reached for Annie and hugged her tight. "Good morning, my dears. I'm glad to see you are awake." She dropped a kiss on each girls' forehead. "Hurry now, Father has a fire in the kitchen and we may have time for a cup of tea."

Evelyn whimpered in her cradle, her little face turning red in preparation of an all-out howl. When no one came, Harold took action. He straddled his crib rail, not sure what to do next as he peered at his baby sister. Quickly, Edith rescued him. She held him close for a moment before parking him on her bed and reaching for her youngest. *How am I to manage with two babies on the train?*

Fred had arranged for a wagon and driver to come and take them, along with all their baggage, to the train depot. Another half hour and he should be arriving. The fire in the cook stove burned low; there would be nothing but a few embers by the time they left.

He'd removed the ashes from both stoves in an effort to leave things in order. Mrs. Fillmore had been good to them in the three years he'd rented from her. They owed her the courtesy of leaving things clean. As if Edith would have it any other way. Fred chuckled to himself as he recalled their fight against the bedbugs. Vermin hadn't a chance against his wife.

The children were ready and waiting. Dolly held Evelyn and gently rocked her. Harold stood like a little soldier beside Reginald. Eric peered out the window hoping to be first to spot the lanterns on the wagon. The trunks were locked and strapped shut. Four valises were lined up beside the door.

Fred and Edith took one more tour through the house, checking to be sure they hadn't overlooked anything. The tickets were in Fred's pocket. He'd returned the house key to Mrs. Fillmore the day before.

There would be no family to see them off on this adventure. Friends, neighbors, and townspeople had already told them goodbye. No one wanted to be out in the cold and dark before six o'clock in the morning if they didn't have to be.

Strong arms hefted the trunks into the back of the wagon. Reginald, Cecil, and Percy gathered up the valises and picnic baskets. Edith took baby Evelyn from Dolly and carried her out the front gate.

Knowing her children were safely settled, Edith didn't look back as Fred helped her onto the wagon seat, but kept her eyes trained straight ahead. No one heard the soft sigh that escaped her lips.

The driver picked up the reins and clucked to the team. It was time to go.

CHAPTER 24

Amy smothered a giggle as she encouraged Annie to follow along behind Dolly. It wasn't the thought of leaving Melita, or departing on a train trip that caused her amusement. Rather, it was the thought of how they must look, lined up in a long row, just like so many dumb sheep following a leader down a familiar path. Like lambs, they didn't question, but simply followed.

Since this wasn't a regular passenger train, but a modified freight line, no porter welcomed commuters. This was what most folks referred to as the milk and mail run. One passenger car generally sufficed for people going to Winnipeg.

Father stood by the steps, watched and waited to help as one by one his family approached. Mother bit her lip and handed their youngest treasure, baby Evelyn, barely three weeks old, to Fred. Edith climbed the steps and turned. Father handed Evelyn up to her waiting arms.

Dolly, carrying Harold, followed close behind Mother. Amy held tightly to Annie's hand and waited their turn. They watched as Father reached for little Harold and swung him aboard. Like playful kittens, Eric and Leslie didn't wait for help, but scrambled up the stairs, behind their sisters.

.Following close behind his little brothers, Percy carried a large lidded basket; his cap hid the cowlick he generally sported. Next in line, Cecil managed two valises. Reginald brought up the rear with three more satchels, and another picnic basket.

"Choo choo," said Harold from his place on Amy's lap.

"Yes, choo choo," whispered Amy in his ear as the train began to shudder and clatter, wheels grinding on rails, cars lurching forward. Smoke billowed from the engine stack, a bell clanged, followed by one long lonely-sounding whistle and two short toots. They were underway.

Amy looked around, surprised to see she and her siblings, plus Mother and Father, were the only passengers in the car. A giggle escaped her as she reached across Annie and poked Dolly in the ribs. "We must be royalty; we have our very own coach."

Dolly smirked, and whispered a pithy reply, "Pretend we're royalty if you like, but sitting on this hard seat, your bottom is going to be just as numb as any commoner's."

A quick look to see if Mother might be watching and Amy stuck out her tongue at her sister.

In the east, reds and pinks stretched across the horizon. The dawn promised a sunny day. Sunshine also meant the temperature would dip. Involuntarily Amy shivered and hugged Harold a little tighter. Harold squirmed in protest and wriggled his way to the floor.

A fire crackled and blazed behind the isinglass window of the tall round stove in the front left corner of the coach. Mother and Father sat closest to the heat. Baby Evelyn slept on a blanket spread on the bench between them. "You children sit up here as close to the warmth as you can," admonished Mother.

The conductor came through; he stopped to collect tickets from Father and replenish the fire with more coal. Harold stared at the stranger, stuck a thumb in his mouth and ran to big brother. Reginald smiled and set Harold on his lap.

The train chugged along the track and the day wore on without too much to break the monotony. The younger children soon tired of the sameness and their limited ability to run and play. Changing seats and walking up and down the short aisle helped. Amy and her older siblings looked for ways to entertain Annie and the little boys. Farfetched, made-up stories had them snickering and games like hide the button served to pass the time. A horsey ride on Reg or Cecil's foot kept Harold giggling for some minutes.

Dinnertime came as a welcome break. All eyes were on Father as he pulled back the lid on a picnic basket. "Anyone here want an apple?"

Eight voices chorused, "Yes, please, Father."

Not waiting for help, Harold turned in the seat and gathered his knees under him. His head almost touched the bench while his round little bottom stuck up in the air. He wriggled his way to the edge, legs dangling, feet searching for the floor. Owning success, he trotted over, clutched his father's knee, stuck out his hand and said, "Pease."

"Pease is it?" Fred winked at Edith, and smiled at his son. "Well, you shall have your apple. Do you want it whole? Or shall I cut it for you?"

"Ho..." Big eyes looked up at his father. When Fred didn't immediately hand an apple to him, Harold blurted, "Want big!"

Edith placed a gentle hand on Fred's arm. "If he doesn't finish his apple, I'll eat it. It shall not go to waste."

For the moment, Evelyn slept on the blanket-padded seat between her parents. Edith rose from the bench and smoothed her skirt. She bent over the wicker basket and withdrew sandwiches enclosed earlier in a tea towel. Glad for the opportunity to stretch her limbs, Edith marched down the aisle and handed thick ham sandwiches to her children.

An apple followed the sandwich with their mother's admonition, "An apple a day, keeps the doctor away." Mother had a jug of tea if they were thirsty, but they would have to drink it cold.

"Enjoy," Dolly whispered to Amy as she bit into her sandwich. "We don't have to do the dishes."

All morning long Amy and her siblings swapped places to sit, and found all seats equally hard. It was now Amy's turn to sit by the window. Annie, still munching on her apple, climbed onto her sister's lap and pressed her nose against the glass. "Lookit," she squealed, "It's snowing." A few flakes swirled willy-nilly in no hurry to reach earth. "Will snow stop the choo choo train?"

Amy giggled and hugged Annie tight. "No, I don't think so. It would have to snow a whole bunch." *So much for our sunny day,* she thought. Clouds darkened the sky and black cinders from the smokestack mixed with pristine snowflakes floated past their window.

A smile tugged at Edith's lips as she surveyed her family. She covered herself and Evelyn with a shawl as the baby nursed. Chin on his chest, Fred snored on the bench beside her. His ability to sleep in less than ideal situations served him well. If Edith didn't understand how he could so completely relax, she nevertheless welcomed his snores as cover for Evelyn's greedy sucking noises.

Eric squiggled his way to a seat by the window and was first to spot a prairie dog amongst the waving grass. The furry little creature sat upright on his dirt mound, sharp eyes watching for danger. "Hey—lookit there! Bet he's barkin' at this old train," Eric quipped.

Percy boosted Harold so he could see. "There he is! See him?" Harold giggled, clapped his hands and pointed.

"I'm surprised he hasn't hibernated," said Reginald. "He's going to freeze his whiskers."

"Oh, he's going to freeze more than that if he doesn't get back down in his burrow. Or maybe he'll get his head blown off." Fred treated himself to a long leisurely stretch and grinned at his offspring. "You children can think he's cute if you like, but I'm here to tell you, the farmers hate them. They destroy a lot of grain."

The train slowed and started across a lengthy trestle. A long mournful blast of the whistle gave notice to man and beast this giant smoke-belching iron monster wasn't to be trifled with. Amy sighed. *No doubt Father is right. But I like the furry creatures anyway.*

Once across the trestle the tracks curved and followed along a broad stream. Alder and yellow aspen grew along the banks leaving occasional open spaces where one could glimpse the clear flowing water.

Amy relinquished her seat next to the window and settled again next to Dolly. The two girls leaned against each other for support. Lulled by the sway of the train and the monotonous click-clack click-clack of the wheels on rails, Amy's eyes drooped. She'd lost track of how many times the train had stopped at some little hamlet. It seemed they would never reach Winnipeg.

Eric shattered the quiet when he hollered. "Look! Look there!" A white-tailed deer bounded from the trees and loped along beside the rails. For a little while it seemed the deer might outdistance the train. Everyone got a good look at the four-point buck before he veered off across a field.

"Oh, he is pretty isn't he?" exclaimed Mother. "But what is that I see at the edge of the trees?"

Fred stretched to peer out the window in the direction Edith indicated. He quickly stood for a better look. "Children—look there! Be quick now!" Fred pointed. A bear left the cover of trees and ambled out to have a look at this curious beast on the tracks. Apparently he didn't like what he saw; he turned and shuffled back to the brush.

"That's one big bear," exclaimed Fred. "I do believe that was a grizzly. Too big, I think, for a black bear."

"Father, will we have bears where we are going?" piped Eric.

"Bears in Paddle River? Yes, I expect so." Fred grinned. "But they'll be holed up in their dens by the time we get there this winter. Spring's when we'll need to watch for them."

The train slowed and pulled into the station, Winnipeg at last!

"Stay together now and don't dally," instructed Father. "Our train for Edmonton leaves in one hour. If we step lively we'll have time for tea." Fred led the way to a nearby teahouse. If they looked like a small invasion entering the shop, the proprietor took it in stride and served them without delay.

A nice surprise awaited Amy and her sisters on the Edmonton train. Not only were the seats nicer, but Father had purchased a sleeping berth for their mother and for them. A grin split Amy's face as she scrambled to the top bunk and settled beside Dolly and Annie. Below them, Mother softly crooned to baby Evelyn and little Harold.

Amy tried to listen to her mother's soothing voice, but the hypnotic click-clack of wheels on rails became the more dominant sound. The repetition put her to sleep.

CHAPTER 25

Edith lay still on the narrow bunk, baby Evelyn on one side of her, little Harold on the other. She shivered, but not from the cold. Her body longed for sleep, but her mind raced ahead of the train. She couldn't shake the sense of foreboding that enveloped her like an icy fog. *I can't let my family know I'm afraid, but how am I to manage in a wilderness? What if one of my babies becomes really ill?*

"Ma'am," the porter called softly through the curtain, "perhaps this will help with your little one."

Edith inched the curtain aside. Immaculate in his cap and white coat, the porter handed her a blanket-lined basket for her baby. White teeth gleamed in a dark face as he smiled down at her. "I have five of my own," he said. "It's not easy traveling with little ones."

His simple act of kindness undid her. Thankful her children slept, Edith let the tears course down her cheeks. She didn't tell the porter she had five more boys, nor did she tell him her heart hurt for the little girl left behind in England. After all this time, Norah wouldn't even remember her.

Fred had said he'd go after Norah in two years, but two years had come and gone. They simply didn't have the money. Edith worried the berths she and the girls now enjoyed were an extravagance they should have forgone, but it felt so good to lie down. Added to the mix was the fear her milk might dry up if she didn't get enough rest. She hadn't fully regained her strength after birthing Evelyn.

In the parlour car Fred wrestled with his own doubts. Contrary to his usual pattern, he couldn't sleep. He had squirreled away money in preparation for the eventuality of homesteading. But would it be enough? Fred squirmed in his seat and stuffed the pillow the porter had given him earlier behind his back. A glance around told him his boys slept. Or if they weren't actually asleep, they rested quietly, eyes closed.

He'd more or less promised his wife he'd go after Norah before now. What he hadn't planned on were two more babies. All-around expenses were greater than he'd figured on. Well, they'd just have to make the best of it. Children were an asset, arrows in his quiver and all that. Once he got his homestead established, he'd go for his daughter.

A house awaited their arrival in Edmonton. Fred had made certain of that with a healthy deposit to the landlord while on his previous visit there. With any luck they wouldn't be in Edmonton long. He'd get his land claim and they'd go on to Paddle River.

෭෨

After three days of nothing much to do but sit and stare out a window, boredom overtook the Watts children and settled on them like cinders on fresh snow. Even baby Evelyn fretted more than usual. Games the older children instituted to entertain the younger ones fell flatter than a hard-shelled beetle squashed on the railroad.

Harold resorted to sucking his thumb. Annie and Leslie poked each other until Dolly pulled Annie onto her lap and sent Leslie to sit beside Reg. A look from their father warned the children they'd better not fuss.

Edith's smile reassured her brood. She placed a gentle hand on Fred's sleeve and spoke for his ears alone. "How much longer before we reach Edmonton?"

"Tired, Dearie?" Fred pulled his watch from his vest pocket and made a show of checking the time. He smiled at his wife. "I figure another twenty minutes or so, we should be reaching the depot." He placed an arm around her shoulders. "Tonight you can sleep in a real bed."

The train slowed. The conductor walked through the car and announced, "Strathcona Station ahead, twenty minutes till arrival."

Fred beamed, Edith smiled and lifted baby Evelyn to her shoulder. The children sat up straighter and stared out the windows with renewed interest. Nearly dark at four in the afternoon, lights twinkled in houses and businesses located beside the tracks. After living in Melita, the children were in awe of Edmonton with its population of over 8,350.

Edith accepted assistance and stepped from the train onto the station platform. She clutched Fred's arm and gazed in astonishment at the station house. "Fred, this is quite grand! The building is as lovely as anything I recall seeing in England. Of course I'm partial to the Queen Anne style, but it's really the red brick and stone façade that sets it apart, is it not?"

Fred opened the door to the station house and ushered his family inside. "Ah, yes, that's Tyndall stone from a quarry in Winnipeg. This station is brand new you know, started last year and as I understand it, they are still putting finishing touches to the building." Fred cleared his throat and continued, glad for the opportunity to enlighten his family.

"The building is 135 feet long and 38 feet wide. I read in the *Winnipeg Free Press,* the total cost was $24,382.00. I'd say it's quite grand! They certainly didn't skimp on materials, only the best lumber, brick, and stone went into the construction.

"Edith, I want you to stay here with the girls and little boys until I come back for you. The ladies and gentlemen's waiting rooms are separate. You can have a modicum of privacy in the room set aside for women and I won't have to worry about you and Evelyn staying warm."

Fred looked to his boys but continued to address Edith. "Reginald, Cecil, and Percy can go with me. I'll hail a wagon and we'll get the trunks to our residence. The house is likely to be colder than ducks' feet. I'll get fires going as quickly as I can. The boys can take charge once that's done; then I'll come back and get you. With any luck, Reg can have tea ready by the time I get you and the children home."

❧

The horses pulled the hack to the curb in front of the two-story house. The first thing Edith noticed were the windows. Her hand flew to her mouth as she stifled a gasp of surprise. Had Fred or the cabdriver made a mistake? This house seemed much too grand to be a rental. Lights blazed from every visible windowpane. Only electricity could pour forth this much brilliance.

Edith maintained her skepticism until she saw Reginald open the door and hurry toward them. Fred looked at her face and laughed outright as he helped her down from the cab. Her obvious delight in the house acted as a springtime tonic to his soul.

Cecil followed close behind Reg and the two boys helped their sisters alight. Amy, Dolly, and Annie stood on the brick walk and stared at the house. "Is this where we're going to stay?" questioned Amy. "This house looks new. And it's big!"

Fred's chest expanded with pride as he took baby Evelyn, the only child who seemed unimpressed, in his arms and led the way to the front door with its ornate-looking frost-paned glass. "Well, don't get too comfortable," warned Fred. "If I have my way, we won't be here long."

Immediately beyond the front door, they stepped into a lighted entrance hall from which a stairway led to rooms upstairs. Off to the right of the foyer a door opened into a wainscoted formal parlor with a fireplace. The upper walls were papered in a pleasing green and peach striped pattern. Edith noticed wood had been placed on the grate, ready for a match to set it ablaze.

To the left of the hall another door led to a parlour the family would use every day. Though not quite so grand, it looked cozy with adequate chairs and a worn leather couch. A potbellied stove at one end of the room radiated a warmth that drew the children like cats to cream. Edith hesitated and held her hands out to the heat.

"Mother, there's a fire in the kitchen range as well," said Reginald. "I put the kettle on and I think the water is hot enough for tea."

Edith smiled in approval and followed her eldest through the door leading to the kitchen. Another pleasant surprise awaited her in this electric-lighted room. A hot water tank stood directly behind the stove. Coils ran through the firebox heating water easier than anything they'd dealt with previously. The fire hadn't been going long enough to heat the cold water in the tank, but by tomorrow after breakfast they'd surely have hot water aplenty. *Imagine turning a faucet and getting hot water with which to wash dishes.*

"Fred, this is marvelous," exclaimed Edith, "a large kitchen and a sink with running water. And is that a pantry I see through there?"

"It is, and there's a cellar too. But as I said, don't get too settled in, we won't be here long." Fred led the way from the kitchen to the adjoining dining room, which also sported a stove, and from there to the formal parlor. The smaller children giggled when they found themselves back in the entranceway and realized they had gone in a circle.

As if anticipating their thoughts, Fred warned, "No running through the house and banging doors. When you open a door close it gently behind you."

Eric, Leslie, Annie, and Amy covertly eyed the polished banister as they climbed the stairs. They wouldn't slide down it while Father watched, but he couldn't be present all the time.

Four bedrooms opened off the upstairs hallway and wonder of wonders, at the near end of the corridor a door opened revealing a modern bathroom. A claw-footed tub with room for adults to stretch their legs graced the room. A pedestal sink hugged the opposite wall. Overhead, a polished wooden box, very near the ceiling, clung to the far wall, a pull chain hanging down from it. A commode was bolted to the floor beneath the overhead contraption.

Amy eyed it with remembered embarrassment. At least she now knew if she pulled the chain the house wouldn't be flooded.

The upstairs rooms were not as icy cold as they might have been; nevertheless, no one wanted to linger overly long unless they could crawl beneath bed covers. Edith nearly wept with gratitude when she discovered the boys had managed to get the proper trunks upstairs and they had made up the beds.

Unlike their previous house, bedbugs did not inhabit these rooms or beds. Everything appeared squeaky clean. The mattresses were not of feathers, but the gray striped ticks were cotton-stuffed, solid and thick enough to be comfortable for bodies weary of travel.

"Come children," Edith urged, "we'll have our tea and retire early. Tomorrow is another day and even with all this luxury, I'm sure our hands will find plenty to do.

CHAPTER 26

Reginald, Cecil, and Percy occupied themselves with trips to the market and post office each day. Father had warned their mother not to buy commodities too far ahead as they would not be in Edmonton long. As a result, the boys brought home only enough groceries for one or two days. One exception was flour. Flour would keep and Mother made bread several loaves at a time. Bread, they could take with them; if it froze, it wouldn't matter.

Eric and Leslie watched their older brothers button their coats. "Can we go with you today?" piped Leslie. "I can keep up and I can carry something too."

Reg grinned at his little brother. "Sure half-pint, you can go; get your coat, cap, and mittens. It's cold out there, so don't complain if you freeze your whiskers."

Eric snickered as he and Leslie dashed away to get their wraps. "We don't have whiskers," he hollered.

"Eric, please don't shout in the house," admonished Mother. "Your baby sister is napping. And Leslie, it's *may* I go." Edith smiled. "If you'll come here, I'll wrap your muffler nice and tight around your neck."

Edith smiled when she wanted to cry. How could they leave this nice house with all its conveniences and start out for an uncertain future in the middle of wintertime? Secretly, she prayed Fred's land grant wouldn't come through until spring, but she knew it was a prayer likely to go unanswered. No doubt, her husband prayed daily the necessary papers would be there when he went to check.

Thankfully, the younger children were unaware of her fears, but she could see the same apprehension she felt reflected in the eyes of her older offspring. She knew Reginald, Cecil, Dolly, and Amy thought their father unwise for starting out in the bitter cold of winter. She had heard their whispered consultations, though she'd pretended she didn't. To hear would have been to reprimand, and how could she scold when she herself thought it less than wise.

Annie played with little Harold in the parlor while Dolly and Amy helped their mother in the kitchen. Amy stood at the sink and peeled enough potatoes for the Irish army, or so it seemed to her aching arms and cramped hands.

Tears rolled down Dolly's cheeks as she peeled and chopped onions. Mother smiled at her girls as she fried bacon in a big black iron skillet. "I think you've peeled enough potatoes now, Amy, no doubt that's enough onions too, Dolly. You girls may do whatever you would like now; I'll finish up with the soup."

The girls washed and dried their hands at the kitchen sink, and then together they climbed the stairs to their room. "What shall we do now?" asked Amy.

"I don't know," huffed Dolly. "What I really want to do is go to school, but Father says no—we'd just get started and we'd have to quit. I wish he'd let us go anyway; maybe we'll be here longer than he thinks."

"I wanta go to school too. But you know Father won't let us, not until we get to Paddle River." Amy grimaced. "Reg says maybe we can't go to school when we get there either—sometimes it's just too cold."

" Kings and cabbages!" spewed Dolly. "How are we ever going to learn anything, if we can't go to school?"

Amy bounced off the bed and waltzed to the window. "Oh, hurry, look—the boys are back and Percy is carrying a cat—looks like maybe a half-grown kitten. I hope it isn't mean like that old 'Bleed-'im' cat he dragged home back in England." Amy rubbed her cheek. "That nasty ole cat scratched me good."

"That he did! I think you have a little scar there yet." Dolly wrapped an arm around her sister and gave her a little squeeze. "But you know our Percy; if there's a stray cat wandering around, he'll drag it home. If anyone can make a pet out of the contrary things, it's Percy. Felines take to him like horses to hay."

"I wonder if Father will let him keep it. You know our father says we won't be here very long. Can we take a cat in the wagon? Maybe we should say a cat would be good for catching mice in our new homestead." Amy sighed and turned from the window, letting the lace curtain drop. "Come on; let's go see Percy's new kitty."

"Okay, it's too cold up here anyhow; my fingers and toes are starting to feel like frozen bangers." Dolly clutched the banister and slowly led the way down the stairs. Her teeth started to chatter as she mumbled, "I wish Percy would find a stray dog. Dogs mind better, and a dog might help keep us warm."

Everyone had gathered around the stove in the parlour. Amy's mouth dropped open when she saw Mother seated in the rocker—the half-grown kitten lay curled and purring in her lap. Percy wore a grin bright enough to melt hoarfrost on the grass.

Listening to Mother's admonition to be gentle, Leslie, Annie, and little Harold took turns stroking the furry head with two or three fingers. Reginald, Cecil, and Eric had retreated to the kitchen to warm milk for the scruffy-looking kitten.

"Percy," said Mother, "as soon as the milk is warm, you'd better take the kitten to the barn. If she intends to stay, she'll snuggle down in the hay."

"Well, well, my dearie, and what have we here, eh? Adopting more strays are we?"

Amy jumped. Intent on watching the kitten, she hadn't heard her father walk in and stand directly behind her.

"Ah, Fred, you're home." Mother looked up and smiled. "Yes, our Percy found the little animal. I do believe the kitten is gentle; she hasn't stopped purring since I placed her in my lap. The children will take her to the barn as soon as they've warmed some milk for her."

"Well, the cat will have to decide if she's staying or going." Fred's face split in a huge grin as he waved the papers he held in his right hand. "Dearie, we have our homestead, the southeast quarter of Section 27, Township 59, Range 3, and Meridian 5."

Edith handed the kitten back to Percy. She stood and shook out her apron—her blue eyes appeared enormous as she faced her husband. "So then, we'll be leaving soon—or dare we wait for spring?"

Thinking she must surely be joshing, Fred started to laugh, but when he read the look of apprehension on the face of his wife and on his children's faces too, he cut it short. His voice came out harsh and clipped,

"Of course we'll go now! We have a homestead to start proving up on."

Edith paled and started for the kitchen. "I'll get dinner on the table."

Fred softened his tone as he seated himself at the dining table, "That's fine then, eh? Soon as I've eaten, I'll be off to buy a wagon and team of horses. I've been asking around and I believe I know where I can purchase sound animals and a topnotch wagon.

"Reg and Cecil can go with me—I can use a strong back or two. We will have a good many supplies to purchase, grain for the horses, axes, saws, shovels. Food enough to last us awhile, barrels of flour, beans, salt pork, salt cod, corn syrup, soda crackers, and tea for sure." Fred looked down the table. "I won't forget your yeast for bread making, Dearie, and you needn't fret—we'll have plenty of game for fresh meat."

Fred returned thanks. Except for Father, and little Harold in his highchair, everyone kept their eyes downcast as they sat around the dinner table and quietly ate hot potato soup. Amy gently blew on a spoonful to cool it before raising it to her lips.

Even the excitement of a new kitten paled in comparison to Father's declaration of a homestead secured. Percy, however, hadn't forgotten. Amy held her breath when her brother dared raise the question.

"Father, did you mean I could take my kitten to Paddle River with us?"

Fred stopped eating and stared at his son. He artfully wiped his mouth and dabbed at his mustache. He laid aside his napkin, before scanning the faces of his family. Taking his time, Fred cleared his throat and let a small smile hover about his lips. "Well son, I'll leave it up to you and the cat. My belief is the cat will refuse; felines don't generally like riding in bumpy wagons over frozen ground. I'll not make any special concessions for a cat, but if you and your pet can agree to that—she may come along."

"Thank you, Father," said Percy as he picked up his spoon and quickly finished his soup.

Mother excused the children from the table as soon as they finished eating. Reginald and Cecil left with their father. Percy and Eric ran to the barn to check on the kitten. Dolly, Amy, and Annie cleared the table and prepared to wash the dishes. Released from his highchair, Harold scampered to the parlor to resume playing with his carved wooden animals. Baby Evelyn let out a howl from her basket on the kitchen bench.

Dolly lifted the baby from her bed and dashed away to change her nappy before giving her to their mother. Amy ran warm water and began to wash the dishes. Edith turned around twice in the kitchen, hands on her hips. "I hardly know where to begin," she confessed. "My routine is interrupted yet again. Well, we'll manage won't we?"

The household became a flurry of activity as Edith and her girls emptied cupboards, drawers, the pantry, closets and chiffoniers. Once more all but immediate necessities were crammed into trunks.

By the first of December, 1908, Fred Watts and his family were ready to leave for Paddle River. Trunks and barrels of provisions were secured in the back of the wagon. The children were swaddled in their warmest clothes until they waddled like fat penguins on ice. Numerous blankets awaited them on the floor of the wagon along with more than one lit lantern.

Mother clasped the heavily wrapped Evelyn to her bosom and pulled a thick wool blanket close around herself and the infant to protect them from the cold.

A few clouds scudded across an otherwise clear sky. The sun made a weak attempt to shine, but the temperature hovered around the zero mark.

With reluctance, Percy clambered into the back of the wagon, lower lip sticking out. His kitten had run away the night before and he had had no time to look for it.

Fred climbed onto the seat of the wagon, pulled his fur hat well down over his ears and took up the reins with hands encased in fur-lined gloves. He looked back over his shoulder and called out, "Everyone set back there?"

Reginald yelled back, "All set."

Fred released the brake and smiled at Edith beside him. "Well then, it's time to go!"

CHAPTER 27

Harnesses jangled a happy cadence as Minnie and Moe pulled the conveyance over solid frozen ground. "Boys," Fred shouted. "I'll give you a quick history lesson here. We're following the old pack trail built by the Hudson's Bay Company from Fort Edmonton to Fort Assiniboine back in 1824. This is the very trail the Klondikers used in 1898. You can be thankful it won't take us as long to travel ninety miles to Paddle River as it did back then."

For the first mile or so the children chattered and giggled as they bumped along in the back of the sturdy farm wagon. They made nests for themselves in blankets, wrapped more covers around their shoulders, and huddled close together for warmth. Shielded by trunks on three sides, a canvas draped over the chests for a ceiling, the siblings laughingly called it their cave.

Eric puffed out his chest, wrapped his arms tight around himself, snickered and pointed to a small hole in the ceiling. "Ha, we're Indians," said Eric. "Me heap Big Chief. This is our wigwam and that's our smoke-hole."

The girls ignored him and cuddled closer. Harold crawled onto big brother Reg's lap, pulled a mitten off and stuck a thumb in his mouth.

"Hey, little brave," admonished Reg. "Put your mitten back on, Indians don't suck their thumb."

Leslie snickered and wiggled closer between Cecil and Percy.

Cecil frowned. "All right, Big Chief Red Nose, don't hog that lantern—pass it along, my hands are colder than winter well water."

The children had a small window on the world from out the back of the wagon. Amy watched a hawk swoop down and grab a rabbit she hadn't seen until the predator flapped wings and lifted the animal in his talons. Too cold to feel much sympathy for the rabbit, Amy pulled the blanket up over her head and reached for the lantern closest to her.

For the most part, they had the road to themselves. They did meet a couple wagons and one man on horseback. No one seemed inclined to stop and talk; folks waved, called a greeting, and hurried on.

Periodically, Father halted the team, climbed down and walked a bit stiffly back to check on his brood. Mother too, with a bit of assistance, alighted from the wagon to stretch her limbs and see for herself how her children fared.

Happy to see a grove of trees on both sides of the roadway, Amy and Dolly took Annie by the hands and scurried off to the left. Mother, always modest, waited until her girls returned and then handed Evelyn to Dolly.

Not entirely sure how trustworthy Minnie and Moe might be, Fred looked to the right and stayed with the team until his older boys returned. Glad to be of help, Percy and Cecil stroked the warm noses of the horses and held on to their bridles while their father headed for the trees.

Business taken care of, Amy was more than happy to crawl back into the relative comfort of the wagon. Mother looked thoroughly miserable, but she uttered no complaint as she hurried to take her place beside their father.

Colder than before, Amy pulled Annie onto her lap. Dolly reached for Leslie. The girls wrapped their arms around their younger siblings and pulled their share of the blankets close around the four of them.

Sidling in close to the girls, the boys scrunched so tightly together one couldn't poke a finger between them. Reginald held Eric. Percy drew Harold onto his lap and wormed his way between Cecil and Reg. Blankets were gathered and drawn around them.

They took turns warming their hands on one of the two lanterns and passing it on to the next person. Talk between the brothers and sisters fell to a minimum. All their energy went into keeping warm. Relay stations were posted along the trail and it was there the Watts family aimed to spend their nights.

౬౩

Not quite halfway on their trip to Paddle River, it began to snow hard. The tarp stretched above their heads sagged under the weight. Reg and Cecil knelt on their knees, lifted their arms and shoved hands upward. Most of the snow slid off over the sides of the wagon, but in moments, it would need doing again. What should they do? Could they take turns shoving the snow off?

The wheels turned slower and slower as Minnie and Moe struggled to pull the loaded wagon through ever-deepening snow. Alarmed the wagon might become completely bogged down, Reg nudged Cecil and together the boys bailed out the back. Percy scooted Harold to Dolly and jumped out behind his brothers.

Reginald slogged his way to the front of the wagon and spoke to his father. Fred didn't answer him. He stood, feet braced apart, lines clenched in his gloved hands. A deep scowl worried his face as he strained to see through the swirling snow.

One hand braced on the wagon, Reg kept pace and peered at his mother. She turned her head and looked at him—her lips were blue from the cold. "Fred!" she shouted as she yanked on his coattail. "The boys!"

"Whoa! Whoaaa!" Fred halted the team. "What are you boys doing up here? What do you want? Why aren't you in the wagon?" Fred shook the snow from his hat. He swiped a finger across his mustache, removed his glove and quickly rubbed his eyes. "I can't even tell if we're still on the road. The wagon is bogging down. We've gotta get outa this storm."

"Father, I thought we might help—at least lighten the load."

Fred shook his head. His breath a frosty cloud on the air, he stared at Reginald as though he had suggested they put wings on the horses and fly. "*What?* ... How?"

Reginald shrugged. "Break trail maybe? Keep us on the road?"

The horses tossed their heads, blew, and stamped their feet.

"I doubt you boys can see any better through this snow than I can—but if you do see anything that looks like a barn or a house, holler—we'll head there."

Fred judged they traveled maybe half a mile with the boys breaking trail when two things happened that seemed like minor miracles. The snow lessened, then stopped, and a man approached them on horseback.

"Howdy, Sir, Ma'am." The stranger tipped his hat to Edith. "Looks like you're having a bit of a rough go there. What you need is a sled. I've got one you can borrow. Follow me to my place, it's not far, you can leave your wagon there and pick it up later."

෫෪

While the wagon wheels had broken through the snow, the sled runners skimmed over the top as smooth as butter over hot bread. Fred had left a few of their belongings behind in the wagon. Thankful for a tad more room on the sled, the children once again wrapped themselves in blankets, and warmed their hands on the glowing lanterns.

Amy watched her mother struggle to change Evelyn's nappy quickly and get her covered again. The baby screamed and kicked her legs. Mother bit her lip—Dolly moved forward to help. *Mother looks as unhappy as a cat forced to swim the river*, thought Amy. *Things have to improve when we reach our homestead; at least there, we will be warm.*

Before nightfall, they reached the relay station established by Gordon MacDonald at Lac La Nonne, the halfway point along the Klondike Trail. Fresh horses and supplies were available if needed.

Icicles a foot long hung from the steep-pitched shake roof over the two-storied log house. Six narrow small-paned windows graced the front of the dwelling. "Fred, if we have a homestead like this, it will be quite grand, won't it?" said Edith.

Fred only grunted as he assisted his wife from the wagon. Reginald and Cecil helped the younger children alight and together with their mother they approached the house while father drove the team on to the barn.

A stout middle-aged woman, with twinkling blue eyes and gray hair twisted into a bun on the back of her head, answered their knock on the door. She wore a black dress with a white apron tied at her waist. "Come in… come in, and warm yourselves. I've coffee on the stove. Or, if you prefer, there's hot water for tea. Myself, I prefer a good strong cuppa coffee. It'll warm your gizzard clear down to your toes."

Introductions were made, wraps were laid aside, and Mrs. MacDonald led the way to the kitchen all the while exclaiming over Evelyn. "She's adorable and so tiny."

The kitchen and dining area were all one big room, filled now with the scent of cinnamon. A large cast-iron range heated space at one end and cooked the meals. A decorative potbellied stove with bright fenders warmed the region closer to the dining table. Gleaming wood floors, scrubbed almost white, gave evidence of a meticulous housekeeper. Bright rag rugs in reds, blues, and greens added touches of color.

Fred and Mr. MacDonald came in from the barns. After more introductions, they sat down to tea and hot cinnamon buns.

Mr. MacDonald produced a cradle. Their hosts exclaimed yet again over the baby, handing her from one to the other. Edith excused herself to tend to the baby's needs; after which Evelyn fell asleep in the little bed.

Edith smiled when she saw the upright piano in the parlour. Her eyes sparkled and she lovingly ran her fingers over the keys.

"Do you play?" asked Mrs. MacDonald.

"Yes. Yes, I do. I had to leave my piano behind in England. I hope to eventually have another one once we get settled in our homestead."

"Oh, that's grand," gushed Mrs. MacDonald. "Please, won't you sit down and play something for us?"

The children gathered round as Mother began to play, "A Mighty Fortress is Our God," "Amazing Grace," and hymn after hymn all by ear. Edith paused, turned and winked at her children. She began to play the lively tune they knew so well.

Amy giggled and she and her siblings started to sing, "Froggy Went a Courtin.'" Another family with children had arrived. The youngsters soon caught on (or maybe they already knew the song) and things got a little wild. The adults laughed and joined in.

"Mrs. Watts, it's a real treat to hear you play. Please don't stop."

"Thank you!" Edith smiled, and after about ten verses of "Froggy," she closed with the hymn, "Abide With Me, Fast Falls the Eventide."

CHAPTER 28

A black cat with four white boots and a patch over one eye tiptoed through the parlour and dashed up the stairs. The adults didn't notice, but four little boys did. Eric, Leslie, and their new friends, Henry and Billy, crept up the stairs after the little creature.

They found the kitty in the first bedroom on the left side of the hallway. The cat had jumped onto the bed and now lay curled on top of the patchwork coverlet. The boys petted the furry feline from head to tail and listened to her purr.

Why Billy started stroking the fur backwards, Eric and Leslie didn't know, but the results made their eyes bug out. Henry and Billy giggled. The electrified cat yowled and leaped off the bed.

"*Billy*? What are you boys doing to that cat?" called the boy's mother.

"Sparks, Mother. Sparks!" Static electricity had indeed caused sparks.

"Well, stop it!" Their mother reprimanded her boys quite severely.

Obeying their parents, all the children quickly hustled off to bed. Amy reached for her sister's hand. Where were they all going to sleep? There were eighteen children, and six adults. Evelyn had the cradle, but that left only six beds for everyone else.

"Are you worried, little one, where you're all going to sleep?" Mrs. MacDonald smiled at Amy. "Well, it's true we don't often have this many people all at one time. But we'll manage. We'll manage just fine. You won't have to sleep on the floor. No siree! You'll be all comfy and cozy in a warm bed."

Mrs. MacDonald led the way with a lighted lantern. She opened the door and ushered them into a small bedroom where she hung the lantern on a wall peg. The room held a double bed, a commode, a cane-bottomed chair, and little else. White ruffled curtains covered the window. A matching ruffle around the bottom of the bed, topped with a cornflower blue counterpane and fat blue pillows edged in lace completed the decor. A blue-flowered pitcher and matching bowl sat atop the commode.

"You'll find all you need behind that little door there," said Mrs. MacDonald as she pointed with her chin and pulled back the covers on the bed. Their hostess smiled; her eyes twinkled. "Tonight, instead of sleeping lengthwise, you little girls are going to sleep crosswise in the bed."

Amy took a place next to the foot of the bed. Annie squeezed in between her two sisters. Three more little girls filled the rest of the bed. The girls whispered and giggled until their mothers came to tell them goodnight and extinguish the light.

∽

After much hustle and bustle between stove and table, twenty-three people sat down to a hearty breakfast of fried potatoes, ham and eggs, bread, butter and jam, milk for the younger children, tea or coffee with sugar and pitchers of thick cream.

Mr. MacDonald cleared his throat, bowed his head and offered a prayer of thanksgiving for another day and bountiful food. The adults ate and exchanged information in quiet tones while the children cleaned their plates and listened.

Fred pushed his chair back from the table. "That was a wonderful breakfast, Mrs. MacDonald. Thank you!" Following his lead, everyone either nodded in agreement or verbally thanked their hosts.

The men-folk left for the barn to care for the animals and prepare to continue their journey. It wouldn't be daylight for a couple more hours; by then, Fred and his family would be on their way.

Mother excused herself to care for Evelyn. Little Harold, released from his highchair, went looking for the kitty. Amy, Annie, and Dolly began to clear the table. The other girls followed their mother up the stairs. Eric and Leslie looked at each other and shrugged. Dolly whispered in Eric's ear. Eric grinned and the two boys trotted to the woodshed to gather wood and fill the woodboxes.

"We'll do your dishes," said Dolly to Mrs. MacDonald. "Amy and I can take turns washing, and Annie will help dry them."

"Bless you, child. I can see you are all good helpers. Your mother has taught you well. You will find a dishpan and soap under the sink. I'll pour the hot water for you; the teakettle is pretty heavy."

The dishes were done and the kitchen tidy when Father returned to briefly warm himself at the stove and tell his family to prepare to leave.

"I hope to see you all again," said Mrs. MacDonald. "And if you girls ever need a job, come see me. I'll hire you in a minute." She beamed on Dolly and handed her a basket laden with ham sandwiches, tea biscuits, and dried apple slices. "Keep your lanterns close and perhaps the food won't freeze."

The other family had taken their leave only moments earlier. Amy would wait until later to tell Mother those girls hadn't lifted a finger to help, and they had left empty-handed too. Mrs. MacDonald had been quite cool when she told them goodbye.

Amy settled on the sled with her sisters and brothers. Cocooned in blankets, their eyes shown with excitement.

Fred took up the reins and slapped them gently on the backs of the horses. "Giddyap there, Minnie, Moe." He turned his head and grinned at Edith. "Well, Dearie, we'll reach our homestead today. You'll soon be back in a home of your own."

Edith smiled, glad her husband couldn't read her thoughts or feel her apprehension. "That will be nice," she murmured as she clasped baby Evelyn a little tighter.

They crossed the Pembina River on the ice and somewhat later the Paddle River also on the ice. Amy swiveled her neck—looking first one way and then another. In every direction, all she could see were trees, snow, and more snow. Even the birds knew enough to fly south and leave this bitter cold behind. Amy had a notion if birds tried to sing, the notes would freeze in their throats.

Reg unwound an arm from the blankets and pointed. "Look there, in that tallest tree. That's an eagle! … I wonder what they eat in the wintertime. Rivers are frozen, can't get fish."

"Cats and packrats," grumped Cecil. "They eat anything that's small and moves. You tadpoles better watch out." He leered at Eric, Leslie, and Harold.

"Stop scaring them!" warned Dolly. "Just because you're cold you needn't be mean."

"Yeah, you're right! Sorry!" He grinned at his little brothers. "No ole bird would want you blokes, you're way too tough."

Father stopped the horses and looked all around.

"Why are we stopping here?" Amy whispered to Dolly.

Dolly shrugged. "I don't know. Maybe this is our homestead."

"It can't be—there's nothing but trees and brush here." Poplar trees, birch trees, willow, black spruce, and tamarack trees in abundance—but no house. No barn. No shed. Nothing.

Fred's shoulders sagged and his head drooped. For moments he just sat there saying nothing.

"Fred?" Edith laid a hand on his arm. "There is no house is there? We have just the bare land don't we?"

"I was promised a house," Father asserted. "At least I though so," he muttered into his mustache.

Trying to sound more hopeful than he felt, Fred picked up the lines and clucked to the team. "We'll drive on to the neighbors, perhaps they can advise us."

They drove a mile farther east and came to the Barker place well before noon. The four Barker brothers, George, Jack, Ernie, Albert, and their sister Evelyn had come from Norwich, England in 1906. They were quick to lend a hand to their new neighbors.

Evelyn invited the family indoors to warm while her brothers hitched their own team to a sleigh. She fixed tea and they huddled around the stove to drink it. Glad for the company of another woman, however briefly, Edith made a valiant effort to smile and converse.

The Barker brothers led the Watts' to a nearby little shack. It was the shelter they themselves had lived in until they could build the house they now occupied. Not wanting to seem ungrateful, Edith commanded herself to smile and thank the brothers before they drove away. Indeed, where would they be without the kindness of these fellow countrymen? They must have shelter in this frozen land.

For the sake of her children, Edith held back the tears as Fred and the older boys carried their provisions into the 14ft by 16ft shack and set the trunks and barrels on the hard dirt floor. The roof was made of poplar poles with a layer of hay laid over them and about six inches of dirt atop the hay. All were now covered with a layer of snow. As quickly as possible, Fred got a fire going in the small cook stove that dominated the room. In doing so, he noted dry wood was in short supply.

"Come on, Reginald, Cecil, Percy—you boys will have to help me. Reginald, grab another ax, we have to cut trees for wood. Poles, too. Five bunks aren't enough—we'll need to nail up at least one more."

Edith looked askance at the pole bunks. *Don't tell me people really sleep on those hard things. They look like torture racks.* Aloud she said to her children, "Others have managed; we will too."

Harold clung to her skirts and stuck a thumb in his mouth. Eric's lower lip hung low enough for a bird (if there were any) to perch on it. Leslie clambered onto a trunk, sat down and sniveled.

Annie, Dolly, and Amy moved closer to their mother and encircled her waist with their arms. Only baby Evelyn did what they all wanted to do. She howled.

Before bedtime, Father and Reginald had one more poplar-pole bunk nailed to the mud-chinked log walls. Though spread with thick blankets, these had to be the hardest beds in all of Canada. Amy doubted she'd ever fall asleep. *I wonder what Grandmother would say if she could see me now.*

Her dire prediction of a pallet on the floor came too close to the truth. Amy squirmed, but the bed remained unyielding. In truth, a bed on the floor might be more comfortable.

Photo Section

Back row from left to right: Dolly, Lesley, Annie, Amy
Front row left to right: Percy, Eric, Cecil, Reg, Harold on his lap

CHAPTER 29

Edith placed a large pot of navy beans on the stove to cook. She lifted a corner of her apron and wiped the perspiration from her brow before adding more wood to the fire. How one could perspire and be cold at the same time, she did not know. She only knew it to be true.

It seemed an eternity since they left England. And almost that long since they'd left Melita. Could it be they had now lived in this primitive shack in the frozen wilderness of Paddle River for nearly two months? Every day was a battle against the cold. They were fast learning what they could and could not do when the temperature dipped. Some days they simply huddled closer to the stove and prayed for the weather to warm.

One thing amazed Edith; news traveled around the settlement faster than smoke from a brush fire. Within days, folks had known about the new people in the Barker's old shack. They welcomed the Watts like well-beloved family. Neighbors came to visit, and never empty handed. Men brought hay for the horses. Women brought an onion, or a few carrots and potatoes from last year's garden.

Caring generous people, they shared what they had learned in the time they'd been here. It was often knowledge gained the hard way. Many were former city dwellers, as were the Watts, intent on carving out a homestead in this imposing land.

"Mother, may we go outdoors for a little while if we bundle up good?"

Edith turned from dipping flour from a wooden barrel into a crockery bowl and smiled at her eldest daughter. "Yes, but only for a short while. We don't want any frostbitten faces, fingers, or toes. Remember to keep a scarf wrapped around your face, and breathe through your nose, not your mouth."

It hardly seemed worth the effort of getting coats, caps, scarves, mittens, and boots on for such a short time. Edith, however, understood her children's need to escape the confines of these four walls if only for a short time. A few minutes outdoors could mean the difference between grumpy or happy children.

Keeping her family fed, reasonably clean, and healthy filled Edith's days. It didn't keep her from worrying though—what would happen if one or more of her children became seriously ill? Doctors and good medical help were so far away.

Edith bent over to add more wood to the fire. Suddenly, she clutched her stomach and groaned. Her upset tummy hurt worse. *Have I eaten something that's upset me?* Gripping her middle she shuffled to the nearest bunk and sat down. *Oh Dear God, I don't know if I can stand this—the pain isn't letting up. What am I to do?*

Feeling nauseous, she searched for something in which to throw up. *Please God, send Fred or the children in. I'm so sick!*

Holding her stomach, crouched over, Edith shuffled to the door when the pain let up a little. Bracing one hand on the wall, she jerked the door open and nearly screamed their names, "Dolly, Amy, go quickly—get your father! He's in the barn."

଼

"Dearie, what's wrong? You're white as a sheet."

"Oh, Fred—I don't know. I hurt so terribly."

"Where? Where do you hurt? Your stomach? Your bowels?"

"I," she groaned. "I …I don't know, I've never hurt like this before."

"We'd better send for the doctor."

Reginald, who'd entered the shack in time to hear his father say, "send for the doctor" turned and headed for the barn to get Moe. He'd not waste precious time with a saddle, but ride bareback. The nearest doctor lived seven miles away.

Wide-eyed children watched their mother in silence. Eric, Leslie, and little Harold climbed to the top bunk and sat like rooks on the highest tree-branch. Harold knelt on his knees and stuck a thumb in his mouth.

Edith lay on the bottom bunk and tried hard not to whimper. Sweat beaded her brow. Fred knelt on the earthen floor beside her; he bathed her face repeatedly with a damp cloth.

଼

The doctor buttoned his coat tight around his throat, pulled a fur hat down over his ears and reached for his black bag. "You stay here with my wife and father-in-law. I don't like the looks of the sky. Could be we'll have a whiteout before I can get back. I'll ride your horse and lead mine. Your horse will know the way there and my horse will bring me back."

Reginald moved closer to the stove in the doctor's house and held his hands to the warmth. He tried hard not to stare at the insane man confined to a cage in the corner of the room. The doctor's wife gave Reg a fleeting look of sympathy, but didn't explain her father's condition. Nor did she offer empty words of sympathy for his mother's illness. "Come," she said. "Sit here at the table. We'll have us a cup of tea. Things always look better with a hot cuppa tea."

❧

Edith bit down on her tongue and managed to not cry out as the doctor probed her abdomen. "A little tender there, is it?" He shook his head. "Well, you have appendicitis." He turned and addressed Fred. "I'll give her some laudanum for the pain, but that's the best I can do. I'm not a surgeon. You'll need to get her to the hospital in Edmonton."

Help soon arrived in the form of Mrs. O'Brien, a well-trained nurse folks in the area relied on. "How much laudanum did the doctor give you?" When told, she nodded and set to work heating rocks on the hottest part of the stove.

How word got around that she was seriously ill, Edith didn't know, especially since the doctor had left for home in a blizzard. The laudanum dulled the pain. Able to relax somewhat, Edith nursed baby Evelyn.

Cecil carried in more wood, poking as many sticks in the firebox as it would hold. He then withdrew to a corner, and stood watching, helpless as a newborn to know what to do to help his dear mother.

A few minutes after the nurse's arrival, Mr. Hooper and his son Gerald arrived with his fast team of sprinters and a sleigh in which they'd thoughtfully placed a feather mattress. Speaking quietly, Mrs. O'Brien tenderly helped Edith bundle up for the long trip to Edmonton.

Fred carried his bride to the sleigh and tucked her in. Hot rocks wrapped in flannel warmed her. Fred lifted the blankets and eased in beside Edith. Mr. Hooper clucked to his team and the horses started down the trail at a good clip.

Mrs. O'Brien sat down as if she hadn't a care in the world and smiled at the children. "Well now, let's see what we have here. If I take your baby and the little fellow here, Harold is it, for a few days, I judge you older bairns can manage just fine."

Amy swallowed the lump in her throat and helped Dolly find Evelyn's nappies. She hugged and kissed Harold and slowly buttoned his coat

Mrs. O'Brien tousled Harold's hair. "We'll have a good time, yes? I've new puppies at my house, and they're just waiting for a little boy to come play with them."

The children stood in the doorway and watched the nurse drive away with their baby sister and little brother. When they could no longer see the sleigh, Dolly led them back inside and closed the door. She held out her arms to her siblings and they gathered close. Forming a tight circle and clinging to each other, they let the tears fall.

Mr. Hooper and Gerald took turns driving—pushing the team for all they were worth—a Herculean effort through a snowstorm and drifting snow. They reached Miseracordia Hospital in Edmonton, a distance of 100 miles, in only two days.

"Hang on, Dearie. We'll get you there. I promise we'll get you there," Fred asserted. They did indeed get her to the hospital. But appendicitis doesn't wait, and peritonitis had already set in.

Too weak to lift her head, Edith clung to Fred's hand. Her voice, now barely a whisper, sounded hoarse and raspy. Fred leaned closer. "I wish I could see my little Norah again … Fred, our babies—" Her hand went limp, and her sentence unfinished. Edith had slipped into eternity.

The tears came. "Ah, Edith, I'm so sorry." Fred kissed her forehead and staggered from the room where he bumped into a nurse. "She's gone!"

"I'm so sorry, sir. I'm sorry we couldn't save her." She touched his shoulder. "We'll get her to the funeral home. It's in the next block going south."

Mr. Hooper walked on one side, Gerald on the other as Fred made his way to the telegraph office. "I'd rather be boiled in oil than send this telegram. Her parents never liked me to begin with, but they'll hate me now." Fred coughed and blew his nose. "Well, there's no help for it. I might as well get it over with. At least I won't have to hear them say, I told you so."

Three solemn men made the trip back to Paddle River. This time, the trip took almost three days, arriving home after dark. Fred wouldn't have minded if it took longer. *If only I didn't have to face my children and tell them their mother is gone.*

One look at Father's face and Amy knew the news was not good.

Fred removed his hat and bowed his head before lifting his eyes and speaking to them. "I'm sorry children—your mother has gone to heaven." He took a handkerchief from his pocket and wiped his eyes. "I had an angel, and I didn't know it."

℞

Reginald, Cecil, Dolly and Amy Gladys made the long sorrowful trip with their father back to Edmonton for the funeral. The younger children stayed with sympathetic neighbors. All the children took it hard, but Reginald took it the hardest. His eyes were red and swollen by the time they reached Edmonton.

An Anglican minister conducted the simple service in the dim parlor of his private home. Heavy frost coated the windows. Mother wore her prettiest high-necked black dress. *She looks like she is asleep,* thought Amy. *But that pin is poking Mother in the neck.* Amy reached out a hand and straightened it. Later the locket-pin was given to Dolly.

Edith Annie Rampling Watts was laid to rest in Edmonton City Cemetery on February 2, 1909.

CHAPTER 30

Amy followed her sister and brothers into the cold dismal cabin. The awful truth hit her like a slap in the face. *Mother is gone! I will never see her smiling face again. How ever—will we manage without our dear mother?*

Reg spoke first as he crumpled paper and laid kindling for a fire. "We're the oldest; we have to take care of our little brothers and sisters."

"*Reginald!*" Dolly wailed. "I can't take care of Evelyn. She's a *baby!* Mother *nursed* her. What would we feed her? We don't even have a cow."

Reg turned and wrapped his arms around his sister. Tears ran down his own face as he tried to console her. "Father will know what to do—and Mrs. O'Brien knows how to care for infants. We can ask her."

Amy wanted to howl as new fears gripped her mind. *What if Father doesn't know what to do with our baby sister? What if Father doesn't want all of us now? What if Father farms us out? What if…*

Father came in from the barn. He drew out his handkerchief, blew his nose, and wiped his eyes, "Well—you're motherless children, and there's no help for that. But I'm your father, and I'm here! Eh? We'll manage!"

Fred cleared his throat. "Reginald, Cecil, you two are my right-hand men. Together we'll get us a cabin built." His eyes swept the room as though really seeing it for the first time. "Get out of this rat-hole. Prove up on our land. Have us a real homestead."

Amy set cups on the table and Dolly poured tea. Father nodded and continued speaking. "Dolly, you are the oldest girl; you'll cook and keep house for us. No doubt the little ones will look to you for mothering. Amy Gladys, I'll expect you to make our bread. You'll help Dolly too, when I don't need you to help me."

Amy knew better than to question Father, but the lump in her throat nearly strangled her before it plunged and landed in her stomach like a bitter glob of unleavened dough.

That night the two sisters shared a bunk, though with most of the family gone they wouldn't have needed to. "I don't know how to make bread," Amy wailed, her voice a hoarse whisper. "Mother made it look easy, but I don't know what she did."

"Well, I don't know how to *cook* either. So there! Oh sure, I fixed a few things with Mother telling me what to do." Dolly sniffed. "Why did Father have to drag us out here in this godforsaken wilderness anyway? What if we all get sick and die?"

"Shhhh! Father might hear you!"

"Maybe I don't care if he does."

Amy clapped a hand over Dolly's mouth. "You'd better care! If you make Father angry, he could whip you."

80

The Watts children had yet to learn how amazing their neighbors could be. With the return of Percy, Eric, Leslie, and Annie, the Barkers brought seven loaves of bread, a large kettle of moose-meat stew, and a three-layer chocolate cake in honor of little Annie's birthday.

Mrs. Mills, a Seventh-Day Adventist neighbor, loaded her six children, along with hot rocks, into a sleigh and drove the fifteen miles to talk to Fred Watts. Without waste of motion or words she said, "Mr. Watts, my youngest is nine months old and can be weaned. I can take your baby and nurse her right away. I'd keep her until she's old enough to eat solid food and then bring her back to you."

Fred studied her, caught himself, and ran a hand through his hair. "Mrs. Mills, that's awfully generous of you. You must have thought this over carefully, or you wouldn't have driven such a distance in the cold to talk to me." Fred fingered his mustache. "If you're sure it won't be too great an inconvenience, I'll gladly accept your offer. It's a worry I've had in the back of my mind since my dear wife passed on—how best to care for Evelyn.

"Right now the baby and my youngest son are with Mrs. O'Brien. She volunteered to care for them for a few days. I can go there today and..."

"I know Mrs. O'Brien and I know where she lives. A fine nurse she is, too, but she wouldn't be wantin' no youngins for very long. With your permission, I can go there and get the baby on my way back home."

"Mrs. Mills, I don't know how I can ever repay you for your kindness, but I assure you, I'm grateful. We'll come to see Evelyn as often as we can. I want her to know us."

In the next few days and weeks offers to adopt or foster the motherless children came from neighbors in Paddle River and as far away as Edmonton. Willing to take one, two, or possibly three children—folks generally first asked for baby Evelyn and little Harold. To all these offers Fred's answer remained the same: "Thank you, but I do not want to break up my family. We'll manage."

Winter wore on and somehow the children learned to cope. It was not always easy for sixteen-year-old Reginald, fifteen-year-old Cecil, and twelve-year-old Dolly on whom the bulk of the burden rested. Amy too helped, and shouldered more responsibility than a ten -year-old should have to. The four oldest children became exceptionally close as they worked together, helped each other, and cared for their younger siblings.

Father pursued his photography as a means to earn some money. By necessity it kept him away from home, often for more than one day. No doubt Fred grieved more over the loss of his wife than his children realized for he did not deal with his pain in a constructive way. He drank.

No matter how hard the older children tried, their father rarely seemed pleased with them. Perhaps in some subtle, or not so subtle, way he sensed their disapproval of bringing them here in the dead of winter and ultimately causing their mother's death. The younger children were innocent of any censure, and to them Fred showed some kindness.

Never a man to show much affection or make over even his youngest children, he didn't start now. For love, tenderness, and someone to dry their tears the younger children looked to Reginald and Dolly. Amy Gladys too, mothered her little brothers and Annie.

This far north, winter didn't release its hold on the land until around Easter. Strange things happened when the temperature plummeted to -50 or -55 degrees. Blankets freeze to the walls. Meat, milk, water, and vegetables freeze in the house even with a fire going in the stove.

Outdoors, frostbite could occur in minutes. Breathing through your mouth freezes your lungs, and even with the face covered, frost forms on nose-hairs. At these temperatures if water touched a window, it broke. Nails popped from wood. Though the children huddled close around the stove, cold feet and cold hands remained a fact of life.

ᴤ

Eric struggled to get up and discovered he couldn't. He tried working his hands beneath him. Impossible! Scared and embarrassed, he started to cry. Tears froze on his cheeks. Close to panic, he let out a scream to startle a banshee.

Alerted to his distress, Reginald guessed what had happened. Eric's bottom had frozen to the toilet seat. As quickly as they could, he and Cecil threw on wraps and went to Eric's rescue.

"Don't cry, Eric! Don't cry! And sit still! We'll get you loose." *But how? Hot water won't work. It'll freeze on contact.* Thinking fast, Reginald noticed the nails had popped from the wood. "Cecil, you get hold of one end of the board he's stuck on. I'll get hold of the other end. When I count to three—lift! But hang onto him with the other hand."

Together they carried Eric to the cabin. With Dolly and Amy helping to balance their little brother, Reg and Cecil held the board up over the stove until frost melted and he was free. Not wanting to make Eric the butt of the joke, but seeing the humor in it and needing a release from tension, the boys laughed. Dolly and Amy were quick to hug Eric, and Dolly handed him a slice of buttered bread.

Later they reported the incident to Father. Fred smiled, but he didn't praise his sons for their quick thinking. He did, however, fasten a rabbit skin to the seat in the outhouse.

Winter temperatures weren't always so bitterly cold and the children ventured out, sometimes with their father and sometimes on their own. A trip to the Paddle River post office for news from the "outside" was cause for celebration. Amy and her siblings loved getting the *Free Press* newspaper from Winnipeg and the *Family Herald* and *Weekly Star* from Montreal. The papers were saved and the comics read over and over.

School district #1771 had been formed in Paddle River in 1908. The schoolhouse consisted of a shed-like room tacked onto Mr. Cason's house, from which he also ran a store. Going to school on any regular basis was impossible for Amy and her siblings the winter of 1909. The older children were needed at home to keep the family together.

In those tough early days, neighbors were a great help to the Watts. The Barker boys checked on the children when they knew Fred was away from home. Often, they took Reg and Cecil hunting with them.

Miss Evelyn Barker coached Amy through her first attempts at bread making and praised the girl when her small hands and arms kneaded the dough.

To reassure the child, Evelyn wrote out a recipe for bread and gave it to her. When the "men" came home with birds and rabbits, she helped the girls scald and pluck feathers from the birds. She showed them how to clean both birds and rabbits and be careful not to damage the meat with bitter bile from a broken gallbladder. When the smelly job was finished they shared a pot of tea and Evelyn rehearsed, "A man's work is from sun to sun, but a woman's work is never done."

ಐ

Rabbits were plentiful and the Watts' family ate their share as did all the settlers in Paddle River. Before spring could edge out winter, rabbits were often all that kept families from going hungry. The Tarplees made up this chant:

"Rabbits young, rabbits old,
Rabbits hot, rabbits cold,
Rabbits tender, rabbits tough,
Thank the Lord, we've had enough!"

CHAPTER 31

Fred Watts knew he needed more money to get his homestead underway than he could possibly make with his photography. He needed a grubstake, and he thought he knew where he could get one. A letter penned to his old aunt now living in Astoria, Oregon, U.S.A. soon produced the desired result.

His aunt Sarah Pickernell, a shrewd business woman, loaned him the requested funds. She said he needn't worry about his debt to her for at least three years, at which time he'd be on his feet. They then could work out a plan of payment satisfactory to both parties. If Fred had any doubts about his aunt's expectations, he buried them beneath his enthusiasm for acquiring oxen. He had the cash, and for now, that's all that concerned him.

Fred bought oxen for the work they could do pulling heavy loads and helping clear the land. That didn't keep Amy and her siblings from making pets of Jerry and Joe. They soon learned they could sit on Joe all the way from his horns to his tail. Not so with Jerry. Not-so-gentle Jerry let them know he hadn't hired on to be ridden by a mob of youngsters. He lowered his head and shook those wicked-looking horns at them.

Her next bread-making day, Amy stirred up a big batch of dough. Before she plopped the dough into the pans, she pinched off a chunk and laid it aside.

"What are you going to do with that?" Dolly pointed to the blob of dough on the table.

"I'm going to give it to Joe. Wanta watch?"

"Are you fooling? Will he eat that?"

"I think so. Come with me!"

"No, you go ahead. Maybe when it's warmer I will. It's too much trouble getting wraps on everyone."

Amy held the dough in her hand and offered it to Joe. He took it. His tongue grew nearly as long as his tail while he slobbered, masticated, chewed, slavered some more, and ran his tongue up each nostril. Amy laughed until her sides hurt. "You are gross, you know that?" She scratched Joe's head and petted his neck before running back to the cabin.

Sneaking a handful of dough to Joe on bread-baking day became a ritual. A weekly event guaranteed to send the younger children into fits of laughter. Reginald and Cecil on rare occasions watched and chuckled too, but for the most part they were much too busy.

Weather permitting, Reg and Cecil cut down trees and cleared brush on their land. Fred helped when he wasn't off somewhere taking pictures. Dolly cooked, cleaned, washed clothes, and rode herd on her little brothers and sister. All the children had chores to do. They missed their mother terribly, but only at night in their beds did they sometimes let the tears fall.

౫

With the arrival of spring and the thawing of the ground came hordes of flies and mosquitoes; enough mosquitoes to carry away each man, woman, and child in Paddle River. Or so it seemed to Amy Gladys. Settlers scrambled to find enough fireweed to keep a smoky smudge going in front of their cabin doors.

Bulldog flies nearly drove the horses mad. Learning from their neighbors, Dolly and Amy sewed little cloth bags to slip over the horses' ears. Fred fashioned wire netting to fit over the horses' nostrils to protect them from bulldog flies. Even more maddening were the heel flies that tormented both horses and cattle.

On a Wednesday Evelyn Barker rode over to see how the girls fared and to offer a suggestion for combating the evil mosquitoes. Dolly, Amy, and Annie welcomed her and the four "women" sat at the table with a fresh pot of tea brewed by Dolly. Since the passing of their mother, birthdays in the Watts' household slid by mostly ignored, but Evelyn's thoughtfulness was cause for celebration. Today she brought cinnamon buns.

"Winter is hard, but spring and summer there is so much work to do we won't know which way to jump first. There'll be scant time for visiting. We'll soon be busier than the poor cow's tail while bossy tries to swat all those flies," said Evelyn. "I wanted to tell you girls, if you'll wrap newspapers around your legs before you pull on your stockings, you won't get quite so many mosquito bites."

Evelyn smiled, finished her tea, and rose to go. "I'm not sure what you can do about your arms and face. Some ladies I know smear on lard or even mud, but I've never liked the feel of it myself."

"I want a well dug right off," said Father. "Reginald, Cecil, you two boys will have to help me dig it. We'll make it four foot square. A square hole is easier to work in and shore up than a round one." Fred finished his breakfast and reached for his hat. "We'll start on it today. It's a big job and all you children strong enough to heft a bucket of dirt will have to help."

Moving dirt and rocks away from the well's edge put blisters on Amy's hands. The tasks Father called upon her to do seemed unending and none of them easy. She dragged away limbs and brush her father and brothers cleared and stacked the debris in piles to be burned. Her arms and shoulders ached at the end of the day for she worked with the intensity of a paid laborer.

Father expected her to help even on bread-making days. Reginald protested. "Father, Amy shouldn't have to work so hard, especially when she makes all our bread. This isn't work for girls; we boys can get it done."

Fred didn't see it that way. "Ah, she's as strong as an ox. She can help." He didn't say much to Dolly, perhaps he thought cooking three meals a day and watching over the younger children exempted her from most outdoor work.

Because it was considered a woman's job, Dolly helped Amy plant the garden. They joked and giggled as they marked out straight rows with sticks and string. "Do you suppose the vegetables will know if the rows are straight?"

They let Leslie and Annie drop a few radish seeds in one row. Percy planted a whole row of potatoes by himself. Not to be outdone, Eric imitated Percy, dug a shallow hole, dropped in a seed potato, and covered it with dirt. Little Harold sat at the end of a row, watched, chortled, and played in the dirt.

"Are we gonna plant tomatoes?" chirped Eric.

"No, Father says we're too far north and the season is too short," said Dolly. "Corn won't ripen and neither will cucumbers. Things that grow below the ground do okay though. We're going to plant a lot of carrots. Miss Barker says carrots are even good in pies."

"Eww! Carrot pie? Yuck! I'm gonna ask Dad if I can plant pumpkins. I like *pumpkin* pie."

With the arrival of spring the younger children had started calling Father, "Dad." It didn't sound right to Amy and Dolly, but it wasn't their place to object. Fred didn't seem to mind, and the little ones had apparently forgotten their mother's genteel influence of calling their parents Father and Mother.

Dolly straightened from planting a row of parsnips and wiped perspiration from her face. "Where's Leslie?" She shaded her eyes and looked around. "Eric, Annie, do you know where he went?"

Eric laughed. "Yeah, he's behind that log over there, studying some wiggly bug or skinning another caterpillar. Maybe he's playing with a garter snake."

৪৩

Amy sang as she swung her bucket and waltzed down the trail to go pick berries. Time alone—time free from picking sticks out of the hayfield, dragging debris to the burn pile, or helping burn stumps so they could be removed from the fields—was as rare as feathers on fish. Helping Father prove up on their homestead meant hard work. Many days by nightfall the only thing white on Amy was her eyes. Smoke blackened her face, arms, and clothes.

Wild sweetpeas and balm of Gilead grew on the hillside where Amy went to pick strawberries. Amy plucked a sweetpea and held it to her nose. *It doesn't have much scent, but they're so pretty. Wouldn't Mother have loved these? I'll pick a bouquet before I go home.* The balm of Gilead did have a pungent fragrance pleasing to Amy. *I'll pick some of these too*, she thought.

Rich red ripe strawberries, how delicious the sunwarmed wild fruit tasted on Amy's tongue as she shoved a handful into her mouth. And so many! Kneeling on the grassy slope, Amy filled her bucket in no time.

Wild raspberries, high bush cranberries, bog or moss cranberries, dewberries, and black currants were to be found in season. Settlers discovered rosehips, gooseberries, and blueberries. Chokecherries grew along the rivers, blueberries in the sandy-soiled hills, but saskatoons were few and far between. All the berries were put to good use, by either being dried or made into jams and jellies, knowledge the neighbors gladly shared with the Watts.

Dolly laughed and groaned all at the same time as Amy presented her bucket of berries. "We'll have fresh berries and whipped cream for supper. Annie, you and Amy will have to help me hull these strawberries.

"I'm glad I thought to ask Miss Barker how to make jam. I just hope we have enough sugar, but one neighbor lady says she uses syrup or honey." Dolly sighed. "If only Mother were here, she'd know what to do. Father is no help, he'd probably tell me to take honey away from a bear."

Dolly and Amy smarted over the retort their father had given them the day before. After poring over Eaton's catalogue and thinking about what "Granny" Sebern of Mellowdale, had said, "Patch beside patch is neighborly, but patch upon patch is beggarly," the girls had made their request.

"Father, we girls need new dresses," Dolly had said. "We have one decent dress apiece, and the others are becoming patch upon patch."

"Ah, paint your bottoms black and go naked," Father had blasted. "You don't need new dresses."

The girls were beginning to understand their father would provide the basic needs, but he didn't acknowledge their desire for other things.

"I wonder what Father would say if we actually did what he said," groused Dolly.

"I don't know, but our mother taught us better," said Amy.

"You're right, little sister. She taught us to be ladies. And it's ladies we shall be."

CHAPTER 32

Reginald stood, hands on hips, and studied the cabin he and Cecil helped to build.

Amy watched a smile spread over his face—as satisfying to see as an early-morning sunrise. It had been an achingly long summer, cutting down trees, limbing them, and dragging them to the site with the oxen. Often the boys had been on their own, deprived of their father's help, as Fred spent several weeks working in Edmonton. The family had desperately needed the money their father sent home five dollars at a time.

The twenty feet by thirty feet log cabin with a plank floor and real windows looked like a mansion compared to the hovel they'd lived in through the winter. Fred added a front porch, giving the house a "Welcome Home" feeling. Best of all, the log cabin was theirs.

"Well, we've work to do," said Father. "Gather all the mud and moss you can. We need to chink between these logs."

Amy giggled and nudged Dolly. "Yippee! We get to make mud-pies again."

"If I'm going to be playing in the mud, that may be what you'll get for dinner," grumped Dolly.

"Well, put some jam on it and serve it with bread," said Amy as she laughed. "I haven't had one of your mud-pies since I was four years old."

છ્

Three days later Amy sighed as she shoved her last glob of mud and moss into a crack between the logs. "I see mud and moss at night when I shut my eyes," muttered Amy to her brothers.

"I didn't know there was this much mud and moss in the whole world," said Percy. "I see this stuff in my sleep too."

"Well, don't look now," said Reginald, "but we get to do this all over again when we get the barns up."

Father mixed up a solution of lime and water to the consistency of milk and handed Amy and Dolly each a brush. "All right girls, hop to, and paint the inside walls of our cabin. This should kill a few bugs and lighten the room as well."

Dolly looked at Amy and shrugged. "This white-wash may be the only way to whiten our dirt-stained hands." She huffed. "I don't think my hands are ever going to be clean again."

As soon as Amy and Dolly finished one wall, Fred set up their bunk beds and a trundle bed for Annie. "When Evelyn comes home—she can share the slide-away bed with Annie, or however you girls work it out," he said.

Hoping for a bit more privacy, Reginald and Cecil had built a small loft overhead for their bedroom. Father and the younger boys would have bunk beds on the opposite wall from the girls. Like Annie, little Harold would have a trundle bed.

Amy waited until Father left the cabin and then she fairly shouted. "Dolly! We have our very own beds!"

Given the tools Fred had to work with, a professional craftsman couldn't have done a better job. He fashioned narrow wooden strips secured to log rails for mattress supports. And wonder of wonders, Father bought new ticking and paid a lady in Edmonton to sew casings for mattresses.

Percy, Eric, and Leslie helped gather wheat straw and sweet-smelling grass hay for stuffing the mattresses. Dolly and Amy still had the daunting task of hand-stitching the ticking closed.

A few residents of Paddle River lived in frame houses, but most preferred log cabins. The log dwellings may not have been as attractive, but they were easier to heat and much warmer in the bitterly cold winters.

What would we do without the help of the Barkers? wondered Amy. George Barker had cut their first wheat crop. Now, the brothers came to help put up the Watts' barns.

On the advice of his more seasoned neighbors, Fred had already dug two wells. Now he would build two barns on his homestead; one to measure 27ft. by 27ft. and a smaller shelter they'd build 16ft. by 22ft. In the event of fire, a second dwelling for the animals and temporary shelter for family could mean the difference between success and failure.

Harold tugged on Dolly's dress and mumbled around the thumb in his mouth. "I'm hungwy! Wanna eat."

Dolly laid aside her brush, blotted her hands on her nearly threadbare pinafore and picked up her little brother. She hugged him tight, kissed his jaw, and tickled his bare feet. Harold giggled and wrapped his arms around her neck.

"Me wuve you."

"I love you too, little britches. Let's go find you some bread and jam."

To Amy, Dolly said, "It's time for me to start cooking dinner. Again! When I'm all grown up, I plan to marry a rich man and never cook another meal."

℘

"Dad, are we going to church tomorrow?"

"You bet we are, Eric. I promised your mother I'd see you rapscallions went to church, and that's one promise I aim to keep." Fred took a bar of soap from the shelf. "You girls can have the cabin to yourselves for your bath. We men will go to the river and rid ourselves of a few layers of dirt."

Dolly grinned, and crossed her fingers behind her back "Even Harold, Father? Will you take Harold?"

Fred frowned and peered at his youngest son. "If I could command a platoon, I suppose I can handle one slippery little eel." He set Harold on one arm before grabbing a washcloth and towel in the other hand. "We'll be going to see your baby sister tomorrow as well."

Dolly fastened the hook on the door of the old cabin so no one could walk in on them while they took their baths in the small galvanized tub. They took turns shampooing each others' hair. "Annie, don't tell

A Time To Go   243

Father we used vinegar in our rinse water. He'll think it's wasteful, but it makes our hair shine. I only use a little. Mother taught us that, but you were too young to remember."

❧

Amy loved going to church. It was pretty informal, but whoever preached said things to make her feel good and want to be a kinder, better person. Her heart swelled too, when Reginald sang with the small choir. Maybe it was family pride, but she knew no one else sang any better. Seeing and chattering with her friends after the service made it the very best day of the whole long work-weary week.

The sun shone in a near-cloudless sky; a light breeze ruffled Amy's hair. Song birds twittered in the trees now beginning to dress in their "coat of many colors." Two great blue herons drifted over the church grounds; their wings flapped in slow-motion while their legs trailed behind them. *What a beautiful world God has created*, thought Amy.

Father exchanged a few words with the preacher, chatted longer with some of the farmers and edged his way toward the wagon. Minnie and Moe stomped, switched their tails at pesky flies and irritating mosquitoes while waiting in the shade of poplar trees.

Dolly poked Amy, and signaled with her eyes. Amy cut her visiting short and hurried to the wagon; Father didn't like to be kept waiting. Already Reg and Cecil were lifting the little ones into the back where they settled onto a blanket.

Mrs. Mills, the lady who so generously took and nursed baby Evelyn, had a heart of gold—of that no one doubted. But Fred and his children grew uncomfortable when they had learned the conditions of her home. She had a twelve-year-old bed wetter and never changed the straw in the mattress until it stank.

Perhaps she just had her hands too full. Her own little daughter had seizures. It was a disturbing sight to watch. Whatever the reason, her house was dirty, and Fred couldn't just ignore that. He had moved his baby daughter as soon as he could.

Evelyn now stayed with Mrs. Lucas. Amy loved going to her house; one could eat off the tongue-and-groove floor; it was that clean. A diminutive woman with white hair and twinkling blue eyes, Mrs. Lucas had no children of her own. When questioned she'd laughed and said, "I grew up in a family of twelve kids. We fought for the drumsticks."

Today Evelyn wore a pretty pink dress made by Mrs. Lucas. A matching ribbon adorned her blond curls and she smelled sweet and clean. Father need not worry his baby daughter's nappy might be wet when the good woman handed the child to him to hold.

Mrs. Lucas directed the men to the parlour. Dolly, Amy, and Annie, she invited to her kitchen. "Come, you can help me," she said. "We'll fry up chicken and have us a Sunday dinner to make our tummies happy."

Two big cast iron skillets held floured and seasoned young fryers. A large kettle of potatoes simmered on the back of the stove. "Dolly, you can open those two jars of green beans and start them to boil. Amy, I know you're the bread maker in your family; I'll let you slice our bread."

Mrs. Lucas turned and smiled at Annie. "And you my dear may help me set the table; we'll put on anything that looks as if it belongs there. Butter, jam, salt and pepper, sugar, cream, pickled beets, and two pitchers of milk should do it, I think."

Dolly turned the chicken in one skillet with a long handled fork. "Mrs. Lucas, I see your braided onions, and is that garlic in long ropes over the stove? I didn't know to do that. Will it keep long that way? We raised onions, but not garlic."

"Well, bless your heart! I'll give you some garlic, and I'll give you a start in the spring. It's wonderful for flavoring meats, healthy too. It probably won't keep all winter, but it will keep for quite awhile."

Mrs. Lucas mashed the potatoes and made gravy. She called everyone to the table and placed Evelyn's highchair between Amy and Dolly.

"Join hands everyone," directed Mr. Lucas. "And don't forget little princess there. She'll be coming home to you before you know it. We'll surely miss her when that happens."

"My dear departed wife could not have done a better job of caring for little Evelyn," said Fred. "My children and I certainly thank you!"

CHAPTER 33

Dolly stood before the shiny new kitchen range, wooden spoon in hand, and stirred thick porridge made from wheat they raised and ground themselves. Amy parked Harold in his highchair and plopped Annie on a tall wooden stool Father had made. She sang a silly little ditty as she set the table for breakfast, "Hey diddle diddle, the cat played the fiddle, the cow jumped over the moon, the little dog laughed to see such sport, and the dish ran away with the spoon."

"Why are *you* so happy this morning?" grumped Dolly. "I sure don't feel like singing. I'm tired as a dog with three bones to chew from hauling all those vegetables to the cellar yesterday. I must have carried a ton of potatoes alone down those stairs—to say nothing of all the carrots, turnips, and parsnips. Today, I need to scrub this floor after all the dirt we tracked in."

"Yeah, I'm tired too," groaned Amy, "but I'm just so happy to have it all done and to know we'll have something besides rabbit to eat this winter."

"Well okay, but remember what our mother used to say, 'Sing before breakfast, cry before supper.'"

Father returned from the barn with a pail full of milk. During the summer he had purchased two milk cows and the family now had all the milk and cream they wanted. Fred poured some of the milk into pitchers. The rest he transferred to a clean bucket to be lowered to a shelf in the well where it could be kept cold.

"All right, Amy. It's your job to put the bucket in the well this morning. Don't dawdle; I believe Dolly has breakfast ready."

"Yes, Father."

Slowly—slowly—slowly, hand over careful hand, Amy lowered the bucket into the well. *Where is that shelf? I should have reached it by now. That must be it.* Amy released the rope. Too late she realized she had hit ice—not the shelf. A whole bucket of milk spilled into the well-water.

Oh, if only Father weren't home. Red in the face, and trembling, Amy entered the kitchen and faced her father. "Father—I'm sorry! It was an accident! I think the bucket hit ice. The milk spilled into the well."

"*What?*" Fred scowled, and rose to his full height. He sucked in his stomach, drew back his shoulders and barked like a drill sergeant. "You were careless! You fouled the well. And you'll clean it!" Eyes ablaze, he glared at Amy. "You hear me? It's your job! Don't ask for help. And you'd better have it done when I get home this evening."

❧

Amy turned the windlass and drew up yet another bucket of water. *How many is that now?* A tear slid down her cheek and splashed into the bucket.

Thankful they had two wells, Dolly brought her a cup of tea. "Sit, Amy, you can't keep this up all day. I'll turn the stupid windlass and haul up a few buckets while you rest. I don't know what makes that old buzzard so mean. Who does he think he is?"

"Dolly!" Amy gasped. "Watch your mouth! You can't help me—Father will punish both of us."

"So how is he to know?" She placed her hands on her hips. "I won't tell him! Eric and Leslie are playing in the barn; I doubt they'd tell even if they knew. And Annie and Harold are napping."

"But he'll ask me, Dolly." Amy's head drooped and more tears ran down her face. "And you know I can't lie."

"Well, he didn't say I can't empty the pails for you, and empty them, I will. So there!"

Amy knew her sister was splitting hairs, but she was too tired and her arms hurt too much to argue. She could only hope Father wouldn't question her too closely.

"I know," said Dolly. "I'll bring the galvanized tubs out. You can dump the water in them; then together we'll drag the tubs away and empty the water; just like on wash day. Then if Father asks, you can truthfully tell him you emptied the water." She huffed. "If Mother were here, he'd never get away with this. What makes him so mean anyway?"

Amy cried a little harder. "Oh, Dolly, I miss her so. Do you suppose Mother knows what's going on down here?"

"Shhh, I'm sorry! Please don't cry!" Dolly hugged her. "If she does, maybe she'll zap him with a thunderbolt and shape him up."

The sun passed overhead and continued to glow in a cloudless sky. Birds twittered in nearby branches, not that Amy noticed as she continued to empty the well one bucket at a time. From hour to hour Dolly came to offer a word of encouragement and help empty the tubs. But she had her own work to do and dared not linger.

Ten minutes before time for Father, Reginald, and Cecil to come home, Amy emptied her last pail of milky water. The bucket hit mud when she lowered it the last two times. Near exhaustion, Amy sat on the porch and tried hard not to cry. If she had to bite her tongue, she wouldn't let Father see her tears.

Fred clomped his way up onto the porch; the sound of heavy boots on planks announced his arrival home. He stopped and scowled at Amy before removing his hat and striking it against a leg of his faded overalls, sending up a cloud of dust. "Well, I see you are sitting. So, is the well emptied?"

"Yes, Father."

"Well, don't think you're finished. You have to clean the mud from the bottom before the job is completed."

Amy blanched, but made no reply as she bit down on her tongue.

The boys, following close behind their father, heard what he said to Amy. Reginald intervened. "Cecil and I will clean the mud from the well as soon as we have our supper."

Fred bristled. "No you won't. Amy fouled the well; she'll clean it. And she'll clean it *now*. You and Cecil can let her down into the well with ropes."

Reginald stared at his father. "Look at Amy! She's worn out! You don't just want the well cleaned—do you? You want to punish her till she's half-dead." He turned away and muttered in disgust. "She's not one of your army grunts to whip into shape."

Fred grabbed him by the shoulder and slung him around. Flesh striking flesh popped like a gunshot. In the house, Dolly jumped and dropped her spoon. Reginald caught himself before falling and lifted a hand to his mouth. His fingers came away bloody.

Amy gasped and leaped from her chair. "No! Please! Don't hit him! I'll clean the mud from the well. Just don't hit him again." Tears flowed unchecked down her cheeks.

Cecil placed an arm around his brother's shoulder and whispered in his ear. "Come on, we just as well do what he says and get it over with. Reasoning with him is like arguing with a bull on the prod. The only thing likely to change his mind would be a rock to the head, and I know you won't retaliate."

Seated in a rope chair, Amy waited for her fearful ride. On the pretext of adjusting the ropes, Reg bent close and whispered to her, "No more than three buckets, Amy; Father won't go down to look." As carefully as they could, Reginald and Cecil lowered their little sister down into the fifteen foot well.

With tender near-blistered hands, Amy gripped the lines till her knuckles turned white. *Maybe if I don't look, I can keep from screaming.* She squeezed her eyes shut and tried to imagine herself anywhere but this cold, dank, dark, hole. It didn't work! Her knee brushed the wet stone. Her eyes flew open. She squealed!

"It's all right," called Reggie. "We've got you! We won't leave you! Keep your eyes open now, you've almost reached bottom."

Not caring anymore how many tears ran down her face, Amy shuddered. Working as much by feel as sight, she scooped sludge until she heard the bucket scrape the rock-lined bed. She didn't notice the mud on her dress, as she tried hard not to imagine what else might be in the well with her.

In the kitchen, Harold tugged on Dolly's skirt. "Dolly, is you mad?"

She stopped her furious stirring of the stew, picked him up and hugged him. "I'm not upset with you, sugar."

Annie, Leslie, Eric, and Percy crowded around her. "Dolly, we're hungry," said Eric. "When do we get to eat supper? How long is it going to take to get the well cleaned?"

Dolly sighed and laid aside her spoon. "Well, my dears, no one said you have to wait for your supper." She winked at them. "Get your hands washed and come to the table. The stew is ready and I'll dish it up."

࿇

Cecil, Reginald, and Dolly spooned stew into their mouths as if they were on the brink of some great discovery contained in the bottom of their bowls. Amy tried to force a bite past the lump in her throat. Appetite had deserted her. She kept her eyes downcast and slowly sipped her hot tea. No one spoke. Father finished his stew and wiped the bowl with a chunk of bread. He scraped his chair back from the table, rose and left the house without a word to anyone.

Dolly heaved a sigh like steam escaping from a boiler. "Well, I guess Father won't get dessert tonight, will he?"

Reginald lifted his eyes to hers and smiled. "You made dessert for us?"

"I did. I made bread pudding." She giggled. "If the small fry aren't asleep lets get them and have a little party." She sobered, went around the table and hugged Amy. "Little sister, I'm sorry you had to work so hard today and we couldn't help you. I could never have done all that work, as you did, without rebelling. You're our angel, and you get the first serving of bread pudding."

Reginald beamed at her. "Amy, you can go to bed whenever you like. I'll help Dolly get the dishes done and the little ones tucked into bed."

"We both will," said Cecil. "Go on to bed, Amy."

෩

The next morning Father whistled as he stropped his razor and prepared to shave. Apparently he'd forgotten the well incident. Amy didn't think she would ever forget it, but she certainly wasn't going to bring it up. She'd pray it never happened again.

"Amy," Father said. "I'm going to take pictures in Paddle River today and I want you to go with me and help me with my equipment. You are getting to be quite the assistant. I don't have to explain to you more than once what I need and when."

CHAPTER 34

Paddle River continued to grow and prosper. Bigger, more modern buildings began to appear. Second-story frame houses went up; not all of which were as comfortable as their owners wished. Residents soon learned houses built in wintertime with green frozen lumber resulted in damp houses in the spring.

"We're livin' in a barn of a place," said the Hoopers. "'Tis mighty cold!"

Still, it was progress and satisfied a longing for the finer things many had left behind when they came to Paddle River.

To record the growth pangs of this emerging community, Fred Watts set up his camera and took pictures. One day it might be photographs of wheat being harvested; another time it could be of large stumps being pulled from resistant ground by sweaty oxen straining to clear land. Barn raisings, land clearing, nothing was too menial.

As it was being built, Fred captured on glass plates the sawmill where Reginald and Cecil would later work. He photographed the bridge Ted and Fred Speck built across Paddle River, from the first timbers felled across the water in early March to its completion in May of

1910. All these pictures were of interest to Canadian newspapers and as far away as England.

In comparison to their first miserable winter living in Barker's little hut, cramped together like sparrows in a nest, life in the Watts' log-cabin appeared grand indeed. Two stoves, a kitchen range and large potbellied heater, with plenty of dry tamarack to burn, kept even their feet and hands warm through all but the bitterest cold.

For a particularly tasty late-winter supper, Dolly fried the pickerel Reg and Cecil had caught early that morning. Fred wiped his mouth with a napkin, laid it aside and addressed his children. "We need supplies, and we best be going for them now. Once we get a spring thaw the roads will be too muddy to travel.

"I hate to take the time from my work to make the trip." He frowned and centered his attention on Reginald. "I'm thinking to send you. You're short of eighteen, but do you think you can handle Jerry and Joe and a heavily loaded wagon? It won't be easy. I calculate it will take you at least two weeks, longer if there's a storm."

"I can do it, Father. I'll go," said Reginald.

"I want to go along," said Cecil. "I can help guide the oxen, and take over when Reg gets tired."

Fred drained his teacup and soon squelched that idea. "I'd consider letting you go, Cecil, if I were going to be home, but much of the time I won't be. I need you to stay here and help Dolly manage with the day-to-day chores." Fred came as close to grinning as he ever did. "You know how Dolly and Amy feel about milking. They're afraid of getting kicked out of the barn. Percy and Eric might handle the chore, but they'd have to get up hours before breakfast in order to finish in time to make it to school."

∾

Reginald spoke in low tones to the oxen as he ran his mittened hands over their backs before fitting the heavy wooden yokes across their shaggy black necks. Their breaths mingled with his and made puffy little clouds in the frosty air. Pink tinged the eastern sky as Reg hitched Jerry and Joe to the sturdy farm wagon. Two sacks of grain for the oxen lay in the back along with a basket of victuals for himself.

"Haw," Reg called as he lightly tapped Joe on the shoulder. Slowly the wagon wheels began to turn as the well-trained team turned left and pulled the heavy farm wagon from the barnyard. Reginald walked beside his team, speaking words of encouragement and sometimes breaking into song as they trudged along the frozen road.

He stopped at the blacksmith shop in Paddle River. A fire blazed on the forge and the smithy, busy shaping iron, looked up. "You're Reggie Watts aren't you?" said Mr. Horn. "Fine looking animals, those oxen your father purchased. What can I do for you this bright morning?"

"Yes sir, Mr. Horn, I'm Reginald Watts. These are Jerry and Joe. I've a trip to make beyond Edmonton for supplies and I'm thinking the oxen need to be shod before we go."

"Indeed. Well, we'll get right to it. Bring one of the animals in here to the chute and we'll put him in the sling. Two shoes to each cloven hoof, sixteen shoes in all; it'll take awhile. Doubt you or I could stand up that long to have shoes fitted. For sure heavy oxen can't. Ox'll be okay though, long as he's got a cud to chew and the weight off his feet."

"Mr. Horn, have you ever had to shoe and ox while on the trail?"

"Ah, yes, lad. It ain't easy. Have to throw 'em and hold 'em down. I'm too old for that now. I'll stick to my shop where I can tie the foot up to a height convenient for my old back."

ॐ

Amy made school lunches while Dolly fixed breakfast. She sliced the bread thin for sandwiches and smeared each piece with freshly churned butter and wild strawberry jam. A piece of fried rabbit and a handful of raisins went into each lunch bucket.

Dolly turned from the stove and heaved a sigh that sounded like it came all the way from her toes. "It's going to be a long two weeks with Reggie gone. I miss him already. I wish it were Father going instead of him. Reg never yells at us and I can depend on him."

"I know," said Amy. "I miss him too. Do you want me to stay home from school today and help you?"

"No, no. Go to school every day that you can, Amy. If Mother had lived, I think I could have gone longer too. I know she wanted all her children to be well-educated. And Father doesn't want us to be a bunch of dunderheads either. He's school trustee and doing what he can to promote education, though I think eighth grade is about the limit for now."

Ready to leave for school, Amy Gladys opened the cabin door and halted mid-step. With a finger to her lips, she motioned for her little brothers to stop. Carefully she moved aside so they could see. There on the wooden bench beside the front door was a little white weasel. His beady black eyes and black tipped tail the only relief in a coat designed to blend with the snow. Probably as surprised to see the children as they were to see him, the little fellow skittered off across the yard.

Eric giggled. "He came to visit us and we didn't even know it. I wish I could have him for a pet. He's pretty."

Percy had a different idea. "I'd rather have the money his fur coat would bring. If I could catch him, I'd skin him in a minute."

Eric stuck out his lip. "That's mean. How'd you like it if we skinned your old cat?"

"Come on boys, don't argue," said Amy. "If we don't hurry, we'll be late for school." The very first day Miss Lila Sinclair had written her name on the chalkboard and explained the rules of discipline. Amy Gladys thought her the prettiest teacher she'd ever seen. She was also the strictest. They'd get a bad mark if they were late.

Eric ran on ahead then turned and called back. "Here comes old Spavins, guess we're not late."

The sight of the old horse shambling along, pulling the sleigh with his head only a few feet off the ground made the children giggle. Eight-year-old Marjorie Critchlow, however, didn't see anything funny about it. She sat regal as a queen, back straight, chin up, and drove the animal as if he were a prize-winner. It was her means of getting herself, her sisters and brother to school each day. With hot rocks at their feet, Marjorie and her siblings were quite comfortable.

The Critchlows opened a store on their property and the post office moved there. Born in 1907, young Connie Critchlow had the distinction of being the first baby girl born in Paddle River. Mrs. Critchlow pushed the child about in her pram and was heard to sigh over and over, "Ehhhh, my dear, suuuch is life! I hope little Connie gets better—Ehhhh, my dear, suuuch is life! I hope little Connie gets better."

Folks thought Mrs. Critchlow nice enough, but a bit eccentric. No one seemed to know what it was that ailed Connie, if anything. The children mocked Mrs. Critchlow behind her back. It became a litany easy to repeat, and for years at the end of a frustrating day Amy might say, "I hope little Connie gets better."

⁖

Two weeks passed; Amy, Dolly, Annie, and the boys began watching the road hoping to be first to spot Reggie coming with the oxen and loaded wagon. Tired of waiting and missing the brother he felt closest to, Cecil took one of the horses and rode out before breakfast to see if he could find him.

An hour later Cecil rode back at a gallop and swung off the horse in front of the cabin. Ears attuned to the sound of the horse, Dolly rushed out onto the porch. "Well, did you see him?"

"Yep, he's comin.'" Cecil laughed. "But you know how slow oxen are; it's like watchin' one of Leslie's caterpillars crawl down a log. He'll get here, but it's going to take some time. Reg won't arrive till after noon. He said to tell you he's hungry enough to eat a bear and he hopes you'll have something good cooked."

Dolly couldn't stop laughing as she dashed out and hugged Cecil. "You're not going to believe this, but a man named Mr. Pilz stopped by and gave us some bear steaks. He wouldn't come in when I told him Father wasn't home, but he kept me standing on the porch in the cold while he rambled on.

"He told me something scratched on his door. He said he opened the door, gun in hand, and this bear stood there. He shot the bear, slammed the door shut and dropped the bar across. When he opened the door the next morning the bear lay there dead."

Cecil laughed. "I know who he is. He's German and a bachelor. He thinks we English are a bit daft with our love of tea. He likes strong beer and even stronger coffee."

Father arrived home in time to help his boys unload the wagon. Most of the supplies could be stored in the cellar, accessible from a trapdoor in the center of the cabin floor. Dolly knew it would take awhile to unload all those heavy sacks of flour, and sugar. She might need to plan supper for a little later than usual. She grinned when she noted lard buckets being carried to the cellar. She could think of many uses for empty pails once she had used the lard. Several cases of dried fruit waited to be unloaded, along with soda biscuits, syrup, and canned vegetables. To Amy and Dolly, as they watched, it seemed like manna from heaven.

Reginald laughed as he tucked into his second bear steak. "I didn't really expect to eat a bear, but this is so good. Thanks, Dolly! You're a great cook."

CHAPTER 35

Proud of the improvements made thus far, Fred continued to work hard developing his land. By summer of 1911, fifteen acres had been cleared. Over two miles of fencing were up and fifteen head of cattle and four horses roamed the pasture. He looked forward to the day the homestead would be his, free and clear.

Fred felt successful, but he wasn't happy. *If only Edith had lived to see this,* he brooded. *I know she would have grown to like it. How I miss her!*

After supper Fred grabbed his hat and prepared to leave. "I'll be back before bedtime," Fred announced.

"Yes, Father," Dolly answered.

Blast them, with their, "Yes, Father. No, Father!" Fred scowled and hurried to the barn to saddle his horse. "They're always proper and polite, the blighters. Their mother taught them well. But I've seen the reproach in their eyes; they needn't think I haven't." Fred grumbled to Floozy as he slipped the bridle over the horse's ears and fastened the strap around the animal's neck. "They blame me, right enough, for their mother's death." The knowledge—along with his own suppressed guilt—irritated him like a shoe rubbing on a heel-blister.

Fred had sold the oxen in the spring and purchased a matched pair of dapple-gray mares named Mona and Floozy. Floozy probably got her name because she liked men but not women. She'd bite the girls if she got the chance.

"Well, there goes Father on Floozy," said Dolly. "He does look striking sitting up there on that horse doesn't he?"

Amy sighed as she wiped another dish. "I suppose so, but I miss Joe. For sure I'm not going to feed that old Floozy my bread dough, no matter how pretty she is."

Barn chores completed, Reginald sat on the porch in the rocking chair. He balanced Harold on one knee, Annie on the other. "Well, and what did you two mischief-makers do today? You both look like Cheshire cats. Did you fall down the rabbit hole?"

Annie and Harold giggled. "We went with Dad to the neighbors," crowed Annie. "We played while Dad helped cut Mr. Strong's hay."

"We no tell," said Harold.

"Tell what?"

Annie swelled with importance, her eyes round and solemn as she looked up at her big brother. "Our Amy Gladys fell in the well! She got all wet. And her hat got all muddy." Annie laid a hand on Reg's cheek to make sure he understood they hadn't told. "Amy said don't tell Father. And we didn't tell him nothing!"

Reg got the unabridged version from Amy later. Unlike their own wells at home, the neighbor's well had no protection built up around it. When Amy started to push the flat covering back away from the opening, it slid easier than she expected. In she went— headfirst. The elastic chin strap kept the hat on her head. Percy and Eric pulled her out and ran home to get her a dry dress. The hat dried in the sun and Amy brushed the dirt off best she could. Father hadn't noticed anything unusual.

৪৩

Harold and Annie were already in bed when Fred lurched through the front door. He kicked the first thing he came to and swore as the chair crashed to the floor. The older children watched in stunned silence as he wove his way across the room and fumbled the gun from its pegs on the wall. His hand groped halfway along the shelf before he stumbled and swore again.

"Whersh the bloody ammo-nation? I'll chust shoot all you older jackanapes."

Though Fred slurred his words, his intentions seemed clear enough. Thinking fast, Reginald grabbed the bullets off the shelf and shoved them down in the flour sack. Fred continued to blunder into things while looking for shells.

The older children hardly dared breathe and they stood as though turned to stone. Not understanding, Eric and Leslie looked from their father to their older siblings and back again.

When Fred again muttered, "Where's the bloody bullets? Eh?" Eric thought he should come forward. "I know where 'tis Fah-thur!"

Reg clapped a hand over Eric's mouth and shoved the boy behind him.

Fred didn't react. He hadn't heard.

As soon as they could breathe again, Reginald, Cecil, Dolly and Amy took to their heels. Out the back door they ran. Reggie watched until satisfied his sisters would be safe before he and Cecil climbed a tall tree and hunkered down on a large limb. Amy and Dolly kept running until they reached the brush. Dropping to her knees, Amy crawled beneath low-hanging branches. Dolly followed. Satisfied they were well enough hidden, the girls wrapped their arms around each other and let the tears fall.

Not sure if his father meant to shoot him or not, Percy hid in the haystack. Eric and Leslie didn't bother to undress, but crawled into bed together and pulled the covers up over their heads. If the commotion woke Annie and Harold, they remained quiet and stayed in bed.

Reasonably sure their father would have fallen asleep in the time they'd been gone, the children crept back to the house. Reggie and Cecil were first, but waited in the shadows for Amy and Dolly. Pausing at the threshold to listen, they breathed a prayer for God's protection. Reassured by their father's snoring, they entered the room silent as cats. Eyes now used to the dark, Reg quickly checked the flour sack. The bullets were still there. Relieved their father hadn't discovered them, the children sought their beds.

Percy stayed away all night. He'd fallen asleep in the haystack.

The next morning the children performed their chores as usual, but they cautiously watched their father for any signs of malice. They saw none. Had he forgotten?

Sober now, Fred made no mention of last evening's incident. With eyes cast down, he ate the breakfast Dolly prepared, pushed back from the table and mumbled, "I'll be clearing more land today. You needn't fix dinner for me; I'll take along some water, bread, and cheese."

&

In June, Reverend Seymour Dallas arrived in Paddle River. The Anglican parish of St. Mary Abbots in Kensington, London, England sent the priest to them as part of the Archbishop's Western Canada Mission. Immediately upon his arrival Reverend Dallas began teaching a day school and weekly Sunday school. He held church services in settlers' homes.

A young man not much older than Reginald Watts, Rev. Dallas soon established himself as a man with stong convictions. His ready smile and willingness to help residents of Paddle River and surrounding areas in practical, as well as spiritual ways soon won him a place in the hearts of the people.

He won Fred Watts over when he purchased a Clyde stallion to improve horse breeding in Paddle River. "I never thought to see a practical priest such as this bloke," declared Fred. "This man has a head on his shoulders and a vision for the future. He can hold services in my house anytime."

Reverend Dallas took part in every community enterprise, freely furnished publicity, and worked tirelessly for the benefit of all. He helped establish a District Co-op Store in Paddle River and served as first president of the Co-op.

Though Reverend Dallas made only $10.00 a month, he managed to establish the little St. Mary Abbots Church at Paddle River, across the road from the Watts homestead.

All the Watts children loved Rev. Dallas. Reginald and Seymour became good friends; when time permitted, they fished together. Who knows if they exchanged confidences? Young Leslie, however, may have been the most in awe of the priest. Or perhaps his fascination centered on the organ in the little church.

Like his older brother Reginald, Leslie was musically inclined and could play by ear. He delighted in sneaking off across the road and popping into the little church. If left alone, he played hymn after hymn.

Occasionally Rev. Dallas heard the young Leslie playing and singing, "Froggy Went a Courtin.'" When that happened, the minister merely smiled and remained out of sight. He delighted in knowing the child enjoyed himself. It didn't take a genius to know the Watts children had a rocky uphill path to trod, especially the older members. He prayed often he could be of help to them. He prayed even harder for Fred Watts and trusted God to work in his life.

ॐ

Dolly wrinkled her nose. "Amy, do you smell smoke?"

"Huh? … Well, sure, there's a fire going in the cook stove."

"No, no. This is different. Something outside is burning." Dolly ran outside followed closely by Amy.

"I can smell it now. There's a sure enough fire somewhere. What do you think we should do?"

Before Dolly could answer, George Barker appeared in the barnyard. "Fire!" he shouted. "Fire! Started somewhere on the prairie. Lightning strike, most likely." As quickly as possible George set about hitching his horses to the plow he'd brought in the wagon. "Is your father home?" he called.

"No, Mr. Barker, he's in Edmonton."

"The boys? Reggie and Cecil, where are they?"

"They're building fence," Dolly shouted back. "Mr. Barker, what should we do?"

"Don't let the little ones wander. Keep them indoors. I'm going to plow a firebreak around your cabin and barns.

"Draw water from the wells and wet down everything you can around the buildings. Soak any sacks you have and keep them handy for beating out sparks that may reach here. Fill all your buckets with water." He shouted his last directive as he began plowing a deep furrow around the cabin. "And pray!"

Frightened out of their wits and wishing Father was home, the girls ran to draw water from the wells.

CHAPTER 36

Alarmed by the smell of smoke and the darkening sky, Reginald and Cecil grabbed their tools and sprinted for home. They arrived in time to see George Barker plowing the last round of the firebreak.

"George," shouted Reg. "Where's the fire? How far away is it?" Out of breath from running, he stopped to gulp air and dispatch another question. "Do we need to go fight the fire?"

"You boys are more needed here. The wind's blowing this way! Help your sisters wet things down. Watch for sparks." George loaded the plow and began hitching his team back to the wagon. "My brothers have gone to fight the fire—other men too. I'll lend a hand to get your roof soaked; then I'll head back home and help my sister watch our place."

❧

Amy fidgeted as she helped Dolly prepare a quick supper. Her sister frowned. "Maybe you could toast some bread-slices on the stove while I scramble these eggs," said Dolly. "If we have to watch for fire outside, I for sure don't want one in here, even if it is in the stove. I'll let the fire die soon as these eggs are cooked."

"Dolly!" Amy squealed. "There's a mouse!"

"Where?"

"There! In the corner—he's trying to climb up the flour barrel." Amy yelped and dropped the butter knife. "There goes another one—he ran over my toe!"

Annie shrieked and climbed to the highest bunk bed. Harold, Leslie, and even Eric took to the bunks. Running to escape the grass fire, critters weren't particular where they found perceived safety. Mice invaded their cabin in droves.

"Do something!" Dolly bleated. "Percy, where are those cats of yours?" Dolly held her ground as long as she could, but when a mouse tried to run up her leg, she screamed and jumped on a chair.

Reginald grabbed a broom and tried to beat the varmints down and sweep them out the door. Crazed by the fire, it appeared for every mouse Reg swept out, three more rushed in.

"I think we have at least a couple traps; I'll see if I can find those and set them," said Cecil.

A man calling from the front yard interrupted Reginald's frenzied sweeping. "Fire's burned itself out! We've got men keeping watch, wind could stir it up again. You'd best keep an eye out too, until we're certain there's no live embers."

"Oh, that's good news! Thanks for letting us know! We'll keep watch," said Reginald.

"It'll be night soon," said Amy. "What will we do then? I'm not staying in the dark with all these mice!"

Cecil, Reginald, and Percy laughed, but soon confessed they didn't intend to sit in the dark with mice either. "We'll leave the lamps lit and try to keep them off the bunks," said Cecil. "We older ones must stay awake and guard against sparks from the prairie fire; playing hide and seek with the mice will help to keep us alert."

Amy and Dolly drew their feet up and watched from their bunks. Cecil set three traps and they quickly heard, *Snap! Snap! Snap!* As fast as the boys could bait and reset the traps, they caught more mice.

ಊ

Reginald yawned, stretched, and muttered, "This has been one long night, but we made it through without a flare-up of fire; I see daylight climbing over the eastern horizon."

Cecil clapped a hand on Reg's shoulder. "Brother, your eyes look like two burnt holes in a blanket. Want some toothpicks to prop 'em open?"

"Huh! I suppose you think *you* look like Prince Charming."

Cecil laughed. "I don't reckon the cows are going to care what we look like as long as we get out to the barn, fork some hay into the manger, and milk them."

Thankful she only needed to strike a match to paper and kindling already laid in the firebox, Dolly cast wary glances around the room as she began to prepare breakfast. "Reggie, are the traps set? I haven't heard one snap in more than two hours. Do you think we caught all the pests, or are they hiding in dark corners waiting to run out and scare me half to death?"

"The traps are set, but I think our mousy visitors have skittered for more friendly habitats. They're field mice, and we didn't exactly welcome them. Forget the traps; you girls' squeals were enough to panic the rodents."

Dolly stuck her tongue out at her brother.

As the day wore on, Amy and Dolly performed their tasks more by rote than conscious thought. Reginald and Cecil excused themselves from fence building for less strenuous work. Cecil mended and oiled harnesses while Reggie cleaned the barns and spread a load of seasoned manure on the garden spot.

By mid-afternoon Fred walked in and found Dolly and Amy napping along with Harold and Annie. "Harrumph," he barked as he stowed his equipment in a corner of the cabin. "I don't suppose there's hot water for tea."

"Father! You're home!" Dolly cried as she struggled from her bunk. "I'll make tea right away. We're a tad discombobulated around here today—we were up all night watching for sparks from the fire on the prairie."

"Yes, I heard about the fire from four sources before I'd made my way through Paddle River. And I met George Barker on my way home. He tells me you children did everything possible to protect our homestead from fire." Fred slumped into a chair. "Sorry I wasn't here."

A blur ran past Fred's foot. "What in tarnation was that?"

"A mouse," Eric announced as though it were a resident house pet. "We had a million of the little beasties in here last night."

Amy hastened to explain about the mice.

"Have you checked the cellar?" Father inquired.

"No, we didn't think to," said Dolly.

"Well, I'll do that," said Fred. "And I'll lay in more traps. Can't have the blighters eating our produce."

At suppertime Fred made an announcement that had the children grinning. "Get a good night's sleep; tomorrow I'm taking you all to the fair in Paddle River."

With the excitement of the fire, the children had forgotten about the coming Agricultural Fair.

ॐ

Folks came from miles around to attend this event, started the year before in 1910. Father unhitched the team from the wagon and staked the horses far enough from other animals that they wouldn't tangle lines. Amy saw friends she knew from school; they waved, and she, Dolly, and Annie headed that way.

"Hi Amy," said Sally Lou, "Are you going to enter something?"

Amy smiled. "No, I just want to see what others have brought."

"I know what you mean; I'm not ready to enter my work either." She laughed. "Come on, lets go see what they are setting out. I hear the cakes, pies, and pastries will be judged and then we get to eat them at our picnic dinner. My mother brought a carrot cake and I know that's good."

The girls strolled together down the long line of tables where numbered entries were being set out. Exhibits included all sorts of canned goods, raw vegetables, grain samples, and fancy work of all kinds. Exquisite quilts with the tiniest hand stitches were draped over clean-papered sawhorses.

"Those are Mr. Pess's baskets," said Sally Lou. "No one makes them the way he does. He weaves them from our native willow, you know. Mother says the Indians can't do better. Those are his horsehair brushes, too. My father won't use anything else for whitewashing our cabin."

Sally Lou wandered off to find her mother. Amy, Dolly, and Annie, tired from all the excitement, went to sit on a blanket in the shade. Leslie ran up grinning like a monkey eating apples and flopped on the blanket beside them.

"What exhibit has you so excited, little brother?" said Dolly.

"Look! Lookit what I found!" Leslie uncurled his palm to display three fat fuzzy black and orange caterpillars.

"Ugh!" said Dolly. "If you have to play taxidermist, please don't do it here."

The men and boys gravitated to the animal exhibits and stood in clusters, supposedly discussing the creatures' merits. Amy did think the lambs were pretty cute, but she didn't see anything about cows and oxen to excite anyone.

The three-legged sack races, women and girls' egg-in-a-spoon, and boys' human wheelbarrow races brought hilarity to the crowd in the afternoon. But by far the most exciting event turned out to be the oxen races.

"Oxen are too slow!" declared one owner of a fine team. "I think we should stick to horse races." The spectators didn't agree.

After some discussion and persuasion, Mr. Armitage was chosen for judge. He announced the rules and Ed

Jensen agreed to race the Thompson's team. A lad named Birnie raced his own oxen.

Birnie sat at the front of his wagon, legs dangling over the front of the box. To get more speed from his oxen, he reached out, grabbed the tail of an ox and began to twist.

"Hey there, Birn! Give that old tail another squeeze," shouted a spectator.

Jensen couldn't keep pace. He began to flap his arms and yell at his oxen. He hadn't considered the forty to fifty dogs that had come with their masters. When all the yelling started they emerged from under their respective wagons and began to herd the teams. The resulting barks and heel-nips startled the animals and Jensen's team careened off into the brush with their driver yelling, "Whoa!—Whoa!"

It took Jensen a half hour to get his team untangled and wagon turned around and out of the brush. Birnie had already been awarded first prize when the red-faced Jensen stepped up to receive a red ribbon.

The main fair events were over by early evening. Dancing for young people, and the young in heart, would go on all night. The music was provided by local artisans with fiddles, accordions, harmonicas, and any other instrument they might bring along.

Dolly giggled. "My feet say dance, but my head says sleep." She grabbed Amy by the hand. "Come on, little sister, it's been a fun day, but it's time to go home. I see Father heading for the wagon."

CHAPTER 37

Dolly made the knitting needles fly as she worked on another wool stocking. She glanced around the room at her brothers and sisters and felt a lump rise in her throat. Glad they couldn't read her rebellious thoughts; she ducked her head before anyone could see the tear in her eye. *I love my brothers and sisters, but being the oldest girl and mothering everyone is hard. I'm tired of always having to be responsible.*

With a mental shake, Dolly pushed aside her knitting and rose to shove another piece of wood in the pot-bellied heater. Snowflakes floated past the unadorned windowpanes as if they had all the time in the world to join those already on the ground. The temperature hovered in the single digits, warm in comparison to what winter's blast had been known to dump on them.

Amy jumped up to add more wood to the fire blazing in the kitchen range. "Dolly, I've about finished this stocking. How many more do we have to knit before Christmas?"

Dolly sighed and shrugged. None too gently, she pulled Amy aside and managed to state her case in a whisper as forceful as though she had shouted it. "It's not the stockings we're knitting that worries me, but what to put in the ones the smallfry are going to hang up on Christmas Eve. I wish Father would come home. Or send some money! Or write! Or something! What is it he's doing all this time in Edmonton anyway? He's been gone nearly three weeks."

With little over a week until Christmas day, could she and Amy do their everyday chores and still finish a pair of stockings for everyone? If Father didn't provide, could she scrape something together for the little ones? These disturbing thoughts tumbled through Dolly's mind like ice pellets driven before a storm.

Amy Gladys stared at her sister and absorbed some of the stress Dolly conveyed. Amy swallowed the growing lump in her throat and tried to smile. In a voice tuned for Dolly's ears she said, "I think Father will surprise us for Christmas. Maybe that's what's taking him so long; he's buying things for Christmas day. I think our father will bring home something to stuff in all the stockings."

Dolly stepped back, planted hands on hips, and gave her sister a look guaranteed to clabber milk. "Don't be daft—Father is just as likely to come home empty-handed and tanked."

Amy looked at the floor and nodded; it was hard to argue with the truth.

Dolly groaned inwardly and looked around the room. Leslie, Eric, and Annie played a game of make believe on the floor close to the potbellied stove. They pretended to be no bigger than a flea that could hide almost anywhere in the cabin— their giggles were evidence it didn't take much to have fun.

Little Harold slept on his cot, rump in the air, thumb stuck in his mouth.

As far as Dolly and Amy could tell, Percy might just as well have been in another province. Totally unaware of anything going on around him, he sat on the lowest bunk and whittled on a chunk of tamarack. Unbeknownst to his siblings, he'd made his little brothers and Annie whistles from pieces of willow. Whistles that really worked. If he were clever enough, he'd have a little horse for Harold.

Percy folded his knife blade and shoved knife and wood into his pocket. He sauntered over to Dolly. "You're worried about Christmas aren't you? You shouldn't be, you know. Father Christmas will visit even if Dad forgets. Reggie is working now and you know we can count on him. I'll bet he comes home this evening with a sack full of goodies for you to squirrel away."

Dolly gaped at Percy. With a laugh that erupted half giggle, half sob, she threw her arms around her little brother.

"Hey! Don't go gettin' all squidgy." Percy grinned as he squirmed and loosened her hold on his neck.

Of course they *could* count on Reggie, but it didn't seem fair to Dolly or to Amy that his hard-earned money should go for needs other than his own. When work on the farm slowed at the beginning of winter, Reg had taken a job at Henry Clemes and Omer Fluet's sawmill. Many homesteaders needed outside employment to earn money with which to prove up their claim. Wages were a dollar a day plus board.

Reginald rejoined his family only on weekends. In some ways it lightened Dolly and Amy's work-load, but they all missed their big brother and looked forward to Saturday nights when he'd come home.

This year Christmas day came on Monday. Reg had told Dolly, Mr. Clemes and Mr. Fluet would shut down the mill Friday evening; Reg would come on home late that day. Family men themselves, his employers wanted their workers to be able to spend the holiday with family if at all possible. The mill wouldn't start up again until Wednesday morning. With an extra day, even the employees that lived a distance away should make it home and back in time for work.

Having distracted his sister and making her think, Percy pushed further. "Let's look in Mother's trunk; I seem to remember she had some decorations for Christmas."

Together, Percy, Dolly, and Amy pulled the trunk a few inches away from the wall. Dolly lifted the lid. All three children frowned as they stared down at the portrait lying there on the very top like some coveted treasure. Why had their father put the despised photograph there? Did he know how they all hated that picture?

Dolly glowered at her image before she turned the picture over and slipped it beneath a garment. "Percy, why didn't you want your picture taken that day, anyway? Because of what Father did to you, we all look like we'd been given a big dose of castor oil two minutes before the shutter snapped."

"I'm sorry I ruined the picture for everyone," said Percy. "I didn't think Father would make such a big deal of it. It's not like I'd be the only kid missing; Norah is in England, and Evelyn isn't here."

Percy's hand lifted to rub the side of his head. "Father nearly pulled my ear off that day—made me forget my bellyache—I can tell you!"

Dolly and Amy hugged Percy. "It's all right, little brother; we love you," said Amy. "We hated seeing you hurt!"

"With a bit of luck, the hateful picture will be lost and forgotten," said Dolly.

Thoughts of looking for decorations faltered when Cecil opened the door and shouted, "Father just pulled into the barnyard, looks like he has a loaded sleigh."

⌒

The man who entered their cabin looked like Frederick Watts, but he sure didn't sound or act like the father they knew. Even now, three days later, he remained cheerful, and actually smiled when he noticed one of his children peering at him.

"You girls may each order a new dress from Eaton's catalogue. It won't arrive before Christmas day, but you'll have it for the New Year." Fred cleared his throat. "Father Christmas will be around, no doubt, to stuff stockings on Christmas Eve. I brought a ham all the way from Edmonton; it's in the cupboard outdoors. We'll have that for our Christmas dinner."

Amy gaped at Dolly. Dolly gave a barely perceptible shrug and rolled her eyes. The girls liked this new version of their father, but they didn't trust the change. What had sparked the difference—and how long could it last?

"You boys bundle up," directed Fred. "We'll hike out to the woods and chop down our own evergreen tree. Christmas trees are all the rage in Edmonton. You children can all have a hand in decorating the tree. I've brought popcorn and cranberries to string and hang on the branches. We'll start a new tradition."

"Me too, Father? Can I go with you to get the tree?" Annie pleaded.

For a second Fred scowled, then his countenance changed to a grin. "Well, I suppose you won't freeze any faster than your brothers. Come along if you like."

∞

Christmas day dawned bright, clear, and cold. The younger children squealed with delight to find their stocking filled with hard candy, nuts, a small toy or two and a bright, round orange. Harold crowed over his wooden horse and whistle. Eric, Leslie, and Annie grinned and added to the cacophony with their whistles.

Percy peeled his orange, stuck a segment in his mouth and grinned the whole time.

As directed by their father, all the children had hung a stocking on the foot of their bed before retiring for the night. Dolly, Amy, Percy, and especially Cecil, and Reginald, thought they were too old to hang up their stocking, but had complied when Fred insisted. Now they gazed in wonder at the orange they found in their stocking. How had their father managed that? This far north, oranges were as rare as paved roads. And sweet oranges had to be expensive.

Dolly and Amy prepared a bountiful Christmas dinner of ham, mashed potatoes, gravy, pickled beets, canned green beans, buttered parsnips, and fresh-baked yeast rolls. Needing to help, Annie set the table and fetched things for her sisters. She placed fresh churned butter and strawberry jam on the table.

"Dinner is ready," announced Dolly.

Fred took his place at the head of the table and watched as his family gathered around. He bowed his head and gave thanks for their bountiful blessings.

When it seemed they couldn't eat another bite, Dolly brought a platter of scones to the table for dessert. Reggie laughed and poured everyone more tea.

"It's been a good Christmas. Eh. What? But I have one more surprise for you!"

All eyes turned to look at their father. Even Harold sensed a change and became unusually quiet. Fred took his time and let his eyes rove over his family.

He cleared his throat, refolded his napkin and placed it beside his plate. Fred looked down once, then lifted his chin and announced, "I'll be going back to Edmonton this afternoon. I'm getting married again at the end of the week. She's a nice lady, a widow woman. Grace Hood lost her husband a year ago. We'll be married in a civil ceremony; neither of us wanted a fuss.

"When I come home again, after the first of the year, I'll be bringing my new wife. I expect all of you to make her feel welcome."

After a deafening silence that lasted too long, Reginald found his voice. "Congratulations, Father. We all hope you'll be happy."

CHAPTER 38

A large kettle of beans, flavored with leftover ham, spiced with onions and a clove or two of garlic, simmered on the back of the stove. Amy picked up a wooden spoon to give the beans a stir. Steam escaped as she lifted the lid on the pot; the aroma of spiced beans permeated the cabin. Amy's stomach growled.

"Oh, that does smell good, doesn't it? Makes me want to eat right now," Dolly said as she turned from hanging a brand new 1912 calendar, courtesy of Critchlow's store. "Well, I now know what's for supper, don't I?" She giggled. "Good job, Amy; maybe we'll just let you do all the cooking."

Amy snorted. "I don't think so."

The girls talked about everything but their greatest fears. From the time their father dropped his bombshell on Christmas day, Dolly and Amy avoided putting in to words what a stepmother in their lives might mean. Of one thing, they could be sure; it meant change. Whether the adjustments could be easily made or not, they didn't know.

The Watts children had heard what you did on New Year's Day you were bound to repeat throughout the rest of the year. Not wishing to test the theory, or be confined to the cabin any longer than necessary, the

Watts clan bundled up, adding layers of clothing until only their eyes peeked out. The snow sported a heavy frozen crust; the children walked on top as if strolling down a city boulevard.

A leaden sky spewed snowflakes intermittently, like a housewife shaking feathers from her fingers while plucking a goose. Amy looked up and felt frozen flakes cling to her eyelashes.

"A team pulling a wagon is coming up the road," called Eric.

Dolly shaded her eyes with a hand in hopes of seeing better. Harnesses jingled and the horses' heads bobbed up and down, evidence they pulled a heavy load. "Could that be Father coming home with his new wife?"

"I don't think so," said Percy. "That's not Mona and Floozy, and Dad left here with the sleigh."

Amy drew closer to Dolly. The two girls wrapped their arms around each other and watched the team advance.

"Is this the Watts' cabin?" a man called out.

Air escaped Amy's lungs in one rapid *whoosh*. Unaware she'd been holding her breath as if she alone could stave off some impending fate, embarrasement added more color to her already cold-reddened cheeks.

"Yes, sir, this is the Watts' cabin. Is that load for us?" queried Percy.

"That it is, son. That it is. Stuff belonging to the new Mrs. Watts, I gather. My orders are to pile it all inside the cabin." The man jumped down from the wagon and tied the team to the hitching rail in front.

"Is there someone here can help me get all this cargo indoors?" He rolled back the canvas. "These trunks and crates are pretty heavy."

Eric took off for the barn to summon Reginald and Cecil.

Amy watched as her brothers and this stranger tugged, hefted, and carried three large trunks indoors. The cabin suddenly seemed a lot smaller, even though Reg and Cecil shoved the chests into a corner, fitted as closely together as they could manage.

Amidst more grumbling from the driver, six wooden crates were unloaded from the wagon and piled beside the trunks. Dolly grabbed for Amy's hand when she noticed a sewing machine crated in one of the boxes. The girls stared at the last item brought into the cabin and piled atop the other things. Never had they seen such a fancy bedstead; fat cherubs were carved into the polished oak headboard.

Unsure what good manners dictated, Dolly looked to Reginald for help. Should she ask this stranger to stay for supper? Should she offer him tea? Or should he simply be allowed to warm himself at the stove before going on his way? He hadn't introduced himself, which seemed a bit rude to her.

As if he read her thoughts, the man turned, doffed his cap and smiled. "Forgive my manners ladies, guess I'm a bit tired and foozled. It's been a long trip, and I'm driving a team strange to me. My name's Mr. Smidgley."

Dolly smiled, but it was Reginald who spoke. "Mr. Smidgley, will you stay to supper? It's pretty simple fare, but you are welcome. We can stable your horses and feed them as well."

"Why, I thank you! Something smells awfully good, and I'll admit I'm a bit hungry." He looked around as though wondering where to wash his hands. "I'll be sure and tell Mr. Watts of your kindness."

ℒ

Dolly scowled at the trunks and boxes piled in the corner. The trunks were double strapped and padlocked. It seemed to her a lot of precaution for a trip from Edmonton to Paddle River. Did the lady think they might snoop through her things?

That thought ran both ways. Dolly didn't want some stranger pawing through her mother's belongings. "Reggie, do you think we could get our mother's trunk up the ladder into your and Cecil's attic bedroom? Would you boys mind having it there?"

Cecil shrugged, but Reginald laughed. "I think, Dolly, that might be a very good idea. If you girls help, we can certainly get it up there."

Percy surprised them by declaring, "I think we should slap a padlock on it first."

To Amy and Dolly's surprise Reginald and Cecil agreed. Percy hunted up a lock. Cecil secured the trunk and handed the key to Dolly. "Hide it where only you girls will know its location."

ℒ

Four days later Father arrived home with his new wife. Dolly hurried to make tea. Amy set out their nicest cups and saucers and laid out white linen napkins.

"Well, children, here we are. This is, Grace."

"Welcome! I'm Dolly. This is my sister, Amy. And this young man trying to hide behind me, is Harold. He's a bit shy, but he'll make up soon."

Amy wished she could hide behind someone as well. *What do I call her? I can't call her Grace, and I certainly won't call her Mother. Mrs. Watts sounds so formal. Oh, I wish I'd asked Reggie.* Swallowing her uncertainty, Amy stepped forward and smiled. "You must be cold after your trip. We've made tea, and there's fresh biscuits. If you'll be seated, we'll serve you."

Fred laughed. "You'll meet the rest of the clan later. Percy, Eric, Leslie and Annie are in school. Cecil is around here somewhere and Reginald will be home the weekend. Reg works at the sawmill in Paddle River."

Grace warmed herself a minute or two by the pot-bellied stove. She removed her rather elegant hat with the green ostrich feather and slipped off her coat. Fred hung it on a peg for her.

Lively brown eyes smiled up at her husband. Grace had hair dark as a crow's wing. A small woman, she wore a pretty pink blouse and a black wool skirt that covered all but the tips of her matching shoes. Amy Gladys noted she barely came to Father's chin, even with high heels.

Fred gulped his tea and announced, "Well, ladies, I must take care of my team. I'll leave you to get acquainted."

Grace sipped her tea and placed the cup back in the saucer. She looked at Amy and then Dolly. "I assume your name is Dorothy and Dolly is a nickname. Is that correct?"

"Yes, ma'am, I was christened Dorothy Mae."

"I thought so. I shall call you Dorothy. You don't look much like a Dolly to me."

Dolly looked at her lap and made no reply. Amy groaned inwardly; the family had called her Dolly as long as she could remember. Did Grace expect them to change?

ଔ

Over the next two weeks Grace established herself as mistress of her home. Routines changed, leaving Dolly confused as to her role in the household. Some days Grace cooked and wanted no help, other days she left it all up to Dolly and Amy.

Never blatantly critical, Grace's suggestions were as irksome to Dolly as mosquitoes in springtime. "Dorothy Mae, perhaps if you didn't fry the meat quite so long, it would be more tender. Dorothy Mae, I know you mean well, but I fear you'll spoil Harold with all your pampering. He needs to do more things for himself. Dorothy Mae, do you think we could do with a little less salt in the potatoes?"

Dolly did her best to bite her tongue and comply until the morning Grace found fault with her clothes.

Dorothy Mae, I know you've had no mother to guide you, but don't you think your dress is a bit too tight? And that skirt is quite short. My dear, proper young ladies strive to dress modestly."

Dolly's face turned beet red and the fire transferred to her tongue. "Mrs. Watts, I'm sorry you don't like my clothes, but I have no money to buy more. I have one new dress that actually fits me. I save that for good. I have two dresses I can wear for every day. You're looking at the best one. This may come as a surprise to you, but Father thinks they are plenty good enough. If you don't like what you see, I suggest you take it up with him."

Struggling to hold back the tears until she could escape to the outhouse, Dolly turned on her heel and dashed out the backdoor.

As quietly and unobtrusively as possible, Amy slipped on her coat, grabbed Dolly's off the peg and followed her sister.

ങ

Two weeks later, Dolly crawled into bed with Amy and shook her shoulder. "Amy! Wake up! I'm so scared! If ever I needed my mother… Amy? Please! Wake up!"

"Huh? What? Dolly! You're crying! Whatever is wrong? You never cry!"

"Father is throwing me out! He says I'm fifteen and old enough to be on my own. Grace doesn't like me, and she told Father I sassed her."

"Oh no! That's awful!" Amy's tears mingled with Dolly's. Careful to keep their voices low, the girls clung to each other. "Whatever will you do? Where will you go?"

"Father says I'm to care for a doctor's children in Edmonton. I leave tomorrow.

CHAPTER 39

Amy soaked her pillow with tears every night for a week, but it didn't bring Dolly back. God alone knew when they might see each other again. On parting, the girls had cried and vowed to keep in touch. Dolly promised to write as soon as she could purchase paper, an envelope, and a stamp.

Father's words rang in Amy's ears and resentment knocked on her heart's door.

"Oh, don't carry on so," said Father the day he left with Dolly. "Your sister will live with a doctor and his wife and care for their four children. She'll be fine. No doubt, she'll soon find some bloke to marry her."

Before Reginald returned to the sawmill that sad day, he pulled Amy aside. In a voice choked with anger, he'd said, "I'll soon check on Dolly if I have to walk all the way to Edmonton."

A month later, Reg and Cecil did walk to Edmonton. It took them two and a half days to make the trip on foot and locate the house where their sister worked.

"Reggie! Cecil!" Dolly launched herself at her brothers. They grabbed her, lifted her off her feet and swung her around by turns. "Oh, I'm so glad to see you! I can't believe you're here! Come in. Come in. I'll fix tea. Doctor Smith and his wife are nice—they treat me like family. And the children are dears; they're taking naps just now or I would introduce you to them."

❦

Reginald replaced the bone china cup in its saucer and stood to his feet. He wrapped his arms around his sister and hugged her hard. As soon as Reg released her, Cecil grabbed her and squeezed even harder.

Dolly swallowed the lump in her throat, giggled and pushed him away. "I can't believe you boys walked all this way to see me! I wish you didn't have to leave so soon."

Reg laughed. "Ah, but I know you, if we stick around here, you'll put us to work." He sobered. "Now that we know you're well-placed, we'll go by City Cemetery and put flowers on our mother's grave, then we'll be hoofing it on back to Paddle River." He hugged his sister again. "Things are changing, Dolly. Like birds, the time comes when we have to leave the nest. I'll keep watch on Amy, but I'll not be staying home anymore."

❦

Evelyn, at two and a half years old, bounced around the cabin, happy as a spotted calf in a field of clover. The child's sunny disposition coupled with her sparkling blue eyes and halo of flaxen curls soon won her a place in Grace's affections. Evelyn, however, preferred her father over any other family member. It was to Fred she scampered as soon as he came in the door, her arms raised and a beguiling, "Up" on her lips.

Home now more than ever before, Fred seemed pleased with the child's attention. He grinned and picked her up when Evelyn called him Papa. Their stepmother watched, smiled, and said, "Evelyn, you may call me Mama Grace."

"Momeegace," said Evelyn as she wrapped her arms around Grace's knees.

The days slipped by faster than a feather borne on the wind. Busier than ever, Amy continued to make the bread, and more often than not she cooked the meals. Grace was an excellent cook when she wanted to fix a dinner, but she couldn't be bothered if she were sewing. Frilly white curtains adorned the front windows and bright blue gingham, trimmed with a white ruffle, decorated the side windows of the cabin.

Grace made aprons for herself and Amy. She made shirts for the little boys and pinafores for Annie and Evelyn.

Life settled into a comfortable routine. Fred Watts spent more time working on his farm and by summer of 1913 he realized his dream. The homestead requirements were complete. Gerald Hooper and Arthur C. Slaughter journeyed to Edmonton and on July 24, 1913 filled out the forms, sworn statements on behalf of their friend and neighbor Fredrick Watts.

ಬ

Amy and Grace worked all day Saturday preparing for a celebration dinner on Sunday. Grace made enough potato salad to feed an army and she killed and dressed half a dozen fryers, now cooling on ice in the cellar.

"Amy, do you think you could make a large pan of cinnamon buns along with the loaves of bread you are preparing?" queried Grace.

"Yes, ma'am. I've mixed extra dough."

❦

Up before dawn Sunday morning, Amy, Grace, and Annie rushed around setting the table, making beds, and generally preparing the cabin for company. Amy gave one last look around and tried to quell the butterflies camping in her stomach before she ducked behind the curtain to change her dress and comb her hair.

Ready at last, Fred beamed on his family as he tucked Grace's hand under his arm and led the way to the little church across the way. Amy sat in the pew beside Annie and tried unsuccessfully to listen to the sermon. Grace's desire for perfection had invaded Amy's thoughts like a swarm of bees driven from their nest. Her mind raced ahead to the anticipated dinner and climbed more than one hill of "what ifs."

❦

The smile on Grace's face and the lift of her shoulders, as friends and neighbors gathered around the table laden with food, told Amy everything was perfect. At least perfect in her stepmother's eyes. It could never be perfect for Amy as long as Dolly remained absent. Dolly, the sister without whom they couldn't have made it. The one who mothered them.

Thankful Reginald sat beside her, Amy reached under the table for his hand. His fingers gave hers an answering squeeze. As heads bowed for the blessing, Reg whispered in her ear, "We know who worked the hardest. And we know who deserves praise. Doesn't matter who is honored today. Father should have gone for our sister."

At Fred's request, Reverend Dallas returned thanks for the food and asked a continued blessing on each member of the Watts family. When he said Dolly's name, Amy felt tears pushing against her eyelids. Did he linger longer over the blessing for Dolly, or was it her imagination?

℘

Gaining title to their land certainly didn't mean less work, and in the weeks following, Amy worked harder than ever. For one thing, they had a larger garden to tend. At Grace's urging, Fred used some of his exposed glass plates to build a cold frame, and previously excluded plants were added to their plot.

Grace did her part, but Amy missed working beside Dolly. They all missed Reggie; Cecil most of all. Cecil and Amy were the two oldest children still at home. Amy shouldered more responsibility in the house and Cecil took on the work of a man in the field, though he longed to work in the mill with his brother.

Fred objected to Cecil working in the sawmill. "You're too young and the work is dangerous," he said. Cecil chafed under his father's authority, but he didn't dare oppose him. "And I suppose he thinks farm work isn't dangerous," Cecil muttered under his breath. "Swinging double-bitted axes all day long isn't exactly child's play."

Cecil didn't mind getting in the hay. He liked working with the horses and he knew he could drive them as well as his father. But today his mood was sour and perhaps he didn't watch closely enough. The horses pulled the loaded hay wagon steady enough until a grouse nesting in the grass took flight right in front of them with a whirr of flapping wings and a distressed squawk.

"Whoa! Whoa! Blast you!" yelled Cecil.

The team raced in circles around the barnyard scattering hay in all directions and knocking over everything in their way. Cecil sawed on the lines and continued to shout *"Whoa!"*

It was no use. Mona and Floozy were crazed. Cecil couldn't hang on any longer. He jumped. Amy watched in horror as the team turned and the wagon ran over her brother's leg. She screamed!

Fred ran, grabbed the horses' bridles and, with brute force, brought the animals to a halt.

Cecil dragged himself out of the way and lay propped against the barn wall. Sweat beaded on his face as he fought down the nausea and tried hard not to cry out.

Tears streaming down her face, Amy rushed to her brother's side. Grace followed with blankets and a cold cloth. "Amy," she directed, "you might get Cecil some water."

Amy ran to obey.

"Cecil," said Grace. "Go ahead and scream! Cry! Or cuss if you want. No one is going to fault you. Your leg is broken and it has to hurt like the very dickens."

As quickly as he could, Fred hitched the team to the farm wagon and carefully placed his son on blankets in the back. Ironic as it seemed, the team responsible for breaking Cecil's leg would now take him to the doctor.

Unfortunately his leg never healed properly, and he ended up with one leg shorter than the other. He admitted it pained him, but Amy never heard him complain. Instead, she heard him singing hymns as he went about his work. It was a lesson she would remember in the years ahead.

ℬ

By summer of 1914 rumblings of war had become a threat the world could no longer ignore. Reginald and Cecil enlisted in the army as did many of Dolly and Amy's friends.

"I'll be enlisting in the Canadian Infantry," announced Fred in August, on Amy's sixteenth birthday. "But first, Amy, I'm taking you to Astoria, Oregon to care for Aunt Sarah Pickernell. She's getting old and needs someone to care for her. I know I can trust you to be obedient and responsible."

A thousand questions assaulted Amy's brain. Butterflies did a polka in her tummy and made her queasy, but her tongue remained mute. What could she say? Of course she would go. Father said so.

Amy poured out her apprehensions in a letter to Dolly.

My dearest sister Dolly,

Tears fill my eyes as I write to you, and my hand trembles, but I dare not ruin this paper. I had hoped when my time came to leave home, Father would take me to Edmonton and we would be together.

Alas, it is not to be. This fall Father is taking me to Astoria, Oregon. I'm to care for Aunt Sarah Pickernell. She's 82, and needs help. You'll understand when I tell you that I feel I'm being traded for a pair of horses. As you know, our father borrowed money from Aunt Sarah to buy Mona and Floozy. I'll be paying his debt.

Aunt Sarah did include, in Father's letter, a word to me. She sounds nice, and she tells me she'll pay me a little wage. I can further my education, and of course go to church. But sister, I'm so frightened. I'll be so far from home. What if she turns out to be mean? Please, please, remember me in your prayers!

Your loving sister,

Amy Gladys

P.S. Charlie Slaughter is enlisting in the army with Reginald and Cecil.

Amy longed to say so much more but she hadn't the paper, and words alone couldn't ease the hurt in her heart. She loved Charlie Slaughter, and she felt sure he loved her too, though he hadn't said so. Would the war and distance separate them forever? Or would they eventually be together? Charlie did say he'd write to her from, "over there."

Why did the future have to be so uncertain? Well, she'd just trust God to lead her.

CHAPTER 40

Every day Amy squeezed in time to go to the post office, and daily she walked home disappointed. After nearly three weeks the coveted letter arrived.

My dearest little sister Amy,

Forgive me for not answering you sooner. This crazy war has upset everything. I am working eight hours a day at the dress shop and spending as much free time as possible with Harold Cruikshank before he leaves to fight.

Harold asked me to marry him now, but I have no desire to be a war widow if things don't work out. I'll wait until he comes home.

I'm so sorry our father is taking you so far away. I wish you were coming to Edmonton. Sometimes I hate Father, but I know our dear mother would scold me if she knew. Surely things will be better for you with Aunt Sarah. You can buy some new clothes and get more education.

I love you so much little sister and you are always in my prayers. I promise to write to you. We must keep in touch.

Your loving sister,
Dolly

8∞

The day for departure arrived in early October. Amy wore her best dress and stuffed her few belongings in a pillowcase. Reggie came to see her off and all her brothers and sisters still living at home gathered around to tell her goodbye and wish her God speed.

Tears ran down Amy's face as she kissed and hugged her siblings one more time. Only God knew when she'd see them again.

"We love you! We love you! We'll write." The promises flew back and forth as Cecil, who would take them to the train station at Westlock, waited patiently in front of the cabin with team and wagon.

Fred smoothed his mustache, settled his hat on his head, and turned to Amy. "Come, Daughter. It's time to go!"

EPILOGUE

Surprises awaited Amy with Aunt Sarah Pickernell; few of them good. Before many weeks passed, Amy felt as trapped as a lamb caught in a bramble thicket. Promises were broken and privileges suspended. Amy became a virtual prisoner in the house, always on call to attend to her great aunt's needs and wants.

Amy received one card from Charlie Slaughter. He told her of his premonition of being killed in the war. Sadly, that came true.

One good thing did take place at Aunt Sarah Pickernell's. John Rathkey came to the door and asked to rent a room from Mrs. Pickernell. At first Amy avoided John as much as possible. She never smiled at him and only spoke when necessary. She didn't know this man, and believed aloofness to be her best defense.

But God hadn't forgotten Amy. A means of deliverance came in the form of help from Mrs. Brown, another renter who liked Amy and perceived the problem. She explained the situation to John Rathkey. An honorable man, with sisters of his own, John began to plan to get Amy away from this old tyrant.

With the help of John's sister, his mother, and Mrs. Brown, John succeeded in engineering Amy's escape, and eventually John Rathkey and Amy Gladys Watts were married.

Many years passed before Amy again saw any of her siblings, but true to their promises she and Dolly faithfully wrote to each other. Occasionally Amy received a card or letter from her brothers, Reginald and Cecil, while they were in the army. Later on there would be letters and telephone calls between Amy, her sisters, brothers, and their wives.

In 1938 Amy took her two younger children, Eldred, sixteen, and Dorothy, seven, by train to Spokane, Washington to visit Percy and his family. Sister and brother, accompanied by family, journeyed on by automobiles to Canada to see Dolly and her family. Then on to Barrhead to see Reg and his wife Kathie. This was the first time Amy had seen any of her siblings since leaving Paddle River.

Amy didn't see her father again until 1946, at which time Fred Watts made the effort, after becoming a Christian, to visit all his children and ask their forgiveness for treating them so badly when they were young. It's believed all did forgive him except Eric. He just couldn't.

In 1976 Dr. Arthur Rathkey, and his wife Roba, took his mother, Amy Gladys, to England to see her sister Norah. It was duly noted that it had been exactly seventy years since they had seen each other. They had much to talk about. As a girl of twelve, Norah had been so proud of her brothers, dressed in their uniforms, when they visited her in England during World War I.

Frederick Watts did offer to bring daughter Norah to America in later years, but Norah wrote to him saying she couldn't leave her family in England and the matter was dropped.

All Fred and Edith's children, with the exception of Norah, revisited the old homestead and their Canadian relatives at some point in later years. Always Reginald and Dolly were there to greet them and show them around. How they hugged, kissed, and reminisced, memories grown sweeter by the passing of time.

LATER:

1. Stanley Reginald Watts (Reg): Came through the war and returned to Paddle River, now called Barrhead. He married (no children) and lived to be more than 100 years old.

2. Frederick Cecil Watts (Cecil): Made it home to Barrhead, but later he had to be institutionalized. He was gassed in the war.

3. Dorothy Mae Watts (Dolly) : Married Harold Cruickshank, lived in Edmonton and had one son and one daughter.

4. Amy Gladys Watts (Amy): Married John Rathkey, lived in Oregon and had two sons and one daughter.

5. Percy Claude Watts (Percy): Married and had one daughter. He lived in Spokane, Washington and was supervisor of a large laundry.

6. Eric Ralph Watts (Eric): He stayed in Canada, married and had a son.

7. Charles Leslie Watts (Leslie): Settled in Pennsylvania, married and had one son and one daughter.

8. Edith Annie Watts (Annie): Married Leonard Craw and had two sons. Lived in Florida for awhile and then in Arizona.

9. Norah Elizabeth Watts (Nora): Remained in England with her beloved aunt and uncle. Married Robert Stevens and had one son.

10. Harold David Watts (Harold): Died at age 21 of a stomach ailment or possibly pneumonia.

11. Evelyn Mabel Watts (Evelyn): Married Wayne Thompson and lived in Florida. No children.